PRAISE FOR JAN

YOUR SON IS ALIVE

JAMES SCOTT BELL

1

Your son is alive.

A scrawl in red crayon. Messy block lettering, across a piece of 8 x 10 white bond that had been tri-folded and placed in a blank business envelope. The envelope had not been sealed.

It had been slipped under Dylan Reeve's door during the night.

Dylan, holding the note, stumbled toward a chair, sat heavily, his bathrobe bunched up under him.

He didn't know how long he sat there. All he knew was he hadn't moved, except to wipe his eyes.

Finally, he got up, went to the kitchen where his phone was plugged in next to the coffee maker. He called Erin.

"Dylan?"

"Can I come over?" Dylan said.

"Now?"

"I need to see you."

"What is it?"

"You're the only one I can talk to."

Pause. "Is this about ..."

"Yeah."

"Aren't you seeing Dr. Reimer?"

"Not for a while," Dylan said. "I––"

"Maybe you should call him," Erin said.

"I got something," Dylan said. "A note. A weird, sick note."

"Note?"

"Please, can I come over?"

Pause.

Dylan said, "Is someone with you?"

"No, Dylan."

He closed his eyes. "Just for a few minutes. I promise."

Pause.

"Give me an hour," Erin said.

It was six-thirty. He could get to Erin's, talk to her, and still make it to the office for his first appointment.

Heading west on the 60 freeway in the half-dark, half-light of another urban morning, with L.A. traffic not yet at the commuter-knot level, Dylan felt as if he were driving in the rain. It was blurry looking through the windshield, even though outside it was dry and warm and the sky was clear as the stars faded against the dawn.

Still, there was something oppressive about that dome of sky, a pressing in. Because of the note. It sat there on the passenger seat like some inanimate hitchhiker, silent.

Dylan thought about throwing it out the window.

No, Erin needs to hear about it.

Or maybe he just *wanted* her to hear about it. Share the pain again, as they had for fifteen years. The first five together, the last ten apart, yet joined forever by cords of never-ending sorrow.

He saw the L.A. skyline then, shadowed in the distance. Soon the buildings would be filled by worker bees—lawyers, bankers, brokers, architects, realtors, wheelers and dealers.

And not one of them could care less about what was happening to Dylan Reeve.

That was life, as his father used to say, in the big city.

He turned his mind toward his own work. This morning his first client would be Mrs. Helen Nussbaum. She was coming in for her monthly soft-tissue mobilization. After that—if he remembered correctly—was Carol Regent, the thirty-something LAUSD elementary school teacher who had been in a car accident a year earlier. Dylan had been adjusting her neck and spine for eight months.

He called his receptionist at home.

"Wow," Paige said. "Early bird."

"Soon as you can, will you call Mrs. Nussbaum and Carol Regent?"

"Reschedule?" Paige said.

"Please."

"Mrs. N's not going to like that."

"Thanks for taking the heat."

"You can double my salary," she said.

"You're worth it," he said.

"Everything okay?"

"No worries," Dylan said, and never sounded so insincere in his life.

Erin opened the door of her North Hollywood condo.

"Thanks for this," Dylan said.

"Coffee?" Erin said.

"Please."

He entered and watched his ex-wife moving toward the kitchenette. Even in loose-fitting pants and untucked blouse, Erin's figure attracted him. It always had. But even more now, lean as it was from her running habit. He felt guilty thinking about that now.

Dylan said, "I wouldn't have called if it wasn't important."

"I know," Erin said.

Dylan sat in a wingback chair and looked around the room. He hadn't been here since April. The lamp he'd thrown across the room last year was gone.

Erin came back with two mugs, handed him one. She sat on the sofa. Her soft, brown hair fell easily to her shoulders.

"Honestly," he said, "I didn't know who else to call."

"You said a note?"

Dylan handed it to her.

Erin unfolded it, read it. Looked up. Her face was tight. "Who would do this?"

"No idea," Dylan said.

"I mean, why?"

"Exactly."

"Do you think …"

Dylan shook his head. "If it was true, why do it this way? After so long?"

"Didn't we used to talk about hope?"

"I had to give up hope ten years ago. The hope was killing me."

Dylan saw Erin's nod, the sadness in it, but the acknowledgement of the truth. Ten years ago he'd seen that same expression when he announced the marriage was over. It wasn't a shock to her. They both had known it to be so.

"I'm sorry," Dylan said. "Maybe I shouldn't have put this on you."

"No," Erin said. "I mean, yes, you should." Erin looked at the ceiling. "But if somebody took the trouble—"

"Not like this. An anonymous note? It's somebody who wants to hurt me. Us."

"But who? You don't have enemies."

"No?"

"Maybe some cracked spines," Erin said.

That almost made Dylan smile. Erin still had her sense of humor. That had always been one of her best qualities. That she could bring it out now was a gift.

Erin wasn't smiling. "It comes back in waves," she said.

Dylan nodded. "How've you been doing?"

"Not bad," Erin said.

"Can I tell you something?"

"Of course."

"You look really good."

"For an old chick."

"Haven't you heard? Fifty is the new thirty."

"Tell that to my knees."

"Maybe you should give them some time off."

"Not a chance," Erin said.

She was a dedicated marathoner now. It didn't take a psychiatrist to figure out why. Erin started training a year after Kyle was taken. She ran her first marathon a month after the divorce. Dylan envied her dedication.

"Whoever did this," Dylan said, "is sick. I guess I just really needed you to know. So I didn't have to be alone with it."

Erin's eyes were warm with understanding.

"Thank you for letting me come over," Dylan said.

"You were there for me, too. Lots of times."

"Seems like forever ago."

Erin said, "One day at a time."

"Today won't be easy," Dylan said.

"If life was easy," Erin said, "it wouldn't be life."

Dylan skipped the freeway and took Cahuenga over to Hollywood Boulevard, turned left, and kept on surface streets all the way into downtown.

His office was in one of those classic L.A. buildings from the thirties that had been preserved and restored. Eleven stories on West Olympic Boulevard, a couple of blocks from Staples Center. Unlike so many urban centers, where demolition and destruction preceded renovation, L.A.'s glorious infrastructure was largely intact. You could see it just walking around a few blocks. Boutique hotels and luxury condos on Broadway, inside buildings Raymond Chandler could have passed. There were upscale bars, like the Edison, housed in the basement of the old Edison Electric company, with the turbine steam generators and utility tunnels preserved. Clothing stores and theaters and sidewalk dining. It was all the right combination of old and new, something Dylan always loved about his adopted home town.

But it was also a city of transience and desperation, of brokenness and lost dreams. That's what Dylan had felt most for the last fifteen years. There had been no reclamation project for his heart.

Paige was at her post at the reception desk as Dylan walked in. Loyal Paige. Single mom, had been with Dylan for seven years.

"Any trouble?" Dylan asked.

"You mean Mrs. N?"

Dylan nodded.

"Let's put it this way," Paige said. "You will get an earful tomorrow when she comes in. At two-thirty, by the way."

"Terrific."

"Carol is fine, will reschedule."

"Great. The morning clear then?"

"There was one phone-in request, if you can fit him in."

"No."

"It's Jaquez Rollins," Paige said.

"Of course."

Three hours later, seven feet of lean, athletic prowess walked into Dylan's office and said, "Hey hey, Miracle Man!"

Jaquez Rollins was the starting power forward for the Los Angeles Lakers. He'd come to Dylan a year ago with compressed vertebrae that the team doctor said might require vertebroplasty. But Jaquez didn't want any "cement" injected into his body. And found Dylan via referral from a bench-warming shooting guard named Max Stevenson.

The timing was perfect, as Dylan had developed a new technique for nonsurgical spinal decompression. Jaquez told him to go for it. His words, in fact, were, "Take it to the hoop." The results, Jaquez kept saying ever after, were a miracle.

Dylan couldn't help but smile now. The Lakers' leading scorer was a kick, a party, always happy, and scandal free. Jaquez Rollins didn't go to clubs. He preferred the company of his wife and two children, watching Disney movies or playing games. He did lots of volunteer work in the community.

And he kept up a string of funny stories as Dylan began to rub his back. Dylan tried to absorb them, as if they were an analgesic for the soul. It helped a little. But Dylan only acknowledged each tale with a monosyllable or the occasional, "Uh-huh."

After twenty minutes, Jaquez sat up and said, "Everything okay, MM?"

"Why?" Dylan said.

"You don't seem your usual self."

"I'm probably more my old self than you know."

"Talk to me, MM. Maybe I can help."

Dylan knew that Jaquez had carried a 4.0 at the University of Kentucky—though he declared for the NBA draft after his sophomore year—and that he was a psych major. Some of the sports writers called him *Head Doctor J.*

"I appreciate it, Jaquez."

"We got time. How much time we got?"

"Seriously?"

"Fifteen minutes at least. It's my time, right?"

It was, and Dylan realized he had not spoken about his son to another man—or woman, for that matter—since he'd stopped going to counseling.

"I don't want you to take this on," Dylan said.

"Pass me the ball, man."

"Do you know about my son?" Dylan said.

"Somebody told me you lost him," Jaquez said.

Dylan nodded.

"How old was he?" Jaquez said.

"Five," Dylan said.

"How'd he die, you don't mind my asking?"

"He didn't," Dylan said. "He was taken."

2

Saturday. The park. Fifteen years ago.

Tee-ball opening day.

Kyle Reeve sitting on the bench for the Cubs.

Dylan watching, hoping Kyle would get a hit the first time he came up. It would be nice for him to get a hit and remember to run to first base. He wanted his boy to feel the thrill that comes from your first hit and hearing your teammates cheer and give you a *Way to go.*

Not the dreaded *Stupid, you're supposed to run fast!*

And then out in right field––the weakest defensive player always got stuck in right field. Would Kyle be able to get his glove on the ball? Would he remember to throw it to the second baseman?

They'd been practicing in the front yard for a week, Dylan teaching his son the right throwing motion. "Like you're reaching for the corner of the doorway. Back and through. That's it ..." as the ball went this way or that. But yesterday, Friday, Kyle got three straight grounders from Dylan (who threw them, not batted them, it was easier to control that way) and two of the three throws had been straight.

Now it was game time. And Dylan was moving around on the hard bleachers so much that Erin said, "Stop. You're making my coffee nervous."

"I'm fine," Dylan said.

She smiled then, the knowing smile, the I-can-read-you-like-arecipe smile. She said, "Need a juice box?" Erin was the refreshments mom for the first game, had the blue vinyl ice chest at her feet.

"You have a beer in there?" Dylan said.

"You'd like that, wouldn't you?"

"I'll take two."

Instead he got a kiss on the cheek from his wife, who said, "Relax, hon. He's going to be fine. He hasn't started taking this as seriously as you."

"Am I one of those dads?"

"You're a great dad. A superstar. And remember what you told him? When he wasn't sure he wanted to play tee-ball?"

"What did I say?"

"You told him it was going to be fun. It was all about fun. He was going to love having fun."

"Did I really say *fun* that many times?"

Erin smiled, nodded.

"What I meant to say," Dylan said, "was you better practice every day so you can get a full ride to UCLA."

Erin punched him in the shoulder.

A cheer went up in the stands. Dylan looked out at the field and saw Richard Fusali running toward first base. The ball he'd smacked rolled through the legs of the left fielder.

It was going to be at least a double.

The Cubs bench was on its feet, jumping up and down. Even Kyle.

He was into it!

The wonderful bonding of team sports.

All would be well. Yes, even fun.

Dylan thought that, felt that.

The feeling lasted fourteen minutes.

Richard Fusali never made it home. The Cardinals, the other team, came up to bat. They were packed with talent, and showed it, scoring four runs.

The next big lesson for Kyle, Dylan mused, was going to be on how to deal with getting pounded by an opponent.

In the top of the third, with the Cubs at bat and behind 6-0, Dylan started his serious squirming. They were getting to the bottom of the order, the Cubs were, and since all the kids got to bat, Kyle would be coming up if enough kids got hits in front of him.

It looked like that just might happen.

Jayson Gillespie, the Cubs spitfire third baseman, got a clean single up the middle. That was followed by a grounder from Travis Millward that the Cardinal shortstop mishandled. Two men on, no outs.

Dylan's right leg started with the jimmies. Erin pressed her hand on his knee.

"Don't let him see you like this," she said.

She was right. But at least Kyle wasn't looking at him. He was squirming, too. But then again, Kyle always squirmed. He wasn't ADHD, so they'd been reassured. But he didn't have the greatest attention span, either. Well, who did anymore? Even among adults. Heck, they had cameras in cell phones now, for crying out loud. Parents were taking digital pictures all over the place. Dylan was happy with his plain old flip phone, thank you very much.

Sergio Varela hit one right back to the non-pitching pitcher, who threw to first instead of going for the force out at third.

Two men on, one out, and two batters before Kyle.

The littlest boy on the team, Neil Brooke, who was about as tall as his bat, came up for his swipes. Though diminutive, he always took a mighty cut. This time he connected, sending a sharp grounder to third base. Jayson Gillespie ran for home and the first really exciting play of the game happened at home plate when the third baseman made a perfect throw to the catcher.

Jayson Gillespie stopped five feet from the plate and just stared.

The Cardinal catcher stared too.

The Cardinals coach screamed, "Tag him! Tag him!"

The catcher started walking toward Jayson.

Jayson turned and ran toward left field.

The catcher ran after him.

It was a race, but the catcher—who wore the gear, even though he never caught real pitches—was no match for the fleet Gillespie.

As the entire bleacher section laughed its head off, the Cards' manager and the lone umpire ran out waving their arms, yelling, until both boys stopped in center field.

After consultation among the ump and two managers, it was determined that Jayson was out and Sergio Varela would stay on second.

Two outs.

As the hilarity died down, and with one more batter to go before Kyle, Dylan had to grip the bench to keep his body from shaking like a washing machine.

He looked to see if Kyle was getting ready to hit.

But he wasn't.

He was waving to Mike, the young assistant coach.

Dylan wanted to shoot down there to see what was the matter. But Coach Mike was on the spot, bending over Kyle, listening. Then, with a knowing smile, Coach Mike looked up at Dylan and winked. Then he took Kyle by the hand and ran him down to the end of the bench and toward the outhouses.

Oh the timing, the terrible timing! Was it the natural course of bladder events, or was Kyle scared before his first at-bat?

Dylan decided it would be embarrassing for Kyle if he ran over to see how his bathroom break went. Erin put her hand on his arm.

"He'll be fine," Erin said.

"But will I be?" Dylan said.

Brandon McNab was walking up to the tee. Dylan cast a nervous glance at the outhouses. What if Kyle didn't get back in time? Dylan was prepared to go down to the field and appeal to the merciful umpire for a slight delay. Maybe there was some obscure rule about five-year-old tee-ball players who had to pee. If not, Dylan was ready to make one up on the spot and appeal to the crowd like some Roman senator.

Then that crowd cheered as Brandon McNab laced a hit through the gap between third and short.

Kyle's turn!

No Kyle.

Manager Dave, coaching at first base, shouted, "Who's up?"

Jared Farmer's mom, the scorekeeper, said, "Kyle."

"Well, where is he?" Manager Dave said.

"Slight emergency!" Dylan shouted.

Some understanding giggles from other parents.

Manager Dave looked at the ump, who looked at Manager Dave, and seemed like he was about to make a ruling.

"I'll check!" Dylan said, and almost twisted his ankle jumping out of the stands. He limp-jogged to the outhouses. Three of them, facing away from the field toward the pathway at the edge of the park.

As he came around to the front, Dylan expected Coach Mike to be standing there, tapping his foot.

He saw no one.

"Kyle?"

No answer.

"Mike?"

Again, nothing.

The first portable said *Unoccupied* on the knob.

Also the second.

"Hey, anybody?"

A lizard skittered out from between two outhouses, and froze.

When Dylan saw the third outhouse also said *Unoccupied* he opened its door.

Coach Mike was on the pot. Fully clothed. Leaning against the side.

But he wasn't moving.

Blood seeped from his head.

Dylan's thoughts split him in two.

Find Kyle.

Help Mike.

As he quickly checked the other two outhouses, Dylan managed to get the phone out of his pocket, flipped it open, and thumbed 9-1-1.

Facing the field now, he shouted, "Help! Over here!"

The 9-1-1 dispatcher answered. A woman. "What is your emergency?"

"Need an ambulance at Hinton Park. Man hurt––" speaking this as he waved at Erin and others, and now they were coming.

"What is your name, sir?"

"My son's missing."

Erin reached him.

"What is it?" Erin said.

"Look for Kyle!"

"Where?"

"He's not in the bathrooms. He might be hurt."

The dispatcher said something. Dylan said, "Hinton Park! Ambulance and police. I have to go."

He snapped his phone shut and said to Erin, "Look up the hiking trail!"

She seemed to know everything then, did not hesitate. But the look on her face broke his heart into a million pieces. He willed his own heart to hold together.

Parents were gathering around now. Jayson Gillespie's father was nearest to Dylan, asking what was wrong.

"The last one," Dylan said, pointing to the outhouse. "Coach Mike's in there."

Then Dylan ran to the dirt path and went in the opposite direction from Erin. Toward the street.

He heard his wife's voice in the distance yelling, "Kyle!"

Dylan stopped where path met sidewalk, looked up and down the street. Saw nothing but the normal traffic flow. His breathing got cold, hard, fast.

A skinny teen––maybe sixteen––rolled up on his skateboard. Dylan put up his hand.

The boy didn't slow.

Dylan grabbed the boy's shoulder.

The skateboard skittered off to the patch of grass by the curb.

"Hey man!" the boy said.

Dylan said. "I have to ask you––"

"Let go!"

"Did you see a boy?"

"No—"

"In a baseball uniform?"

The skinny skater pushed Dylan in the chest, grabbed his skateboard and ran off.

Once, when Dylan was in college, he'd gone backpacking with his girlfriend. He and Linda went deep into the Los Padres National Forest. They had a fight and Dylan stomped off to let Linda stew in her own juices. An hour later he went back to apologize, but she was gone. He called her name, got nothing back. And all sorts of imagined horrors filled his mind. Did she fall off a cliff? Into the river? Break her leg?

Get kidnapped?

He ran along the trail, shouting her name, not stopping until he was out of breath, unable to go on. Then he looked around, realized he was not on the trail they'd come on.

He himself was lost.

He had the same feeling now.

Was Kyle safe?

Parents and kids were swarming around the outhouses now. Dylan's mind tried to comprehend the incomprehensible. Somebody had savagely attacked Coach Mike and taken Kyle.

In broad daylight!

Kyle *had* to be nearby.

Distant sirens now.

Dylan ran to the corner, where the parking lot was. When he got there the wind was completely out of him. His heart was pumping so fast, he thought it might break a rib.

He doubled over, put his hands on his knees.

The ground blurred under him.

"Please God, please," he said, though his relationship with the Almighty was distant at best.

No voice answered him, only the sirens, blaring.

Everybody pitched in to search.

Manager Dave, the ex-Marine who led the Cubs, got some men together and said, "Cover everything from this side, through the trees, down to the street. Go!"

It became a search-party free-for-all. Within his panic Dylan felt a warmth. This was what community was about. This was not a matter of debate, like the time he and Paul Fusali got into a brief shouting match over presidential politics. All that was insignificant now. It was about finding Kyle, a kid, a child, one of their own.

The police arrived, one black-and-white unit. Then another.

Dylan told one of the patrolmen, a big guy, as much as he could. It was probably a two-minute ramble, but it felt like an hour.

It was interrupted by a voice shouting, "I got somebody!"

. . .

It was Roger Millward, Travis's dad. He was coming out of the trees with a confused-looking elderly man. He held the man by the arm, like a cop escorting a suspect to jail.

Dylan and the big patrolman met Roger and the old man halfway.

"He's a witness," Roger said. "Lives right across the street over there." Roger motioned behind him with his thumb.

"What can you tell us?" the patrolman asked.

The old man was dressed in wrinkled khaki pants, a white T-shirt and yellow cardigan, unbuttoned. His white eyebrows needed a major trim. His sallow face needed sun.

"Seen a guy get in a car," the old man said.

"Tell him what else," Roger Millward said.

"Had a big bag with him," the old man said. "Threw the bag in the trunk."

"That it?" the patrolman said.

"He told me it was a big bag," Roger said. "Big enough for a young boy."

"What kind of bag is like that?" the patrolman said.

"That kind," the old man said. He pointed at a black equipment bag a few yards away.

"That's a bag for carrying bats and gloves," the patrolman said.

"But it's big," Roger said.

"You think the bag had anything in it?" the patrolman said. "I mean, besides bats."

"Don't know," the old man said.

"Tell him what else," Roger said.

"Well," the old man said, "this fellow seemed like he was in a hurry."

"Can you describe the man?" the patrolman said.

"He was wearing a baseball hat," the old man said. "I think maybe he had on a uniform-type shirt."

"You *think*?" Dylan said.

The patrolman put a hand on Dylan's arm. "Let me do this."

"I wasn't studyin' 'im," the old man said. "I just came out to water my lawn. I seen this guy across the street. In a baseball hat. Like everybody else around here."

"What kind of car was he driving?" the patrolman said.

"Think it was silver."

"Do you know what make?"

"Nah."

"Four doors or two doors?"

"Not sure. Four I think."

"I suppose you didn't get a license plate number," the patrolman asked.

The old man shook his head. "Why would I?"

"But it's a silver car," Roger Millward said. "You can order stops, can't you?"

"For what?" the patrolman said. "It sounds like one of the coaches or fathers with a bat bag."

"Parked over there?" Roger said. "And not the parking lot?"

"There's no law says you have to park in a parking lot," the patrolman said.

"Time's wasting!" Dylan said. "Can't you do one of those Amber alerts?"

"Not on this information, sir."

"Well, what can you do?"

"We can look. And we will, sir, we will."

Three months later Dylan and Erin filed with The National Center for Missing and Exploited Children. They told their story on the local news and got a national pickup.

They talked to the FBI.

They hired a private investigator.

They put off plans to have more children.

They went to grief counseling.

They began to drift apart.

Kyle Reeve was never found.

3

"Oh, man," Jaquez said.

Dylan felt cold and drained, like he'd run a mile through a snowstorm.

"I didn't mean to go on like that," he said.

"S'okay," Jaquez said.

"It's just that it all came back hard this morning."

"This morning?"

"Somebody stuck a ..."

"A what?"

Dylan, short of breath, sat on the therapeutic chair normally reserved for clients undergoing spinal rehab.

"Come on now," Jaquez said. "We're this far along."

Dylan sighed. Then told Jaquez about the note.

"Wow," Jaquez said. "Think it might be true?"

"I don't see it," Dylan said. "More like somebody trying to get at me for some reason."

"You tick anybody off lately?"

"Not that I know of."

"Aw, man." Jaquez put a hand the size of a bathroom mat on Dylan's shoulder. "I know how you feel."

"Do you?" Dylan said, with more harsh skepticism than he intended.

Jaquez said, "My dad got shot dead robbing a 7-Eleven when I was twelve. Kid at school started giving me grief about it. Kid was a bully. I tried to fight him once and he bloodied my nose. I swore I'd get even with him."

"Did you?"

"Oh yeah. I shot up six inches and a hundred pounds in two years. All I had to do was give him the look and he'd run away."

Dylan said, "I wish I knew who to look at."

"Don't let him work your head," Jaquez said.

"Kyle would be twenty now. Even if he was ... I wouldn't know him. He wouldn't know me."

"You got a security camera at your house?"

"I've been meaning to."

"Let me give you my guy," Jaquez said. "I got security like you wouldn't believe. Squirrel tries to get in my yard, boom, I got his picture."

"Squirrel?"

"I gotta protect my nuts."

Dylan almost fell off his therapeutic chair. His laughter was a relief.

Jaquez said, "My guy can fix you up with a hidden cam at your door. Catch the guy if he tries it again."

"Maybe," Dylan said.

"And it's on me," Jaquez said.

"What?"

"You made it possible for me to hit twenty-five foot fadeaways again." Jaquez mimed his shooting motion. "Least I can do for you."

"Jaquez ..."

"No more about it." He stood to his full, magnificent height. "I'm ready to lay some hurt on the Spurs tonight. I'll dunk one for you."

"Thanks," Dylan said.

"And I'll send a prayer upstairs," Jaquez said. "He's got angel armies, you know."

4

Dylan left the office at 4:30. He pulled out of the parking garage, noting his vision was fuzzy. Or, rather, unfocused. In his chest, the two demon Gs were pounding at him anew.

When he'd first gone to see Dr. Reimer, he was told to keep a journal, write down his thoughts and feelings and fears. It was one prong of their multifaceted dealing with grief. That was one of the demon Gs, grief, and it quickly became apparent that while it was relentless, it was not the most cruel.

The cruel demon was GUILT. And that was how Dylan always spelled it in the journal. All caps. Grief and GUILT, and the latter was the tormentor, the one that kept him up at night. Or, when he managed to get some sleep, it would wake him up, and he would hear himself wailing for a long and torturous minute.

He had failed to protect his son.

He had failed to bring him home.

It was back now, GUILT, and Dylan did not want to rush to the shadows and silence of his own home. Maybe he could hit a sports bar and have dinner, see the first part of the Laker game. Maybe catch that Jaquez Rollins dunk. He'd be with people and surrounded by noise, and maybe that and a beer would start putting the note business out of his mind.

But two minutes after leaving the parking garage, he found himself heading for Hollywood.

Runyon Canyon was a bit of city parkland off Vista Street. Popular with day hikers and dog walkers, it offered a panoramic view of the cityscape between Hollywood and downtown. It was also the last place where Dylan had been with Kyle all by himself.

He remembered every detail of that day. The feel of Kyle's hand in his. His son's joyous dance as he spotted an airplane gliding over the downtown skyline. His giggle at the friendly Labrador who thought Kyle was a new toy to play with.

They sat on the bench on the point at the eastern edge of the park.

It was to that bench Dylan headed now, taking the dirt path instead of the paved one, even if it meant getting dusty. Kyle had preferred the dirt path for just that very reason.

When Dylan reached the point, both benches were taken. But then the couple sitting on the furthest one, the one facing downtown, got up, laughing.

Dylan took their place, not laughing.

When Kyle was a toddler, Dylan and Erin had attended a local Methodist church for a while. Erin's parents were good Methodists, still living in Indiana. But when the minister started preaching more about current events than biblical ones, Dylan stopped going. What was the point? He could hear that stuff on CNN.

Now, looking at the downtown skyline, bathed in the soft glow of an orange sunset, Dylan heard himself say, "God, if he is alive, let him be safe and happy."

The moment he said it, something broke in him, a cracking of the wall of ice erected around his heart. It was rubble now, and then rushed in wave after wave of heaving sobs, relentless.

Traffic was horrendous on the 101. What a shock. But it was okay with Dylan this time, because he listened to soft music on the retro station and that allowed his mind and heart to rest.

The Pomona Freeway—what every Angeleno called the 60—was likewise jammed. It took Dylan almost an hour to cover fifteen miles.

But he felt a strange and wonderful comfort as he pulled into the driveway of his Whittier home. He loved this old house, a Craftsman style from the early 20s that he'd lovingly restored. It was there for him.

He owned it outright. Had paid off the mortgage a year ago. His father would have been proud.

He went to routine by making an omelet—cheese and spinach—and sourdough toast. A little salsa verde over the eggs. Warmth for the soul.

Good prep for the call he had to make to Tabitha Mullaney. They'd met via a dating site—Dylan's tentative step back into the world of mating rituals. They had a second date scheduled and he was supposed to confirm it.

Dating! It sounded so archaic, and yet still mysterious. The nerves of that first meeting, the up-tempo pumping of the heart, and even though you're fifty-one years old, you feel like a high school kid with a pimple on your chin and hair that won't stay in place. It had been that way the first time he asked Erin to go out with him, in high school. He was supposed to be Mr. Popular, at least according to the prevailing social winds that blow through every school hallway that has ever existed. But any bravado he managed to put on was only a costume hiding a fear of rejection. If Erin noticed, she did not let on. She seemed just as nervous as he was. It was like they were meant for each other, and that was how it turned out. For a time, at least.

With Tabitha, though, they'd had a first lunch and both of them worked through the nerves into a comfortable, get-to-know-you conversation.

Afterward, Tabitha offered to pay, but Dylan said he'd take care of it, and she said at least let her leave the tip, and again he said no. He knew she was as nervous as he was, anxious to please, but she didn't overdo it. She accepted his largesse with a simple thank you.

It was the kiss on the cheek that cemented the good impression. Outside in the parking lot, Dylan was as stiff and unmoving as the statue of David, though with considerably more coverage on the old bod. He had planned to shake Tabitha's hand, but it suddenly felt out of sync with what was going on inside him and, he sensed, inside her.

Then Tabitha took the initiative, stepped in and kissed him on the cheek. It was a classy move. And he said, "Let's do this again," and she said, "Definitely."

In a follow-up call Dylan had asked if she'd like to go to dinner at one of his favorite places, and she'd said yes. Set up for Friday.

He entertained the quick thought of canceling, wondering how he'd be acting because of the note business. But no, this was life, as Erin said. You've got to power on or it will lay you flat.

He made the call.

"Hi there," Tabitha said.

"We still on for Friday?" Dylan said.

"Absolutely," Tabitha said. "Clearman's, right?"

"You'll love it. Old school. And my treat."

"Let's split the bill this time," she said.

"Tell you what," Dylan said, "we'll negotiate."

"As long as I win."

"Some negotiator!"

She laughed. He laughed. And that was a good way to end things for the day.

After the call, Dylan clicked on the TV. He felt like diving into whatever TCM was showing. Turned out it was a movie called *Detour*. He hadn't heard of it before. It looked like one of those shoestring budget jobs from the 1940s. A guy with a worried look on his face was sitting in a diner. Dylan caught himself thinking, *I could play that part.*

He arranged the pillows on the sofa and popped off his shoes. He put his feet up on the coffee table. The poor sap in the diner was flashing back to better days.

Dylan put his head back on one of the pillows.

And promptly fell asleep.

When he woke up, the man was walking away from a diner. In a voiceover, as a police car pulled up to him, he was saying something about fate putting the finger on you for no reason.

Cheery.

Dylan got up, stretched, went to make sure the front door was locked.

Then stopped like he was hit in the chest.

And stood there, staring at the envelope on the floor.

5

At night, she goes into the churches, alone.

She has for years.

She's mapped them out like an archipelago in a dark sea.

For the first five years she went every night, to one, two, sometimes three.

St. Mel's Catholic church. St. James Presbyterian. St. Paul's Methodist. The little Baptist church on Shoup and the megachurch in Porter Ranch.

As her hopes of seeing Kyle again dimmed—like dying votives in the vestibules of plaster saints—she did not go as frequently. She felt as though she'd fallen off a cruise ship at night, in the middle of the ocean, her screams for help unheard, the lights of the ship and the laughter of the passengers dancing and drinking and having fun, fade in the distance, leaving her in the dark waters, treading as long as her strength could hold out.

Tonight, with the gossamer thread of thought that Kyle might be alive—though she knows that Dylan is most probably right, that this is a sick joke—she feels drawn to Our Lady of Grace in Encino. She always liked that name.

Inside is the alcove, and the candles, and she takes a long match and lights it by one of the small flames, and then lights a candle. And another. And another.

It's quiet and there is only the sound of a souped-up car on White Oak Avenue, thrumming its engine.

Erin Reeve gives voice to her prayer. "Dear Lord, if he is alive, please bring peace and comfort and protection to my boy, wherever he is. If he is dead, please let him be in Heaven. Please give him a room in Heaven and let him know that I'll be with him soon, if you will allow me. And if he's alive, may we see him again? May we know that he's all right? Please let me know. Please ..."

When she finishes, she is spent, it feels like the last leg of a marathon when your body screams that it can't go on but you make it so, and you fight through all the pain in your legs and the burning in your lungs. Because when you cross the line—or even if you pass out trying to reach it—you know you've done everything you are capable of doing, you don't have to bear any shame for failing to try.

6

Dylan's fingers tingled, little needles shooting out of the envelope like electrical charges. Dizzy, he got to a chair so he could sit and catch his breath.

What if he didn't open it? What if it all just went away? What if whoever was doing all this was sitting outside his house now, watching?

Think, think! It had to be a disgusting joke. No ransom hunter or kidnapper would have waited fifteen years to connect with him again.

So keeping calm was the best way to fight him, the unseen figure, the slimeball.

Slimeball. Of all the words he could have hit on, all the familiar epithets, this was what his mind snapped to. For in his mind it was the worst thing a person could be, because he had decided that when he was ten years old and that bully, Cal Webb, had made Dylan his pet project that year. None of the adult bad words resonated with Dylan. But *slime* did, because Dylan had fallen in some awful goo on a camping trip once, a poorly covered cesspool, and forever after *slime* was the worst possible thing to be associated with. Cal Webb was a slimeball, and picturing that had made things more tolerable that horrible year.

Whoever was leaving these notes was a slimeball.

He wanted Dylan to suffer. He wanted to make him squirm.

The envelope was again unsealed. Slimeball didn't want to leave saliva.

His breath was still short, like his lungs weren't at full capacity.

That made him mad.

And the anger gave him new life.

It was a game, a slimy game, and Dylan was on the defensive.

Time to go on offense. To make a move.

He stood, not dizzy anymore, and walked to the credenza by the window and took out a Sharpie from the miniature golf bag pen-and-pencil holder. He uncapped it and on the envelope wrote, *Nice try.*

He capped the Sharpie and put it back in the holder. He went to the front door and opened it wide. He stepped out into the pleasant March evening, took a couple of strides on his twisting cement path.

Now he didn't care if the guy was out there. Dylan wanted to be seen. Even in the faint glow of the streetlight.

Dylan lifted the envelope into the air. He waved it around.

And then, with a flick of the wrist, he sent it sailing through the air. It helicoptered a few yards and landed on the path.

Dylan turned and walked back inside his house.

He felt strangely exhilarated, though the rush was tangled up with intestinal knots of uncertainty. He had no answer to a mystery that gnawed at him—*who was doing this?* At the same time, he'd given whoever it was a tweak on the nose, a message. *I'm not playing your game. You have no power over me.*

Dylan kept telling himself that. *No power.* But even as he did he acknowledged that the very telling of it proved there was still a hold on him.

Likewise his attempt to get to sleep.

There was no way.

A few minutes after midnight Dylan went to the pantry and took down the bottle of brandy. He carried it to the kitchen, got a juice glass from the cabinet and poured a healthy snort.

Still with the lights out, he took the drink to the living room and sat in the dark. The faint yellow of the streetlight seeped past the curtains of the front window, giving the room a foggy, moonlight feel.

He sipped the brandy. It warmed him. He started to relax.

But he knew it wouldn't wipe out the thoughts roiling inside his head.

He knew, too, that he would get up and go to the door, go outside and see if the envelope was still there.

After another swallow, Dylan put the glass down on the table, stood, and made for the front door—and suddenly wished he had a gun.

Good God. Kill somebody? Over this?

He was about to reach for the handle when his eyes, adjusted to the dark, picked up a whiteness near his foot.

The envelope.

He picked it up, his body now abuzz with anger and fear, with the swarm of disquiet that comes from the feeling of being violated.

Not wanting to give the slimeball any indication he was awake, Dylan took the envelope to the pantry, closed the door, and turned on the light in the windowless space.

There on the envelope, below his notation *Nice try* was a red crayon response:

His favorite toy was ...

Dylan opened the envelope. A tri-folded piece of paper. He unfolded it, read the block letters:

... Lego Harry Potter and the Chamber of Secrets.

7

Thursday morning, Erin was at her desk trying to thread the needle, as usual. As the head of admin for the valley campus of the nonprofit DeForest University, she was the one who had to juggle the delicate sensibilities of the faculty as she scheduled both class times and classroom space. Since the entire faculty was made up of a mix of working professionals and tradespeople teaching mostly in the evenings, and retired professionals seeking slots that would not interfere with golf outings and spur-of-the-moment vacation opportunities, her job was almost entirely made up of a daily round of herding cats. Or, in some cases, lions.

Like Alan Sharperson, a retired VP from Northrop Grumman, who was used to ordering around a staff tasked with billion-dollar arms deals. Naturally, he expected every single person at DeForest, up to and including the janitor, to bend to his every wish. Which today involved a total rescheduling of his fall class in Business Management for the Entrepreneur. His latest salvo had been a terse, ten-second phone call to Erin that was made up of seven seconds of tirade ending with a terse "Make it happen" just before he clicked off.

Hers was not to reason why ... and so she stared at the faculty and classroom grid on her computer monitor and tried to concentrate.

It wasn't working. Within the swirl of times and class sizes and rooms and connections, she kept seeing, as if in a kaleidoscope, a multiform pattern of disquiet.

Because of Dylan and the note.

She pondered wistfully what it would be like to tell Mr. Alan Sharperson to go to the devil.

And knew it would be only a momentary pleasure, a short-lived respite. It would take about fifteen minutes for Sharperson to go over her head and for her to be ordered upstairs to HR for a dressing down or her two-weeks' notice.

Reality intruded by way of a tap on her cubicle.

Yumiko Ota, who handled the front desk, was standing there.

"Sorry to disturb you," Yumiko said, "but there's someone here who'd like to see you."

"Not faculty, I hope."

"A student," Yumiko said.

"See me about what?"

"I don't know. He asked for you by name."

"What class is he in?"

"Real Estate."

"Jill Kenelly's class," Erin said.

Yumiko nodded.

"What could he possibly want?" Erin said.

With a shrug, Yumiko said, "I kind of wished he asked for me."

"Huh?"

"He's pretty hot, and he's not wearing a wedding ring."

Erin's laugh was more of a snort. "I'm not in the market."

"You should be," Yumiko said.

"How old is this hottie?"

"Probably thirty-five."

"Definitely not in the market. You take him."

"I'm not sure my boyfriend would approve."

Boyfriend. A word from the distant past, from a happier time.

"All right," Erin said. "Let's check this charmer out."

He was sitting in the reception area, looking at a *Golf Digest*. He was dressed in business casual, all of it sharp. His black hair was thick and neatly trimmed, and he had one of those square jaws you found in old westerns. She recognized him. She'd passed him in the halls a couple of times.

He looked up from the magazine, tossed it back on the table, and stood. Smiling, he came over with extended hand.

"Anderson Bolt," he said.

Really?

Erin shook his hand.

"How can I help you?" Erin said.

"Can we talk somewhere?"

"Here."

Bolt cast a quick glance at Yumiko. "Can we find a place to sit for a moment?"

"The conference room is open," Yumiko said. Erin wasn't sure if Yumiko winked at her or not.

The conference room was just off the reception area. Erin flicked on the lights. The room had a black, artificial wood table in the middle with six black executive chairs around it. On a whiteboard on the wall, someone had scrawled, *Action without motivation is like a squirrel in a wheel.*

Erin pulled one of the chairs out and sat. Anderson Bolt did the same with the chair next to her.

"Thanks for seeing me," he said. His voice was smooth and deep, like a morning-drive radio host's. Which put Erin on edge. What was this guy selling? He was in the real estate class, after all.

She tried to ignore the blueness of his eyes.

"I'm in the real estate class," he said.

"Everything okay?" She hoped he wasn't going to complain about the instructor, Jill Kenelly. She liked Jill and thought her the best instructor in the whole school.

"Oh yeah, fine," he said. "I'm learning a lot. I hope to get my license in the fall."

"Great."

He nodded.

Erin waited for him to go on.

"Anyway," he said, "Ms. Kenelly had a very intriguing class the other night, on salesmanship. A theory. About rejection. She talked about this guy who did some internet videos, and then wrote a book, about how he went out and tried to get rejected. You heard of that?"

"Was that the donut guy?"

"Yes! He went to a Krispy Kreme and asked if he could get five donuts joined together in the shape of the Olympic rings. And they did it for him."

"I did see that. I remember Jill ... Ms. Kenelly, talking about that."

"It's a pretty amazing theory," he said.

"Okay," Erin said.

"So, that's why I wanted to talk to you."

"About the class?"

"About rejecting me."

She looked at him. He seemed a bit nervous, but without guile.

"You want me to reject you?" Erin said.

"Not really, but I'm ready for it."

"You're going to have to explain."

"I want to take you out to dinner," he said.

Erin turned her head, as if hard of hearing.

Quickly, he added, "I know, I know. Out of the blue, right? But honest, I've been thinking about this for at least two months, and you probably have no idea why."

"That would be an understatement," Erin said, trying to process her reaction through a heavy gauze of shock.

Anderson Bolt smiled. "It was more than you realized at the time, I'm sure. See, you were in the lunch room one day, you were eating with the woman out there."

"Yumiko?"

He nodded. "I was getting a Hershey's from the vending machine and I heard you guys talking about art, and you said, 'Picasso was a genius, but Jackson Pollock was a fraud.' Something along those lines."

"I may have said something like that. I have a few opinions about art."

"I liked it. Because I feel the same way about Pollock."

"You know his work?"

"I took a class in college. I remember thinking a three-year-old could spill paint and produce the same thing."

Erin smiled.

"I liked your honesty," he said. "And I thought you're someone I'd like to get to know."

She could not deny it. She was flattered. Absolutely. And, for one small and embarrassing moment, attracted to him. It was both exciting and disconcerting. She had not felt any kind of charge of the raw attraction kind since being drawn to Dylan. The term *one-man woman* certainly applied to her. Even after the divorce.

But now, suddenly, here was an electrical charge.

"Wow," Erin said, "I'm floored."

"You can reject me now," he said.

"Okay, if it will make you feel better, I—"

"It won't! I don't want you to reject me. I want you to say yes."

"Mr. Bolt, you—"

"At least call me Andy."

"I'm not sure about that," Erin said.

"One dinner. To see."

"See what?"

"If there's something to be pursued."

"Mr. ... Andy, I don't know if you picked this up, but I'm a bit older than you are."

"That doesn't matter to me," he said. "I'm attracted to you and I want to get to know you better."

"But it could never ..." She stopped, hearing Dylan's voice. *Fifty is the new thirty.*

"We won't know unless we give it a shot," Anderson Bolt said. "Maybe we'll end up like those Olympic donuts, linked together."

Smooth, she had to give him that.

But was that all she wanted to give?

8

All Dylan knew about Gadge Garner was that he was an ex-Marine who did high stakes security work for celebrities like Jaquez Rollins. And that his nickname was short for Gadget.

Dylan met him at the office at noon on Thursday, at Jaquez's insistence. Garner actually came in two minutes after twelve and said, "Sorry I'm late. I was getting my car towed."

"Getting?" Dylan said.

"It's cheaper than parking around here," Garner said.

Dylan smiled. "You should do standup."

Garner said, "I used to, actually. When I was in my twenties. But then I heard something that made me stop."

"What was that?"

"Crickets."

Gadge Garner was in his mid-forties, stood around five-ten, all of it solid. His hair, buzzed short, was the color of steel. He sat in one of the chairs in front of Dylan's desk, leaned forward with his elbows on his knees. He looked ready to spring at any provocation.

"Jaquez says you got a guy playing a mind game."

"It seems that way."

"Slipping things under your door at home?"

"That's right. Notes. About my son being alive. How much do you know?"

"That much. And that you have no idea who would do that."

Dylan nodded.

"So let's talk about catching this guy and scooping out his entrails."

Dylan froze.

Garner smiled. "The second part is optional. Now, first thing we do, we optic-mize your place. Hidden cameras so you'll be able to look at your phone anyplace you are and see what's going on, plus tap into the digital stream on your computer, which'll record as long as you want. We can also code it to flag certain parameters so you don't have to scan eighty hours at a time."

"That's a lot of coverage."

"What it takes these days. Even then, this guy may not be back. He may try other ways, other places."

"That's troubling."

"Life is troubling," Garner said, "if you only look at it from the wrong side. Me, I try to find the things that make me laugh. That way I can laugh when I fight."

"Fight?"

"You got to fight. No choice. You can fight this guy."

"How?"

"Information."

"I haven't got much of that."

"So get some."

Dylan looked at Garner's implacable face and said nothing.

Garner smiled. "Dylan ... may I call you Dylan?"

"I fear for my health if I say no."

Garner threw his head back and laughed. "That's the ticket!" he said.

It felt good to hear the man laugh. Maybe there was something to his philosophy after all.

Garner said, "This note said your son is alive. Two possibilities, right? True or false. If true, he is somewhere, and he's about, what, twenty?"

"Yes," Dylan said, even as his head tightened at the actual prospect. He couldn't help his mind forming pictures of what Kyle might look like at this very moment, if he was breathing. It was an idealized picture, a good-looking young man, smiling. People around him. A college scene.

"Did your kid ever get fingerprinted for school?" Garner asked.

Dylan shook his head. "Some kids did in Kindergarten. We opted out."

"Why'd you do that?"

"It just seemed intrusive to us at the time. I guess it was a mistake."

"It's never a mistake to put on the chain lock when the government comes knocking," Garner said. "How about DNA?"

"Kyle's?"

"Any items from his childhood you maybe have in a box or something?"

"My wife might have some things."

"Worth a try, matching with a database."

"But isn't that only if Kyle went to prison or something?"

"Also the military, a hospital stay, some school systems."

"Can a private citizen tap into those?" Dylan asked.

"There are ways," Garner said.

"Do you want to fill me in on those?"

"Do you want to know if your son is really alive?"

"Yes."

"Then no," Garner said. "I'll leave the vertebral subluxation complexes to you, you leave the security to me."

9

Despite the notes, Dylan was determined to have dinner with Tabitha Mullaney. He wanted that part of his life to stay on the upward trajectory it seemed to be heading. The only question was when he would tell her about the notes.

He met her at Clearman's, a classic L.A. steakhouse. He'd fallen in love with the place when he moved to Whittier from the San Fernando Valley ten years ago. He liked the low lighting, the tableside service, and the kitschy decor.

But pulling into the parking lot, he didn't know what to do when he saw her again. Should he be the one to kiss? On the cheek? The cheek was still safe. Lips would be after this date, right? Would she expect that? What if she turned her head or backed away? Would that mean she didn't want to yet, or ever? How does anybody deal with this anymore?

She was waiting for him by the hostess stand. Smiling, she stood and said, "Hello!" and moved toward him.

Dylan made a snap decision to go in for a fast hug, bypassing her cheek, taking his out of range, a nice neutral gesture. But when they hugged he felt a tenseness in her. Was she as nervous as he was? Or was it his palpable edginess passing through him to her?

"Your table is ready," the hostess said.

. . .

A waitress greeted them at their table and asked if they'd like a cocktail. Dylan wanted a double bourbon, but decided that wouldn't be such a hot idea under the circumstances.

"Shall we have some wine?" he asked Tabitha.

"That would be nice," she said.

"Let's have the wine list, please," Dylan said, and felt a small measure of relief. He was with a woman again, a woman he liked, and was going through normal dating motions in a nice restaurant.

Maybe life could recalibrate itself.

Maybe Tabitha Mullaney would be the one to do it. At forty-nine, she was two years younger than Dylan. Like him, divorced. They'd spoken of it only briefly at their first meeting, in a let's-get-it-out-of-the-way manner that pleased them both.

She had shoulder-length auburn hair, blue eyes, and tonight wore a black dress that was perfect for the venue. Not tight and strapless as if going to an Oscar party, but with cap sleeves and high neckline that showed off a modest necklace of silver and turquoise beads.

"I love this place," Tabitha said, looking around. "I never knew about it."

"Been here since 1947," Dylan said.

"And I want you to know, we're splitting the bill."

He'd anticipated that. "Thank you," he said. "But not tonight."

"Please."

"Let's discuss after we've had our dinner," he said, smiling.

Tabitha smiled back.

The waitress returned with the wine list. Dylan took it, wondering what the new protocol was. Having a woman offer to pay was new enough. He didn't want to blow it by being too assertive over the wine.

"What sort of wine do you like?" he said.

"Hm, I suppose that depends on what I'm eating."

"Ah, good," Dylan said. "James Bond won't take us for Russian spies."

Tabitha laughed. "What?"

"Did you ever see *From Russia with Love*, the James Bond movie?"

Tabitha shook her head.

"I like Daniel Craig," Dylan said, "But Sean Connery was the best Bond, most fans will tell you."

"Fascinating," she said, as if she really meant it, which was another couple of points in her favor.

"So Bond identifies a Russian assassin because he orders red wine with fish."

"Ah ha."

"We must order carefully," Dylan said. "This place is dripping with secret agents, and we don't want them to spot us."

Tabitha laughed again, an easy laugh.

They decided they both wanted meat, so Dylan suggested a Duckhorn cabernet. Tabitha said it sounded good.

And it was. Dylan did the tasting and approving, and the waitress poured and took their dinner order. Filet for Tabitha. Dylan ordered the bone-in ribeye, medium rare.

Dylan raised his glass.

"To the newness of things," he said.

Tabitha said, "Indeed" and they clinked.

And spoke of childhoods. Tabitha was from El Paso, or as she called it, "Hell's stove." Her name came by way of *Bewitched,* the old TV show that her mother loved. It gave her some amount of teasing in school, but she learned how to stand up for herself that way.

After high school she went north, to the University of Michigan.

Dylan told her about growing up in Stockton, going to U.C. Davis, and then to chiropractic school in Los Angeles. He stayed in the city because he wanted to work with sports teams. And what was Tabitha's dream job?

"I'd like to be in charge of a fleet of fishing boats," she said.

"That's your dream job?"

She nodded. "You asked. My father used to take me fishing. I've always loved it. But the fishing profession is not one that many women go into. So I went to paralegal school instead."

"That sounds a little more practical."

"Oh it is," she said. "But then that means putting aside the things you really want to do. The adventures you might go on."

Over salads they spoke of adventures. Dylan had always wanted to go to the Alps and walk around. Tabitha wanted to see the Great Wall of China. When she said that, Dylan could see the two of them walking it together, holding hands.

Slow down, boy.

The meat was presented tableside, with a bit of flambé for show.

And by the time the waitress left the dessert menu, Dylan wondered if he might be falling in love. The thought filled him with a certain kind of fear—a delicious, wonderful fear, the kind that tells you your heart is still beating and thrumming with hope.

Only once did Tabitha ask if anything was bothering him. He had to make the decision. Tell her about the notes then and there? Or hold back so as not to ruin the best night he'd had in months?

He said, "The only thing that's bothering me at the moment is figuring out how to make this meal last as long as possible."

She reached out and took his hand. No words. They weren't needed.

They decided they were too full even to share a dessert. Tabitha ordered a cappuccino. Dylan a regular coffee.

It was after the first warm sip that Tabitha said, "This has been so nice."

"It has," Dylan said.

"May I tell you something?"

"Of course."

"No Russian spies around?"

Dylan leaned in. "Better keep it low, just in case."

"Okay," Tabitha said, leaning forward herself. "If you want to see your son again, do exactly as I say."

10

Erin said, "Did you feel that?"

Monica said, "What?"

"A bump."

"Bump?"

"I felt it here." Erin touched her chest.

"Have some more wine," Monica said. She held up the bottle of chardonnay. They were on Erin's balcony looking out at the lights of North Hollywood. Her complex on Vineland was part of the NoHo hipster renewal. She'd decided to move here after the divorce to recapture a slice of her artistic youth. Paint again, maybe.

Which is why she liked Monica so much. She was in her late twenties and was a freelance illustrator for the movie studios, and dressed and spoke with a wild abandon that seemed to always cheer Erin up. Which she needed tonight.

"Bring it on," Erin said, holding out her glass.

"Shall we get drunk?" Monica said.

"Just buzzed," Erin said.

"Like Pearl."

"Who?"

"Pearl," Monica said. "From that Will Ferrell vid about the landlord?"

"I guess I'm out of it," Erin said.

"I'll show it to you later. You'll crack up."

"I'd like to crack up," Erin said.

Monica said, "What's going on?"

"Oh, just little things," Erin said, feeling like the lousiest liar in the world.

"You know I was supposed to go out with Sean tonight."

"I didn't know that. I'm sorry—"

"A poker game came up," Monica said. "He said he had to go, his old college roommate. And did I understand?"

"Did you?" Erin said.

"Oh, I understood all right. And I'll have my revenge."

Erin laughed again.

"All to say," Monica said, "that I've got nothing but time, so tell me what's going on, will you?"

Erin took a sip of wine and looked at the lights, silent in the distance.

"I saw Dylan the other day," Erin said. "He had some disturbing news."

"Is he okay?"

"I don't think so," Erin said. "Neither am I."

Monica held her wine glass with both hands.

"There's something you don't know about me," Erin said. "I never talked about it. I had a son."

"Had?"

"He was kidnapped."

"Oh," said Monica, the word drawn out and full of sympathy.

"Fifteen years ago," Erin said.

"God, I can't imagine."

"It's the not knowing that gets you," Erin said. "You have to learn to live with it. The first couple of years, your insides burn up and you're hoping that he'll be found. And then you turn to hoping he's alive. That he'll be found. Then you start to wonder if he's dead. Then you have thoughts that he's being hurt, abused, and you start hoping he's dead, and then you feel guilty for hoping that and ..."

Erin's throat closed up. Then she felt Monica's arms enfold her, and she let herself lean on Monica's shoulder.

11

It felt as if his skull had been reduced to sand and spilled down his neck into the pit of his stomach.

Tabitha sat there as if nothing had changed. Her smile was easy, though no longer warm.

"I know it's a shock," Tabitha said. "But it doesn't have to ruin our evening."

Same voice. Same lilt. Same eyes. No, the color of the eyes wasn't quite the same. The shadows behind them were new, having just been revealed.

Dylan had no idea what to say or do. He imagined himself reaching over and grabbing her by the throat and choking her until she told him what was going on.

But of course he couldn't do it, not here.

Clever girl.

Evil girl.

"Is he ..."

"Alive? Yes, he is. He's twenty now."

"Dear God."

"Don't bring God into it," Tabitha said. "That will just complicate matters."

Bile rose in his throat. Incipient love had turned to hate in a matter of seconds. He thought he was going to retch. He breathed, slowly, in and out.

As Tabitha batted her eyes at him.

"Is everything all right?" It was the waitress. She was looking at Dylan. He tried to regain composure.

And failed. He couldn't even move his head to look at the waitress.

"He's all right," Tabitha said. "Just had some news. Maybe a little air will do him good. Will you bring me the check, please?"

12

"You're going to need money," Petrie said.

"You gonna give me some?" Jimmy said.

"Sure."

"How much?"

"Ten."

"Grand?"

"What, you think I'm cheap? You think I don't pay for a good job?"

"What job?" Jimmy said.

"You know what job," Petrie said. He and Jimmy were sitting at the far outside table at the barbecue place near the freeway. Jimmy was still working on a rack of baby-back ribs, his mouth rimmed with brown-red sauce.

"I wanna hear you say it," Jimmy said.

"Not here," Petrie said.

"Nobody can hear us," Jimmy said.

"You never know these days," Petrie said. "You been in the joint too long. You don't even have a phone."

"Don't want one," Jimmy said.

"I got no problem with that," Petrie said. "How about a movie tonight? I'm running a couple of Preston Sturges screwball comedies. *The Palm Beach Story* and *The Lady Eve.* What do you say?"

"So who is it?" Jimmy said.

"What?"

"Who!"

Petrie laughed. "What are we doing here, Abbott and Costello? Reminds me, I want to run *Buck Privates*."

"Tell me who I'm supposed to do!" Jimmy said. "A guy or a chick?"

"A guy, of course," Petrie said.

"How come?" Jimmy said.

"How come what?" Petrie said.

"How come you want him gone?"

"You don't have to know how come," Petrie said. "You just have to get it done. Hey, that rhymes!"

"Maybe I wanna know how come," Jimmy said.

Jimmy picked up a soggy napkin and made it soggier by scraping it across his mouth.

Jimmy licked his fingers and took a sip of his Coke. The Coke cup had barbecue sauce stains on it.

"Have we got a deal?" Petrie said.

"Ten large?"

Petrie nodded.

"Paid how?" Jimmy said.

"Two up front. The rest after."

"Half up front," Jimmy said.

Petrie wanted to shove a bone in Jimmy's pie hole and make him swallow. Maybe Petrie could've done it when he was younger. He had wiry strength once. But now the skin under his biceps was beginning to sag. Jimmy's skin was tight over his muscles.

"I'll give you half," Petrie said. "Which is generous."

Jimmy smiled. "Okay, Captain America. We got a deal. Who is it?"

"All you have to know now is, he's a chiropractor. I fill you in on the whole thing later."

"When do you want it done?"

"No more talk now," Petrie said. He was starting to wonder if there was a microphone planted in the coleslaw. He was getting too nervous, he told himself. But it was good nervous because he was closing in.

The whole thing was going to come together just right.

13

"Dear, I've just given you some good news," Tabitha said.

"Good?"

"Your son is alive, and you are going to see him again."

Dylan forced himself to speak. Each word was a brick pushed through mud. "How can I believe you?"

"Why should I want to lie?" she said. "I like you. We like each other, obviously. Didn't you enjoy dinner?"

"Where is my son?"

"He's a handsome young man," she said.

Dylan pounded his fist on the table. A fork bounced up, hit the table's edge, tumbled to the floor.

"Please, dear," Tabitha said.

"Don't call me that," Dylan said.

"But I want to," she said. "This is how love begins."

"How can you"—he lowered his voice—"talk about love?"

"You were going to kiss me tonight, weren't you?"

"Why are you talking this way?"

"Why should this change anything?"

She was cold and crazy! "Tell me about my son. Prove to me he's alive!"

"Why won't you take my word for it?"

"Did you leave those notes?"

"Notes?"

"You know what I'm talking about."

She shook her head. In the dim lighting, Dylan tried to read her face. Then knew it was fruitless. She was only going to let him see what she wanted him to see.

"Honest, honey, I don't," Tabitha said.

The waitress appeared with the check. She placed it on the table in front of Tabitha and said, "No hurry, take your time."

Tabitha smiled and said, "Thank you."

Dylan stared at the salt shaker. That was him, reduced to granules, shaken and under glass, held and controlled by this woman.

Control. That was the issue. He had to take it back.

"Listen," Dylan said, "you can't expect me to swallow all this. Right now I think it's a sick game you're part of, and I am just blown away. You have got to be one of the coldest con artists ... ever."

It sounded lame, but at least it was something.

"Calling me names isn't going to help anyone," Tabitha said, without a flicker of change in her frozen-nice expression. "Especially not Kyle."

"I refuse to believe you without proof," Dylan said.

Smiling, Tabitha said, "You know what let's do? Let's have an after dinner drink. I'll signal the waitress."

"No."

"Yes. Then I can give you some of what you ask for."

"Give it to me now," Dylan said.

"Oh no," Tabitha said. "I really feel like a drink. And then, as we sip together, I'll tell you what Kyle was wearing the day he was taken from the baseball field."

14

Monica went inside to call Sean. Erin poured more wine, liking the easy, cool chardonnay buzz she was feeling. She knew she had to tread carefully. She'd come very close to developing a drinking problem in the second year after Kyle's kidnapping. She'd learned from a counselor that it was the second year, not the first, that was the hardest. You spent the first year doing what you could to cauterize the wound. And then just when you thought it was getting closed up, the anniversary comes and the whole thing is ripped open again. He was right. That ripping was more painful than the original gash to the soul.

Early into that second year, Erin noticed Dylan growing impatient with her tears and unabated anguish. For the first time in their marriage, she felt him drifting, staying away from home longer, not talking to her as much.

She knew full well the stats on divorce for couples going through the trauma they were experiencing. But she'd never, ever thought they could be one of those stats.

They'd met in high school, in Stockton. Dylan was a senior, Erin a sophomore. He was a defensive back for the football team and wanted to do something sports related, maybe coach. She was shy and studious and wanted to be a writer. They didn't seem like a match, but one day Dylan walked by her locker and said, "I'm your density."

She laughed. It was a line from *Back to the Future,* which everyone had seen that year. And it worked. They went on their first date that

Friday. Date! Erin had never been on one. She could hardly believe she was starting at the top, with one of the popular guys. But she was a little wary. She hoped he wouldn't go for a touchdown.

He was a complete gentleman. Plus, there was a surprise. They saw *Witness*, the Harrison Ford movie, and afterward over burgers and fries Dylan mentioned that the movie's style reminded him of *The Grapes of Wrath* and she said, "The movie?" and he said, "And the book."

A football player who read books!

Speaking of which, it was a storybook romance after that, including a knight-in-shining-armor moment. For a few ugly weeks a boy everybody called Weezer was bothering her, chattering at her that she had to go out with him just once, not leaving her alone. He followed her into the girls' bathroom once after school and pushed her against the wall and put his hand under her blouse. Dylan had seen them go in—even the timing was out of a book—and when Weezer tried to get away, Dylan caught him and knocked him out with one punch.

For which Dylan was suspended, but at least Weezer was forced to leave the school. And for the rest of the semester she and Dylan were treated like Robin Hood and Marian.

Yes, storybook, through prom and graduation and a summer of sweet promises.

But then Dylan was off to U. C. Davis, an hour's drive away. The weekend visits grew scarcer. So did the phone calls.

Erin knew what was coming. It started with the old "Let's feel free to see other people" from Dylan. Erin did not want other people.

She cried for a week.

And then it was over, replaced by that uncomfortable silence that pretends you are still friends but will never be filled by the sound of real conversation again.

After graduation, Erin went to UCLA as an English major, and then to Long Beach State for an MFA. Which naturally led to a job at Burger King.

A year later she was a receptionist at a law firm. At least the firm was in Beverly Hills where she could pretend she was doing research for a novel on the rich and famous.

There were some other men in her life. Like the sensitive hipster poet whose free verse ended up costing her $600. That's how much she loaned him that he never paid back.

Then at the firm there was the associate who wanted their affair to be both legal and brief. Erin objected. The associate's wife sustained the objection.

Erin quit the firm and got a job teaching fourth grade at a private school. She began dating a single dad who worked for a music company in Los Angeles. It lasted a year. Then the dad got back together with the mom, and Erin decided to forget men for a while and finish her novel.

Which she did. And began the arduous process of finding an agent.

Seventeen of them turned her down. She got a little bit of encouragement, and one major suggestion: *Can you Danielle Steel this up a bit?*

She was in the process of figuring out what that meant when she took her manuscript and pen to try out the new coffee place everyone was raving about. Yeesh! One small cup of drip coffee cost a dollar twenty-five!

Who drank here? Bankers? Lawyers? Trust-fund babies?

Erin coughed up the dough and settled into a soft chair and began looking over her manuscript.

She was at page ten when she heard someone say, "Small world."

She looked up.

Dylan Reeve said, "Or a big Starbucks."

Erin almost did a spit take.

The chair next to her was open.

They talked for two hours. At the end of which he asked her to dinner.

At the end of dinner, he said, "I was right the first time."

Erin said, "About what?"

Dylan said, "You and me. It's our density."

Six months later they were married.

A year and a half after that, Kyle was born.

What Erin noticed first was the nose. Kyle had the Reeve nose all right, like Dylan and Dylan's father, Rick. And even his grandfather, as family photographs showed. It was what some would call a Roman nose. But Erin liked to call it imperial. As in authoritative and confident. That would be her boy.

"The nose knows," she told Dylan as she breastfed Kyle for the first time.

And in those first years, when Kyle went from baby to toddler to little boy, at odd moments Erin found herself kissing that nose.

Like at bedtime, when Kyle would want her to sing to him. He always wanted "The Star Carol," which Erin sang low and slow.

Long years ago, on a deep winter night,
High in the heavens, a star shone bright ...

Often, at the end, he would be asleep and she would kiss his nose again and imagine it fully mature, on an honor student's face, a handsome face ready to take on any challenge, including which girl to choose from among the many who flocked to him—

Erin, on the balcony, felt her chest constrict. The pictures were coming too fast now—from birth to kindergarten, to tee-ball, to that day, that day ...

"You okay?"

Monica was beside her.

"Hm?"

"You moaned," Monica said.

"I did?"

"A little."

"I guess I'm woozy," Erin said.

"Is that all?"

Needing to get out of the onslaught of images, Erin put up a picture of Anderson Bolt in her mind.

"A younger man has asked me out," Erin said.

"Exsqueeze me?"

"Yeah. At the school."

"How young is younger?"

"Thirty-five."

"Looks?"

"Very nice."

"Define *very*."

"Perfect soap opera doctor," Erin said.

Monica touched Erin's shoulder. "Go for it!"

"I don't know."

"What don't you know? What else do you have going?"

"Do I have to have something going?"

"Of course! Without something going you're just stalled on the side of the road. Plus, you're giving me incredible vicarious pleasure. I want this to play out."

"Maybe *you* should go out with him," Erin said.

"You do the groundwork," Monica said. "We'll talk about handoffs later."

15

"It was a Cubs baseball uniform, of course," Tabitha said. Then she took a sip of her cognac.

Dylan's cognac sat untouched in front of him. Tabitha had placed the order for both of them.

"You were there?" Dylan said.

"Now, dear, let's get a few things out here on the table." She smoothed her hand across the table's surface. "No questions. I will give you the information you need. I know what will make you happy."

How could she be talking like this? "Why are you—"

"Now that's a question." She sipped between smiling lips.

"Well then what ... how am I supposed ..."

"I know it's difficult," she said. "And I'm not being mean, really I'm not. You've been hit with a pretty big shock. I'm well aware of it. But you've been dealing with your loss for fifteen years. A few more weeks won't seem that much."

Dear God, weeks? After some credible evidence that Kyle might be alive, just as she said?

He would explode in days, not weeks. What she was asking was impossible.

"I can read your eyes," Tabitha said. "They are lovely eyes, you know. Even in this light. Troubled, but still lovely. I want to take the trouble away, Dylan. I want you to see that."

She was crazy. But she didn't talk crazy. She spoke with the cool assurance of someone at home, as his grandmother used to say, in her own skin.

"Go on," Tabitha said, nodding at his cognac. "Have a drink."

He shook his head.

"I insist," she said, the smile disappearing for a moment, then returning like a cautious snake peeking out of a hole.

Dylan reached for the glass. His hand was shaking. He couldn't stop it. He put his other hand on the glass and forced some cognac down his throat. It burned.

"That's better," Tabitha said. "Now, I want you to know some things. First of all, Kyle has been well taken care of. He's healthy. He's happy. He's working. He has a girlfriend. He's planning on going to college in the fall."

Dylan said, "Please, let me see him."

"Now, dear, let's—"

"Don't call me dear!"

"What would you prefer?"

"I prefer you not call me anything, just—"

"That's not the way love works," Tabitha said.

"Don't you dare talk about love," he said.

"Don't you dare tell me what I can and cannot talk about."

A cold, steely silence walled between them for a long moment.

Tabitha broke it with a warm voice. "Let me lay things out, dear. I know you're suffering. I do. And I don't want that. I want you to feel hope. Something you haven't felt for a long time, I'm guessing. You've lived with terrible uncertainty, I know. I'm going to help you get over it."

A counselor from hell, Dylan thought.

She said, "Now, some things up front. I am going to assume that you'll want to go to the police or the FBI or some desperate move like that. Should you do so, you will never see Kyle again. Nothing will happen to me. I will have all the evidence I need to convince anyone that you snapped and started accusing me of laying out an unbelievable story. I have the waitress here, who saw that you were acting strange. I have a record of our emails and texts, demonstrating my sweet spirit. I will be able to convince them that you hit me, because we both know the climate in this country gives women all the leverage with such an accusation. Understand?"

Hell wasn't low enough for this woman.

"Further," she said, "I am going to assume that you will try to get a recording of my voice when we speak. So when we're together I'll not say a single thing to implicate me until I'm sure you're not wired or activating your phone. If I suspect at any time that you have told anyone, including your ex-wife, about any of this, I will disappear and you will never see Kyle. You see, I want you to see him. I want you to know him."

"What do you want from me?"

"Again with the question. But I will answer it, so you know my motives are pure. I do want you to be happy."

"Why?"

'That's one question too many," Tabitha said. "And we have had a very heavy meal. Both the food and the conversation, right?"

She finished her cognac, closing her eyes and savoring it.

"Now I will pay the check," she said. "Then I'll walk you to your car. I will kiss you on the cheek and tell you that I can't wait to do this again."

"You can't leave it like that."

"Why not, dear?"

He had no answer. Of course she could leave it like that, or any way she wanted to. At this point, she had a death grip on his subclavian artery. She could squeeze and squeeze. Sure, he could break away, but that would mean never seeing Kyle.

If she was telling the truth.

He had to know.

In the parking lot she did just as she said she would. Kissed him on the cheek. Quickly, so he couldn't pull away. It was more like her lips were a dart and his cheek the dartboard.

"Now don't you worry," she said. "And don't do anything impulsive, like try to follow me. Just trust me. Everything is going to be all right."

16

Driving home was like hurtling through a dark tube in one of those water parks. Nothing visual registered around him, nothing but the strip of asphalt illuminated by his headlights.

He managed to park in his driveway without smashing the hedge. As he made his way toward his door, he smelled the familiar acridity of his next-door neighbor's Camel cigarette.

Cesar Biggins sat on his porch nearly every evening. He would smoke and sometimes play the spoons. Real spoons. Silver. From his dead wife's set. A way, he once told Dylan, of connecting with her through vibration.

"Cesar, you got a second?" Dylan said.

The shadowy form leaned forward on his wicker chair and said, "Hours I got." And then coughed.

Dylan guessed that Cesar Biggins was in his mid-seventies. Dylan never met the late Mrs. Biggins, as she had died some five years before Dylan moved in.

Cesar Biggins had been a clown for the Ringling Bros., Barnum & Bailey Circus. Now he was a wizened and rail-thin widower, grieving with silverware, and smoking himself to death.

Dylan sat in the other wicker chair on the porch. The chair creaked and crackled. It was only a matter of time before someone's rear end would break through.

"You been to the doc lately?" Dylan asked.

"What for?" Cesar said. "I'm in the pink." He coughed again, then took a drag on his cigarette.

"Let's switch you over to vaping?"

"To what?"

"Water vapor."

"Eh. I heard of that."

"It has all the nicotine you want. What it doesn't have is the tar coating your lungs. What would you think about that?"

"Water? You kidding?"

"It's perfectly healthy and helps people live longer. So naturally California wants to regulate it out of existence."

"This crazy state," Cesar said.

"I need to ask you a question," Dylan said.

"So ask."

"Have you been out here much this week?"

"Every night," Cesar said.

"Have you noticed any strange people wandering around?"

"All the time," Cesar said. "All we seem to have any more is strange people."

"How about the last couple of nights? Someone alone."

"You looking for somebody in particular?"

"I thought I heard some strange goings-on outside my front door."

"Salesman. Or Jehovah's Witnesses. Can't tell the difference anymore. People want to sell you solar panels, stucco your house—can you imagine stucco on this house? Or they paint your address on the curb and then knock on the door and expect you to pay 'em. My answer to that is just don't answer the door. Can I offer you a beer?"

"Another time," Dylan said.

Cesar stubbed out his Camel in a stuffed ashtray on a small table. He removed a fresh one from the pack and lit up.

"You know why I got out of clowning?" Cesar said. "I got tired of taking the pie. In circus world, you are the pie taker or the pie thrower. They liked me to be the taker because I had the sad face. Oh, I got my licks in, rubber hammer and all that. But sitting there taking it night after night, being the set-up man, I got tired of it. And you know what I decided? I'm gonna be the one that throws the pies first. That didn't go over with the star clown, and he got me fired."

Dylan nodded politely. "I better get home," he said.

"Remember that," Cesar said.

"Remember?"

"Throw the first pie. If somebody is worrying you, throw the first pie."

The wisdom of clowns.

And somehow it made sense.

17

Dylan flicked on the lights, half expecting to see another envelope on the floor.

Nothing. The hardwood floor was mockingly clean.

He tossed his car keys on the hall table and went to the family room. He plopped into a chair. What irony. As if there was a family to share this room. Or ever would, now. He'd started to allow himself a little hope that Tabitha might be someone he could share his life with. Yes, it was early, but you get a sense of these things from the start. It had been that way with Erin. She wasn't one of the popular girls in school, but there was something about her, an intelligence and vulnerability, that drew him.

He'd had that same feeling about Tabitha Mullaney until she played him like a prime sucker.

He looked at the fireplace. And at the wrought iron tool set that stood on the hearth. The set his grandfather had owned, passed down to Dylan. A shovel, poker, and brush. Black, with shepherd's handles. Tools, yes, but in a pinch the poker could be a weapon. Dylan was aware of a strange sense of exhilaration building within him. Powerless as he was at Tabitha's game, he sensed the voice of Gadge Garner. Fight. You have to fight. And in that very acceptance comes a deep, atavistic, natural attention of the nerves and the senses, an aliveness. In a crude way he was almost thankful this was happening. He'd not felt this kind of fighting spirit for a decade, since he'd given up hope of ever seeing Kyle again.

Cesar was right. You can't sit around and wait to get hit with a pie. You have to hit first.

But what could he do? Tabitha—if that was even her name—held all the pies. He didn't know where she lived, what she drove. He had her phone number and a voicemail.

He also had a feeling—one that told him she was perfectly capable of making things worse.

18

T. J. Petrie was a man of many loves.

He loved the Three Stooges. And Schopenhauer. And a good hot dog, the kind that snaps when you bite into it and it sends fatty juices over your tongue. He put that right alongside *duck l'orange*, when the skin was crisp and chewy but not tough. He loved a chef who knew his art.

He loved the theater, the legit theater, which was not the overpriced and ubiquitous Broadway musical revivals, usually starring some hack television actor trying to sing for the first time.

He saw David Suchet in *Amadeus*. Loved it. That was some great acting! And the play itself, magnificent. It asked the profound question, why would God allow artistic genius, so rare in this world, to be possessed by an unworthy slob like Mozart? Why not Salieri, who worked so hard and lusted so deeply for recognition? Salieri had declared himself the enemy of God. That was what made him a chump. T. J. Petrie had merely declared God his competitor.

He loved winning, did T. J. Petrie.

Most of all, he loved the movies. Especially the silents. And especially the god of all actors, Lon Chaney.

T. J. Petrie also loved identity theft. When he started using it twenty years ago, he could not anticipate the high it gave him. To actually take someone else's life, suck most of the financial juices out of it and never get caught, that was the ultimate in theatrical.

And now as he sat at the upscale bar, sipping a gin martini, paying for it with cash, T. J. Petrie reflected on his ability to control his emotions and adjust his plans accordingly. For that is what he had to do now.

His immediate reaction had been anger, the kind that he had long ago learned to subdue. He had studied Greek tragedy. He had seen Patrick Stewart as Oedipus Rex. He knew what a tragic flaw was, and that he was stronger than any flaw.

He also knew that he had to tread carefully, which is why he would allow himself only one martini before going on a long walk in the evening air.

Outside he would think about how everything was coming together now. And he would rehearse in his mind how he was going to reveal it all to Erin Reeve.

19

"So tell me about yourself," Andy said.

"Oh my gosh," Erin said.

"What?"

"I should be asking *you* that. You could be my younger brother. Way younger."

Erin was still processing this whole thing. She was actually on a lunch date with Andy Bolt. The question was why? Was it because she was curious? Actually attracted to him? (This was the leading contender.)

Or was it simply because she wanted to feel something other than the dull ache of being alone in her condo?

She did feel something of the rush she got when starting a race. But did she really think this had any possibility of turning into a marathon?

But come on, that age difference was real. As real as a gap in a canyon. Maybe not Grand Canyon wide, but big enough.

They were sitting at a table in that little bistro on Wilshire, the one near the Los Angeles County Museum of Modern Art. Andy had offered to drive out to the Valley to pick Erin up, but she thought driving herself to neutral territory would be the better option.

And if things went well—she could hardly believe she was contemplating this—they could easily extend this Saturday afternoon by strolling over to LACMA.

Andy said, "I wish you wouldn't bring that up."

Erin said, "But it's true."

"Truth is malleable."

"Malleable?"

"I don't believe in fixed truth," Andy said. "We all interact with the things in this world and our perceptions shape what we think the truth is."

"Whoa! Where did that come from?"

Andy smiled. "I took a little philosophy in college and kept it up after I dropped out."

"Why'd you drop out?"

"To make money. I don't think philosophy majors are buying BMWs."

"Is that what you want? A BMW?"

"You're asking if I'm materialistic."

"Maybe."

"Aren't we all?" he said.

"I don't think so," she said.

"You want a roof over your head. Nice clothes, good food. That sort of thing."

"Sure."

"That's all I'm saying. And if the things I want are nice quality, what's wrong with that?"

"I guess I'd like to know what else you're about," Erin said.

Andy smiled. "And I'm the one who started off asking you to tell me about yourself. You sure know how to turn things around."

A waiter came by to take their drink order and to see if they had any questions.

Yes, young man, do you think I'm crazy for being here? That's my question.

Erin ordered a Diet Coke. Andy asked for an Arnold Palmer.

"I'm from the Midwest," Andy said. "I came out here to get into the real estate market. I aim to be a top producer."

"Good," Erin said. "That's what we like to see coming out of DeForest."

"Maybe you can put me on your home page. I'll be your cover boy."

Boy.

"Andy, I'm really very flattered that you asked me out."

"Uh-oh. I hear a *but* coming."

"No, I—"

"Go ahead. Cards on the table."

"No cards, really. This is nice, it is, only ..."

"*Only* is just like *but.*"

He said it with a smile. Erin smiled, too. "But nice is really all it can be, right?"

"Am I boorish and ungainly?" Andy said.

"Of course not!"

"Have I got all my teeth?"

"All right—"

"You should know one more thing."

"What's that?"

"I'm a good kisser," he said.

And as his eyes danced Erin felt a burning inside her, a desire to find out if he really was, a deep want to be kissed again, passionately. And just as quickly she jumped over that hunger with an equal desire to run and keep on running, right down Wilshire Boulevard, and not stop until she got to the ocean.

"Andy, I need to tell you something," she said.

"Where we'll go to dinner?" he said.

"Seriously," she said. "I was married for nine years to a man I was deeply in love with. We had a tragedy. Our son, when he was five, was kidnapped. He was never found."

"Oh, Erin." He reached for her hand.

She pulled her hands to her lap, looked at them.

"We ended up getting divorced," she said. "It's all come back recently, the memory of it, and we're going through that together, in a small way, but a way that's deep. I don't know if I can explain it any better than that."

"Which means you're putting your love life on hold?"

"I'm not even thinking about that."

"Maybe you should."

"But I'm not."

"I can be persistent," he said.

"I'm not some prospect you can use sales techniques on, okay?"

"I'm sorry. You're right. I need to know when to back off."

Erin suppressed a smile. But it must have showed, because Andy said, "What?"

"I was just thinking," Erin said. "Sometimes, in a race, if you're in the lead, the runner behind can lull you into a false sense of security by falling back."

"Is that what you think I'm doing?" His voice had a bit more edge to it than before.

"I'm sorry," Erin said. "That was unfair of me."

Andy tapped the table with his index finger. After a long moment he said, "Maybe not. Maybe you have the power of perception. Maybe I have it, too. It's what makes me a good salesman and you a good ..."

"A good what?"

"A good person for me to be with," he said.

20

Dylan spent most of Saturday afternoon with Gadge Garner and his team of two, installing a top-of-the-line camera system. All expenses paid by Jaquez Rollins.

When the installation was finished, Gadge dismissed his team and sat Dylan down in the living room for a tutorial. Everything was covered with cams—front, back, sides. There would be constant digital recording, and live feeds to an app on Dylan's phone.

"A cat chasing a lizard won't go unnoticed," Garner said.

Dylan nodded.

"Anything new?" Garner said.

Dylan knew what he meant. "No," he said.

Garner gave him a long, careful look.

"What?" Dylan said.

"You were warned not to talk to anybody, weren't you?"

Unable to keep a straight face, Dylan said, "Am I that obvious?"

"No," Garner said. "I'm that good. And I don't give up confidences. I don't do things unless somebody wants me to. Okay?"

It was comforting to have him here, an expert like this. Dylan was on a ledge already. What was the risk of a step or two around a blind corner?

"Let's talk," Dylan said.

"Good," Garner said. "Do you have any liquid refreshment?"

Dylan got a couple of Coronas from the fridge. He brought them to the living room, handed one to Garner.

The security man nodded his thanks, took a sip, and said, "Have you talked to your ex-wife about DNA?"

"I'm going to see her tomorrow," Dylan said.

"Those notes you mentioned. Can I see them?"

"Of course."

"Don't touch them with your fingers. You have plastic wrap?"

"Yes," Dylan said. "But I've already touched them myself."

"Of course you have. But let's not add anything."

Dylan went to the kitchen and pulled out a box of plastic wrap from a drawer. He had to fight the roll to get a grip on the edge. Fingernails and a curse word did the trick and he finally had a swatch of the stuff. He put it over his hand like a makeshift glove.

Taking the box of wrap with him, Dylan went to his computer desk and got the notes from the right-hand drawer. He carried them to the living room like they were bottles of nitro.

Garner put his Corona on the glass table. He expertly covered his hands with plastic wrap, somehow giving himself opposable thumbs.

He took the notes from Dylan, unfolded them, read them. Then he held the first one toward the window where the sun was streaming through. He turned it slowly.

"Plain white, twenty-pound bond," he said.

He turned it some more, looked at the edge with one eye, waving it slowly like a fan. "Israeli trick. I can see what are probably your prints. It's where you naturally would have held it. Could be tested, but if the guy was careful not to seal the envelopes, I doubt he'd leave prints on the paper. I'm saying *he* because of the block letters and heavy print. This is a man's work."

"You can really tell that?"

"Ninety percent," Garner said. He repeated the same exercise with the other note. Then he folded them and placed them on the far side of the glass table. He removed his makeshift gloves.

"Ninety-five percent," Garner said.

"There's something you don't know," Dylan said.

"There's lots I don't know," Garner said. "Like why people watch the Kardashians."

"Good point," Dylan said. "What do you know about women?"

"No man knows anything about women," Garner said.

"I just found that out," Dylan said.

"Tell me about it."

And so he did. Dylan told Garner the whole story up to its bizarre conclusion in the restaurant parking lot.

After Dylan finished, Garner did not speak for a long moment. He took a contemplative sip of his Corona, then set the bottle down again.

"It's a team," he said finally. "At least one man and one woman. And they are not amateurs. Think what it took to get to you online, to get you to connect for a couple of dates. What was it that made you say yes?"

"I think it was her sense of humor," Dylan said. "She and I seemed to laugh at the same things in our past."

"Like what?"

"*Saturday Night Live.*"

"Back when it was funny?"

"Eddie Murphy, Joe Piscopo."

"Is there any way she could have learned that about you beforehand?"

"I don't see how."

"Social media. Ever talk about it on Facebook?"

"I don't do Facebook."

"So you're the one," Garner said. "How about other places?"

"Not that I can think of."

"Do you and this woman have friends in common?"

Dylan shook his head.

Gadge Garner took a long pull on his Corona, then said, "She hasn't brought up the issue of money?"

"Not yet."

"She's monkey-dancing you. Pulling a string. This may not be about money."

"What else could it be?"

"Revenge."

Dylan stared at him, the chill of that word working its way up his neck.

"Do you trust your ex-wife?" Garner said.

"Of course."

"You got divorced."

"That had nothing to do with trusting her. Why are you saying that?"

"I did a job for a guy once. His ex-wife was the sweetest little thing you ever saw. Two years after the divorce she claimed he was a rapist and wife beater. Almost went to trial. Turned out she was mad about the prenup, that he wouldn't modify it in any way. If I hadn't managed to get a recording of her talking to her boyfriend about it, she might've ruined the guy's life."

"There's no way," Dylan said.

"Just covering all bases," Gadge Garner said. "Think about it, though. Revenge, I mean. Somebody with something against you."

"I've tried."

"Try harder," Garner said.

21

Erin was about to get into bed when her phone buzzed. The number was private. Normally she would let it go. But things were not normal.

"Hello?"

"Hey, Erin!" A man's voice.

"Who is this, please?"

"Somebody who really, really wants to help you." A tense excitement in the tone, like somebody operating on too many cups of coffee.

She took a chance. "You're the one who left those notes for my husband."

"Your ex-husband."

"What game is this you're playing?

"I am very good at games," the man said, with a lilt that was almost childlike. "You should see me. You know, I think you will."

"What does that even mean?"

"Listen, I'm here to help. Really. You've got to believe me, Erin. I need you to."

"How do you know my name?"

"Listen! Your husband—I mean your ex-husband—may be about to do some stupid things, because he's a man and men do stupid things when a woman begins to wrap them around her little, painted finger. Just so you know. But I am going to look out for you. Both of you."

"What do you mean, both?"

"You will soon know."

"What is it you want?" Erin said. "Money?"

"Money is as money does," the man said. "No, this is the deal. I'm going to call you again. When I do, you may be tempted to try to record the call or something like that. Don't. Please don't. I want to help you. If you do something like that I'll know. I have ways of knowing. I have—"

"Do you have my son?" Erin said.

"Get a good night's sleep, Erin," he said. "You need your sleep."

There would be no sleep. She knew that. She walked around her condo for ten minutes, twenty. Put on music. Poured a glass of red wine. Sipped it outside on the balcony.

When she came back in she was more awake than when she'd received the call.

Games. He was in her head with his games.

Control your thoughts.

Like you told Kyle to do that one time, when he said he couldn't sleep because he kept thinking about a monster. And you sat on the bed and told him he could think a new thought, and he should try to think of the beach and the ocean, because they'd been to a beach house in Ventura that September. Kyle loved the ocean, standing in the wet sand as the waves came up.

Think of the ocean, you told him. Standing there in the sand and hearing the waves. Close your eyes and imagine it. Smell the smell, remember? And the waves, gentle waves, one after the other.

You sat there until his breathing got steady, and soon he slept.

Control your thoughts.

She tried. She even thought of the same beach, the vision of Kyle, but the sound of the waves was interrupted by another sound, and try as she might she could not drown it out.

It was the sound of his voice saying, *"I am going to look out for you. Both of you."*

22

In the morning, Dylan drove to the Valley to see Erin. She'd called last night wanting to get together. Something she wanted to talk about, but in person. He found himself glad to be seeing her again so soon.

It was Sunday and traffic was light. If only L.A. could always be this way. That's how Angelenos thought when their freeways actually moved. No accidents. No slowdowns.

Unlike life, Dylan mused. He was coming through the Cahuenga Pass, toward Universal Studios and all the overpriced distractions up there. That was the way you did life now, wasn't it? Put up enough lights and rides and food courts and movie houses and merch stores and you won't have the time or the quiet to think about how relentless life is.

Driving by the exit for Universal he saw a billboard, and lost breath. A big, new, splashy ad for the latest attraction at the Harry Potter world. Something about night and lights and Hogwarts castle.

The smiling face of the flying boy-wizard loomed, seemed to be staring right at Dylan.

How long had the sign been there? Of course he knew about the Wizarding World of Harry Potter at Universal. It was one of the biggest SoCal attractions in recent memory. It staggered him when he first read about the plans. Another place he would never get to take Kyle. A place that would have lit up his son's face, even at age twenty. It would have been one of those nostalgic trips—*Remember how you loved that Potter*

Lego set as a kid? You wouldn't play with anything else. Let's go see what they've got at Universal. You, me and Mom. I'm buying.

He got off at Vineland and drove to Erin's street, found a place to park. Erin buzzed him into her complex. She was waiting for him upstairs at her open front door.

She was dressed in weekend casual—blue jeans and a long-sleeve Dodgers T-shirt. Her hair and makeup were, as always, attractive. But the face muscles underneath were tight.

Erin had coffee brewed and handed Dylan a cup. She'd remembered he took it black. Then he watched as she poured herself a cup, added a dollop of Half-and-Half and tablespoon of sugar, and stirred. Just like she had virtually every morning when they were married.

They sat on the balcony, and Erin said, "I got a call last night. I'm sure it's the guy who sent you that note."

"There was another one," Dylan said.

"What did it say?"

Dylan hesitated.

"What?" Erin said.

"I don't want to upset you."

"I'm already there," Erin said. "What did it say?"

"It said Kyle's favorite toy was Lego Harry Potter and the Chamber of Secrets."

Erin gasped. She put her coffee cup on the table. Then she interlocked her fingers and squeezed her hands together.

"He has him," she said.

"Or just knew us back then," Dylan said.

"He said he was good at games. And then something about you. He said you were going to do something stupid. With a woman."

Dylan tried to get his thoughts in order.

"Is there a woman?" Erin said.

"A woman I started seeing, yes."

"So what's this stupid thing he's talking about?"

Dylan said, "It's some kind of con. I think in the end it will be about money. I met this woman, her name's Tabitha, through a dating site. She set me up somehow. She seemed nice and all, then hit me between the eyes. She told me if I wanted to see Kyle again I'd have to do exactly what she said. That she could be so cold about it. I've never met anybody like that."

"You don't deserve that," Erin said.

At that moment Dylan wanted to hold his ex-wife, as if they had never been apart, as if all the pain of the last fifteen years was gone and Kyle was with them, visiting from college. The thought flashed through him like a butane flame and went out almost immediately.

"So there's two of them," Dylan said. "This woman I'm seeing and the guy who called you, who sent those notes. He's working you, she's working me. We can't just sit here and let them do it. Do you still have that box of Kyle's clothes?"

A year after Kyle's kidnapping, Erin had carefully folded all of Kyle's clothes and put them in three plastic boxes, with sealing lids. They'd stayed in the garage until the divorce.

"They're at my mom's house," Erin said.

"Did you ever open them since you packed?"

Erin shook her head.

"I'm working with a security guy Jaquez Rollins set me up with."

"The Laker?"

"The biggest Laker," Dylan said. "His guy is Gadge Garner. He thought if we could get DNA maybe it would match from one of the national databases."

"How do you access those?"

"Garner will do it," Dylan said. "But we have to be careful. We have to assume they are tracking us somehow. Seeing if we go to the police or FBI."

"So what are we supposed to do?"

"Go over to your mom's," Dylan said. "See if you can smuggle those boxes of Kyle's clothes into your trunk."

"Smuggle?"

"Exactly. Like you were a drug dealer trying to fool a stakeout."

"You think it's really that bad?" Erin said.

"I don't want to take any chances with these people."

Erin put out her hand. Dylan took it. They said nothing for a long time.

23

Dylan decided to take the 134 to the 5 and avoid downtown. He'd seen enough of that hub. The 5 would take him past Dodger Stadium, another memory of Kyle. It was on his fourth birthday that Dylan and Erin took him to his first major league baseball game. It was against the Cincinnati Reds and it went into extra innings. The Dodgers won in the bottom of the 14th, by which time Kyle, filled with a Dodger Dog and copious amounts of peanuts, was asleep on Dylan's lap.

It was just after he passed Stadium Way that Dylan got a call on his Bluetooth system.

He punched connect without speaking.

Tabitha's voice was measured and cool, like a jealous girlfriend. "Did you have a nice visit with your ex-wife?"

He was in his car, almost home. The day was murky with low-level smog.

"The one thing I cannot take," Tabitha said, "is disloyalty."

Dylan wanted to throw his phone out of the car, into a rain gutter, where it would fall and smash and be nibbled by rats. He wanted the phone to turn into Tabitha before the rats finished eating. He wanted to go full Stephen King on her.

"Are you still there, dear?" she said.

"Talk," he said.

"I know you're very upset now, and that going to your ex you probably tried to come up with some sort of plan of action. Am I right?"

Dylan stayed silent. How could she know all this?

"You're going to have to answer me, honey."

"No," he said. "It's over."

"Excuse me?"

"You can have him."

Silence.

"You can keep him," Dylan said.

"Ah," she said, "you are calling my bluff, as they say."

"Whatever. Good-bye."

"I suppose you want proof he's alive and well?"

"I don't care anymore."

"I think you do."

"Think anything you want."

"I don't like this game you're playing with me," Tabitha said. "I don't like it one bit."

"Tough."

"And you shouldn't like it either, because I can take it up a notch."

"Don't bother calling me again, *dear.*"

Dylan killed the call.

He was breathing hard. But there was freedom in the breath.

She called again.

He didn't answer.

She left a voice message.

He didn't listen.

Until five hours later.

24

Erin's mother lived in Sylmar. She'd moved there after Erin's father, Frank, died of a massive heart attack at age fifty-seven. A former school teacher, Lily Peterson had spent a year in deep mourning, as his death had turned into the second shot from a double-barreled tragedy. He died only two months after Kyle had been taken.

Lily found she could not work, and so had taken time off from Melvin Avenue Elementary School, then decided she didn't have her heart in it any more. She sold the Reseda house that Erin had grown up in and moved to Sylmar, to a smaller place, but one that left her with some equity to invest. Dylan did that for her, and the results had been enough so that Lily could work part-time and get along just fine.

If by just fine you meant walking around with a sadness that was equal to Erin's. But while Erin had started to move upward the last few years, Lily seemed on the downslope. Now it was daughter taking care of mother time.

Except today. The visit here was for one purpose only. And to get back without too many questions.

The first question came from Lily, with the familiar tone of impending doom that seemed to have crept into all her inquiries since the death of Frank Peterson. "How are you feeling these days?" Lily said, placing her hand on Erin's arm.

Lily was now seventy-two. Her hair, once a robust auburn, was ashen-colored and flat.

"Mom, I'm fine," Erin said.

"You sure?"

"Absolutely," Erin lied, and pushed inside the house. It was an odd mix of items from Erin's childhood, like the sofa where she'd spent many an afternoon watching *Happy Days* (she loved The Fonz) and *Chico and the Man* (she loved Freddie Prinze). And the dining room set with laminate table and polypropylene chairs. These, alongside the new things that had no discernible matching qualities. IKEA by way of thrift store central.

"Let me fix you some lunch," Lily said.

"I'm only here for a short visit, Mom," Erin said. "I have to get back. I just wanted to see you and pick something up."

"Oh?" she said, heading for the kitchen. "Just a snack then. What would you like to drink?"

"Honest, Mom, I can't stay. I need to get something from the garage. Can I go out and look?"

"The garage? What is it you need?"

"Oh, just some boxes that you've been storing here."

"Oh my." The sound of Lily's voice was not comforting.

"What?" Erin said.

Her mother faced her, and her complexion matched her hair. She had one hand on her cheek.

"Mom, what is it?"

"The garage," she said "I had it ..."

"You had it what?"

"Cleaned out."

"Of everything?"

"I—"

"Mother, without even asking me?"

"I forgot. I mean, I didn't know."

"I had three boxes of Kyle's clothes. You knew that!"

"I honestly don't remember, honey. I mean, I do. But at the time ..."

Erin cut off the words coming at her by way of a silent scream. She'd filled her head this way often in the first few years after Kyle was taken. It dulled the pain and shut out whatever it was she did not want to deal with. And now it came back to her, full volume, for with the news that the boxes were not there it was like losing Kyle all over again.

As she ran toward the door connecting washroom to garage, Erin thought she heard her mother crying. She did not stop to check.

The garage was pretty much emptied out. A few tools, a coiled hose, the water heater. Up in the rafters, nothing. That was where the boxes had been the last time she saw them.

She had a feeling of falling then, like in those old cartoons with the coyote and roadrunner. No matter what the coyote did, he always ended up dropping hundreds of feet and making a little cloud of dust when he hit bottom.

She got ready to hit bottom.

It didn't come. She made herself hover in the air, again cartoon-like. Hover and figure out what to do.

She went back in the house and found her mother sitting at the kitchen table, head in her hands.

Erin knelt and put her arm around her shoulder.

"I'm so sorry ..." her mother said.

"Me too," Erin said.

"I didn't think."

"Sh."

"It's been so long since ..."

"I know."

"Some poor child will have them, and they'll do good."

"Poor child?"

"Those boxes went to the Salvation Army."

Erin sat back. "How long ago?"

"It was only last week."

Erin stood. "Which one?"

"I think ... Lake View Terrace."

"I wonder if ..."

"It's possible," her mother said. She took Erin's hands. "Dear God, it's possible."

25

Silent movie night at the Bijou. Petrie still got that old feeling in his loins. Something about that world, the silents, dark and mysterious. With its great god Chaney.

Tonight he was screening *Tell It to the Marines*. Not his favorite Chaney. He was too human in this one. But of course he didn't get the girl, and that was reason enough. Those looks on his face. Enough to make you watch the whole thing.

He was standing by the popcorn machine when old Mr. Weathers approached. He came to every single silent movie. He said his father used to tell him about the great silents. Now, here in Lancaster, at a theater that had been marked for demolition, they were back. With a live organist, too.

"Another Lon Chaney, eh?" Mr. Weathers said. He was in his mid-eighties, walked a little stooped over. But he always had a smile on his face.

"The greatest actor ever," T. J. Petrie said.

"Thank you for doing this," Mr. Weathers said.

"You're welcome. Thank you for coming."

"I love what you're doing with this place. I remember when it started going downhill. When it started showing all those arty movies. Who was that Swedish guy?"

"Ingmar Bergman?" Petrie said.

"That's the one. Made me want to hang myself. Thanks for bringing back the classics. Like *Casablanca*."

"My pleasure, sir."

"And another thing, I hate to mention it ..."

"What is it?"

"You always have such clean bathrooms."

"We want our customers happy,"

"Yes, you do. But, well, it's not tip top right now. There's a smell. I just thought you ought to know."

"I do want to know," Petrie said.

"The young man who cleans it, maybe he hasn't been in there yet."

"Oh yes he has," Petrie said. "I'll make sure he goes back in there. Pronto."

"He's a nice boy, even if he's a little slow."

"Not so slow that he won't understand what I tell him," Petrie said. "Enjoy the movie, Mr. Weathers."

26

Dylan, at home, circled his phone as if it were radioactive. It sat on his coffee table, inert and secretive, holding inside it a message he knew he would listen to. Eventually. Because in the end it really was about Kyle. She had the upper hand, the leverage, the aces. His bluff about not caring was mere puffery. He knew he couldn't walk away, and she knew he knew.

Still, making the message wait felt like a momentary victory. But a child's victory, about as meaningful as *I know you are but what am I*?

Then it was time to stop being a child. He sat down and played the message. Tabitha's voice was as clear and calm as the first time they'd met.

"Dearest, I need you to know that I forgive you. I'm not hurt, except for a bruise on my arm. You don't know your own strength, baby. I know you've got some demons in your past and that maybe they come out like this. I don't want this to break us up. One of the things people do when they love each other is work through things, you know? I'm willing, if you are. I'm willing to say it was just a burst of anger that came from stress or something. We can deal with that, I know we can. Call me when you can. One more meeting. Hear me out. You didn't mean the last thing you said to me, about not caring. I guarantee it. And I miss you already."

A thousand spiders spun a web around Dylan's mind, binding his thoughts, sticky and secure. He awaited giant mandibles.

Who was he dealing with here? Someone clever enough to reel him in via a dating service. To pose and charm. And he fell for it like one of those saps in film noir.

He had no doubt she had a self-inflicted bruise on her arm. And now had left a few breadcrumbs in the form of a voice message, which could lead an inquiring police detective to question Dylan.

If they searched his phone.

He could just delete it.

But wasn't the message up in a cloud somewhere?

Could she plant it?

Could he get any more paranoid?

All he had on his side were those two notes, but she could deny any knowledge of them.

If she was this careful, this clever, maybe she did have a lead on where Kyle was.

But if so, why hadn't she asked for money?

And if not, why this elaborate play?

27

The man at the front desk of the Salvation Army said, "May I help you?"

Erin said, "My mother donated some boxes to you about a week ago."

The man was thin and sixtyish, with wispy white hair and glasses that perched on the lower portion of his nose. He looked at Erin over the lenses. "Oh?"

"It had some things in it that I need. Is it possible it's still here?"

He smiled. "You ever heard of the needle in the haystack?"

"That bad?"

"Could be. Cardboard boxes?"

"Plastic, you know, with a lid that snaps on. The boxes were clear and the lids were blue."

"I personally don't recall."

"Is there any way to check?"

"You know, these items are donated. They belong to the Salvation Army."

"I'm aware. I'd pay for it. I'll make a donation. If only I can check."

"That important?"

"Yes."

"You look serious."

"As the proverbial heart attack," she said.

His reserve changed to a sympathetic warmth. "Let's not have one of those. Come on then, we'll give it a try."

He took her to a back room that was stuffed with boxes, bags, books, shelves, clothes on hangers on portable rods, appliances, furniture, toys, and at least one canoe.

"Welcome to my world," he said.

"How long have these things been here?" Erin asked.

"Varies. You're welcome to look around."

"Thank you."

She began making her way around the space, scanning for a visual of the box. But the boxes she saw were all cardboard. Some of them were hidden behind piles of clothes or chairs or some other obstruction. She powered past every one.

At one point she accidentally kicked a paper bag full of books. The bag burst and the books spilled out, sliding like dominoes upon each other. She looked upon them, fascinated, as if the accident were a casting of lots in a cultic ritual.

Amused, she took note of two Danielle Steel novels, a book about the interpretation of dreams, and a chili cookbook.

But it was the last one that kicked her in the heart. It was a big, glossy encyclopedia about the TV series *Lost*.

She almost burst out laughing and crying at the same time.

Lost indeed!

And she wasn't going to take it. She picked up the book and threw it. It sailed over pile of clothes and landed on the other side with a hollow thunk.

Erin followed it.

And there it was, the book of *Lost,* sitting on top of a large plastic box with a blue top.

28

Petrie said, "Biggest thing is, you don't kill him."

Carbona shrugged.

"You want to get paid," Petrie said, "you make sure it doesn't happen."

Petrie had paid a lot of money to Carbona in the past. He was a professional. The consummate pro, he once bragged. So he better be able to follow instructions. To the letter. Or this whole thing, this meticulous and beautiful plan, would crumble at the very end. Petrie could not allow that to happen. If it did, and Carbona was the reason, he would make sure the big man suffered. Carbona, ex-LAPD, had smarts. But he wasn't as smart as Petrie. No one was.

"I better get all the money," Carbona said. In his floppy Hawaiian shirt, Carbona resembled a middle-aged Margaritaville fan. But his eyes were straight whiskey. "I'm hitting the road after this one."

"You'll get it," Petrie said, "if you deliver a live package."

When they first did business together Petrie was running a low-level meth trade out in Mojave. A biker named Steele had recommended Carbona's security services. When they first met Carbona tried to put the fear of Satan in to T. J. Petrie. Having studied the ways of the devil himself, Petrie laughed inside.

He'd agreed to give Carbona two million cash. The one hundred grand Petrie already paid him might never be recovered, but that was a small price to pay for the plan. And Carbona would never see the rest of it.

Carbona said, "How much does that retard know? The one you let hang around?"

"Leave him out of this."

"I don't like him."

"I'll take care of him," Petrie said. "I always have."

"He makes me nervous."

"You're getting paid not to be nervous."

Carbona smiled. He had perfect teeth. Petrie had to give him that.

29

To breathe, to clear his mind, Dylan walked the mile to John Greenleaf Whittier Park in the center of old town. He liked the friendly little swath of green that took up one block. It had a play area for the kids, and even a statue of old Whittier himself, a somewhat forgotten figure in American letters.

When Dylan first moved here and discovered the park, he did some research on Mr. Whittier. He was a poet and devout Quaker who became an early leader of the abolitionist movement in America. He also hobnobbed with people like Mark Twain, Ralph Waldo Emerson, and Oliver Wendell Holmes.

A good and noble man, everyone said. Which, when he thought about it, was all Dylan wanted to be. He was certainly no poet. But he was a darn good chiropractor and he had modeled his life on the idea of decency.

Which was why this whole matter of Tabitha Mullaney was such a swift kick to the gut. Oh, not that he was naive about people's capacity for evil deeds. But that such a person could be as smooth and deceptive as this woman. And he'd been completely taken in.

As Dylan walked around the park, taking deep breaths to pump oxygen into the blood, he passed a church on Penn Street. The people were coming out the door. Some dressed up in their Sunday best, others in business casual, and at least one man in shorts and Hawaiian shirt.

Ah, Southern California.

What were they getting inside? The reason why God allows shootings and kidnappings and leaves grieving parents hanging, never knowing what happened? At least give us a little mercy, a tiny drop of it, the ability to sleep without nightmares. Just that cup of water in the desert.

The only hope was that there was some sort of balancing act going on. That the scales would get righted somehow. He'd been waiting years for proof that it could be so. He hadn't seen it yet.

Maybe hope was not the best word after all.

What about love?

Dylan had been in love three times in his life, and only once deeply.

The first time was high school, when he'd dated Erin for half a year.

The second was a girl named Cara Rennie at U.C. Davis. She was a volleyball player and majored in sports medicine. They were together for two years, even talked about marriage. But when she made the Olympic team, she went off for training and met, surprise surprise, a trainer. Who she married right after the Games.

The third time was Erin again, ten years removed from high school. And that was the deep one. The sure one. The one that lasted, until it cracked under the strain of losing Kyle.

There would be no more deep ones, he was sure. The universe had taught him not to expect anything good. But in the last year or so he'd allowed himself the possibility of finding someone to share some life with. A companion, to fend off the loneliness. He'd tried a couple of times with the dating site. But it was one disappointment and one disaster.

He almost gave up.

Then he met Tabitha. And despite his caution at their first lunch, he thought he heard the furtive tiptoeing of love coming up the back stairs of his mind, reaching for the doorknob ...

It wasn't reaching anymore.

Never again, he thought. He would not be stupid. He would not be a schoolboy. He would not let anyone get to his soul again.

His phone buzzed.

It was her.

30

I mustn't touch the clothes, Erin thought. I can't disturb the DNA, if it's there. The TV shows all tell us that.

But I can smell them.

The box was on the dinette table in front of her. She'd placed it there when she got home from the Salvation Army but didn't immediately open it. She wanted to pray first. She even recovered a birthday candle from a kitchen drawer and lit it. God wouldn't care if it had come off a cake now, would he?

Now she was ready. Or so she hoped.

Erin popped the corner of the lid. It unsnapped easily, the box being overstuffed with Kyle's clothes.

Erin put her nose to the crack and inhaled.

And went back in time, covering a span of Kyle's childhood all at once. The smell of the clothes was a time machine. She was back there now, the pictures in her mind more vivid than photos or movies. The shirt that was on top, red flannel, she remembered when she bought it at Costco because it was on sale and it looked warm and Kyle did not like being cold.

That shirt she saw on Kyle when they went to 31 Flavors, just the two of them, because Dylan was at a seminar. Kyle was three then and wanted a rocky road cone and that's exactly what he got. Erin got mint chip like always, that was her favorite. They sat at a table by the window looking out at the parking lot and Kyle was in his flannel shirt and smiling.

"My mouth is happy," he said after a good, sturdy lick.

It was the perfect thing to say. And then the inevitable dripping over the cone began, and Kyle's tongue, not yet as skilled in ice cream maintenance as older kids, tried to keep up with the trickle. But a dime-sized drip of chocolate found its way onto the flannel shirt. Erin moved with motherly precision with the extra napkins she'd placed between them. She went for the cone first, wrapping two napkins around it then handing it back to Kyle perfectly straight and over the table.

Kyle understood and went back to his work in earnest. Erin took two more napkins to the drinking fountain near the back. She wetted the napkins and came back and wiped the chocolate stain with downward strokes, without interfering with Kyle's enthusiastic anti-drip program.

"There," she said, sitting back. "No harm done."

Kyle smiled one of his big smiles, the kind he would put on when any picture taker would instruct, "Smile!" or "Say pizza!" But this time the smile was just for her benefit, because Kyle said, "That's what moms are for!"

And Erin, now remembering it all, and even more, the flashing of memories of Kyle in that shirt, closed the lid of the box again and pounded it with her fist.

Again and again and again.

31

"Isn't the view gorgeous?"

Tabitha Mullaney made a grand gesture with her arm. Presenting the San Fernando Valley! From the top of Topanga vista point. As if she were trying to sell a view lot to a wealthy buyer. She leaned against the split-rail fence. The sun on her face gave it a sheen like the skin of a rattler basking on a rock.

"You better get right to it," Dylan said. "Or this is the last time we meet."

It was Monday morning, and Dylan had cleared his appointments because Tabitha was insistent they meet one last time and he felt compelled to do it. Only part of it was about Kyle now. He was just as driven to find out what was inside this woman. He wanted her with the police. He was looking for an opening of any kind.

The Topanga view area was at the apex of the boulevard, coming from the beach through the canyon before descending into the massive maw of suburbia below.

Tabitha said, "First, if you'll just do something for me, dear. Raise your arms."

"Excuse me?"

"So polite!" she said. "I love that about you."

"What, you think I'm packing heat or something?"

"You're also cute. Packing heat! But yes, something like that."

"Come on, you don't really think I would, do you?"

She laughed. "It's just a fashion thing. I love that outfit. Go on." She made a gesture for him to raise his arms.

"Why should I?"

"Because I have some good news for you. You'll see. Please."

He'd come this far. He raised his arms. The moment he did, Tabitha's hand came out of her purse holding something. A gun? No. Some other kind of device. She waved it in front of him, scanning him up and down.

Impulse. Sometimes you just follow it. Dylan, who in high school had prided himself on being able to take a football right out of a receiver's hands, snatched the item from her grasp.

The look on her face was not so much one of surprise but of disappointment. She didn't make a move to get it back, whatever it was.

Feeling he had the advantage now, Dylan looked at the gadget. It resembled a handheld recording device. But it wasn't recording anything that he could see.

Tabitha said, "It's just to tell me if you have any active electronics on you. And it appears that you're clean. Your phone isn't doing anything but sitting in your pocket."

"Fantastic," he said. "Why don't we take this little thing to the police and talk about it?"

"That would be inconvenient," she said. "Especially for you. Whose fingerprints are on it?"

"Both of ours."

She shook her head, raised her hands and wiggled her fingers. There were small squares of what appeared to be clear tape on all of her fingertips.

Impulse again. Feeling the heat in his cheeks Dylan turned and threw the device as hard as he could. It whirligigged through the air and disappeared into a clump of brush.

"You owe me fifty dollars," Tabitha said calmly. "I'm giving you a discount."

"I'm done with you."

"You don't really mean that," Tabitha said.

"I'm prepared to walk away," Dylan said, wondering if he really was. He wanted to be. But like a steel shaving on a magnet he couldn't pull away. Yet.

"I don't think so, dear," Tabitha said.

A cool breeze was blowing from the ocean side, pouring over them, down toward the warm valley where it would die.

"You haven't seen what I have," she said.

"I don't care—"

"Or heard."

"Heard?"

"So many things. You can be happy. We can be happy."

We? It was a word that was poison now, transformed from the promise it once held. That she could throw it out with any kind of sincerity was enough to get him to say—

"Tabitha, you must know you need help."

"Sexually?"

What a strange and off-putting answer. What was in this woman's mind?

"I know people," Dylan said. "I can get you help. I'm willing to forget all of this, if you'll just once and for all tell me everything you know about Kyle, and back it up with proof."

She cocked her head and gave him a half smile. "Not just yet."

"Because for all I know he's dead and I'm not willing to be played anymore."

"Dylan, can I say something, with all sincerity?"

"Sincerity?" he said. "Are you kidding?"

"That hurts."

Dylan almost laughed in her face. His mouth formed an open smile, the kind that communicates *unbelievable.*

Tabitha Mullaney certainly could pool earnestness in her eyes. "You are not being played. I know it seems like it, because I'm being coy."

"You call all this coy?"

"A woman's charm, then?"

"I'm not calling it that."

"Listen," she said, "I'm being totally open with you. I want you to be reunited with your son, and for the three of us to be happy."

"The three of us?"

She nodded.

"I want photographic proof," Dylan said. "I want something solid. You and whoever wrote those notes."

"Notes again? I told you—"

"You're working with someone. A man. You're trying to shake me down for some reason, and my wife."

"Your ex-wife," Tabitha said.

"Who is he?" Dylan said.

She came to him and put her hand softly on his chest. The move repulsed him, but he let it stay in order to keep her talking.

"Can I be truthful with you?" she said. "Oops, there I go again, huh?"

Dylan said nothing. Her hand pressed harder.

"It's true there was a man involved in this," she said. "But not anymore. I want you to know everything. But I need you to know it on my terms. I've waited a long time for this."

"Just tell me now."

"You won't believe me," she said. "But tonight, you will."

"Tonight?"

"I want you to come to my house."

"Not a chance," Dylan said.

"Even if it means seeing Kyle?"

He grabbed her wrist.

"You're hurting me," she said.

Dylan said, "You're a liar."

"Let go."

"What do you want from me?"

And then, shocking him more than if she had produced a live dove from her sleeve, Tabitha began to cry. Softly at first, and yanking her arm away, turning on him, going back to the fence. She put her hands on the fence and lowered her head. Her shoulders shaking.

Just an act, Dylan told himself.

But it was a good one. He was tempted to say something even-handed, then reminded himself that she was pathological when it came to anything resembling truth.

He waited.

Finally, Tabitha turned around, wiping her eyes. "There's so much I want to tell you. So much that will heal you. Won't you give me one last chance?"

"After all this?"

She nodded. "I live in a house in a very quaint residential neighborhood."

"Where you could kill me," Dylan said.

"I'm not the one who wants you ..."

"Wants me what?"

"He, the man, he is the one who wants you dead. Not me. I can make this right. If you don't come ... it's dangerous for you."

"This is all so crazy."

"Look at me now," she said. "He is alive. Your son is alive. And you can see him. Tonight."

32

"Well, this could get interesting," Yumiko said, smiling at Erin as she looked up from her keyboard.

Yumiko cradled a long, gold-colored box in her arms.

"Are you kidding?" Erin said.

"I take it your lunch the other day went swimmingly?"

"It was just lunch," Erin said.

Yumiko lifted the box. "Oh really?"

"Hand them over."

"Did you lip lock?"

"No! Now gimme."

"Okay," Yumiko said, handing Erin the box. "But I'm going to want details."

"Nothing juicy happened."

"Well that's a major letdown."

The second wave of afternoon students were on their way to classes. Erin knew Andy's schedule—had checked it when she'd first come in to work—and he didn't have a class on Mondays.

"It's still highly romantic," Yumiko said.

Erin used her fingernail to slice the tape on either side of the box, then lifted off the top.

Revealing a dozen long-stemmed red roses.

Yumiko sighed. "This definitely looks like love."

"Will you stop?" Erin said, reaching for the small envelope on top of the stems.

"What's it say, what's it say?" Yumiko curled around behind Erin's chair.

Erin pulled the envelope to her chest. "Will you let me, please?"

"Come on, this is so rom-com. I'm the best friend character."

"It's private," Erin said.

"No way! In the script, I snatch the note and read it." Yumiko made a half-hearted move to take the envelope.

Erin pulled it away. "This is not a movie."

"How do you know?" Yumiko said. "Maybe everything we do is being filmed."

"That's a comforting thought. Now step back and I'll read it and let you know."

Yumiko returned to her previous spot, saying, "There goes my best supporting actress nod."

Erin opened the envelope, took out the card. It had a floral pattern on the edges, with a blank middle for a message. In blue, felt-tip marker was written, *It's you I can't replace.*

No signature.

"So what's it say?" Yumiko's chin rested on the edge of Erin's cubicle partition.

Erin gave her the card.

"It's you I can't replace," Yumiko said. "Wow. That is some serious romancing."

Erin felt an odd friction inside her. Part of it was as Yumiko described—the spark of romance. She wanted it to be that spark. But offsetting the desire was a streak of disquiet. It ran through her like a discordant note in an otherwise pleasant musical piece.

"What's wrong?" Yumiko said.

"I don't know," Erin said. "It's kind of a strange message, don't you think?"

"It's poetic."

"Replace?"

"He must be referring to something you said at lunch. Did you talk about replacing anything?"

"I don't think so."

"Tires? Dishwashing liquid?"

"No," Erin said. "We didn't talk about replacing anything."

"Maybe it's a line from a poem or something," Yumiko said. "Google it."

Erin reached for her trackball mouse.

"Don't forget to put quotes around it," Yumiko said.

"What are you, my teenage daughter?"

"Your quirky and fun-loving coworker."

Erin typed *"It's you I can't replace"* into the search box and hit return. The top hit had a video thumbnail.

"The Police," Erin said. " 'Every Breath You Take.' "

She looked at Yumiko, the unease inside her now a full-on chill.

"Oh, no," Yumiko said. "Is that ..."

Erin nodded. "The stalker song."

"That's kind of creepy," Yumiko said.

"Ya think?"

"Maybe he doesn't know it's a stalker song."

"Maybe it wasn't Andy," Erin said.

"What? Who else?"

Erin heard the voice in her head.

I am going to look out for you. Both of you.

33

"He is alive. Your son is alive. And you can see him. Tonight."

Dylan, tired from the long drive home, couldn't get the words out of his head. They could be one giant lie, one huge come-on for some other sort of plan. Yet he knew he'd give her this chance.

He got a root beer from the refrigerator. No alcohol tonight. He would need to be sharp. Especially since he'd have a gun.

Sitting in the front room, Dylan couldn't help a wondering what Kyle would be like now, if indeed he was really alive. Would he be an extension of the boy he had known and loved with all the fervor that's possible to know and love another person?

Or would he be a complete stranger? Some other being, from another life, as separated from Dylan as a random box boy in St. Paul or an honor student at Princeton?

He'd be the smarter one, right?

Dylan recalled the first time they'd gone to Disneyland, the three of them. Kyle was three, his eyes full of kid wonder at the Magic Kingdom, but also inquiring eyes, and full of questions.

As they walked toward the carousel, Dylan paused to show Kyle the window above the Snow White ride. The curtains opened and the Wicked Queen peered out for a moment before the curtains closed. Kyle wanted to know who she was. Dylan told him she was a mean lady who didn't like Snow White.

Kyle wanted to know why.

Dylan started to go over the story, how the queen wanted to be the fairest one of all. Then he had to explain what *fairest* meant. But how do you explain jealousy and vanity to a three-year-old at Disneyland?

But Kyle got it. He seemed to, at least. His little brow furrowed as he looked up and saw the queen's appearance once more.

"She needs help," Kyle said.

What an answer from a three-year-old child. Not *She needs to be hit by lightning.* No, he saw she had … issues. And he wanted to get her help.

Dylan and Erin had talked about Kyle's heart, how innocent and sensitive it was.

Would he have that same heart now?

Or was it ripped out of him forever the moment he was taken?

Did that tear his soul so completely that he would cut off all wonder, all joy?

Well, one thing was sure now. Dylan's own heart, pounded by grief over fifteen years, was perfectly capable of revenge. Yes, Tabitha needed help, just like the Wicked Queen. But if it came down to it, Dylan would be the source of the lightning bolt.

It would come from a gun.

He owned a Beretta M9, a semi-auto pistol he bought several years ago from a retired Ventura County police officer at a gun show in Oxnard.

Dylan had never been into guns. But with home invasions on the rise in Los Angeles, he'd finally decided to get something that would be a last resort but a winning hand.

He took the requisite training and got his Handgun Safety Certificate from the California Department of Justice. He remembered the day he got it, how he laughed and said to himself, in the Dirty Harry voice, "I got your justice, right here."

Two years later, he got a Derringer with the thought of getting a conceal-and-carry permit. A late night in downtown L.A. was not the proverbial walk in the park. Or even parking lot.

But he never pursued it. Instead, he'd installed a wall safe for both guns, and they hadn't been out for exercise at the range in over a year.

Dylan opened the safe and took out the Beretta. The magazine was next to a box of Winchester 9mm bullets. Fat lot of good all this would have done him in an emergency. He'd have to load the magazine, shove it into the gun, and chamber a round. Enough time for the invader to take his laptop and have a cup of coffee, too.

Maybe he should take the Derringer. But that was a weapon for emergencies and close quarters, and of course he had no idea what the setup would be.

Was he really thinking of doing this? Holding the Beretta, testing the heft, Dylan was hoping he'd feel like Bruce Willis.

Instead, he felt like a mall cop in a mediocre comedy.

Who was he kidding? He wasn't a gun-toting hero.

Not yet, anyway. But he was morphing into someone not entirely himself. If not a hero, at least a father who did something for his son, long lost, maybe dead. But *something*.

Dylan placed the Beretta on top of the safe and began to load the magazine.

34

The night lights of the Valley always looked so benign from Erin's balcony. In the past she would take comfort from the sight, the way most people do at a cityscape under the stars.

Now Erin was fighting her thoughts, thinking about what was happening under those lights. Was somebody breaking into a car in the parking structure at Universal? Was there a killing taking place in that nice little apartment building on Ventura? A rape behind a liquor store on Lankershim?

She hated thoughts like that. They came from what she called the shadow corner of her mind.

When she was six she accidentally killed a rabbit. She was visiting her grandparents in Acton, California, a place of desert and dust and sun. Nana and Papa were old-school Californians, with a home and a big backyard with a rabbit pen. Nana raised the rabbits, she said, because their droppings were the best kind of fertilizer for her garden. She called it composting. She even put the pellets in jars and sold them at open markets!

Erin took one bunny to heart. One of the small ones. She named it Happy. She got to hold it sometimes when Nana was there. But Erin liked it best when Nana wasn't there. Because then it was just her and Happy and she could talk to it and pretend they were having a conversation.

One afternoon when Nana was working on her quilt in the living room, Erin told Happy that she was going to get the rabbit something to eat, to help it grow bigger. To keep up with the other rabbits.

There was a magic food, Erin told Happy, that her grandmother told her about. Nana called it "the perfect food."

It was the avocado. You could eat it with some salt and pepper, or you could smash it all up and make something called guacamole.

Erin got an avocado from Nana's refrigerator and fed some to Happy. That night Happy died.

Erin was inconsolable. Nana held her and rocked her and between her sobs softly asked Erin if she had done anything to Happy.

Erin said no, only fed her some good avocado.

Which was when Nana stopped rocking her. And told her that avocados are toxic to rabbits.

Erin didn't know what toxic meant.

"Poison," Nana said. "Something that causes death."

Erin wailed at the horror of it. She was Happy's killer. She was bad inside. And if she was bad so was everybody else, except maybe Nana.

Though she never spoke about it to anyone, ever after Erin's imagination would take off of its own volition, wondering about all the bad things being done by people when no one was looking. In the shadows.

Those thoughts became little pictures, and the pictures took up rent-free space in a corner of her mind.

By the time she married Dylan she'd become self-aware enough to be able to assert a little control. When a shadow thought materialized, unbidden, to her she'd pause and try to imagine the coastline of Big Sur, which she found overpoweringly beautiful. She'd hear the waves crashing on the rocks and smell the salt air, and usually that would do the trick. The shadows would diminish, go and crouch somewhere in her mind waiting for another opportunity.

Their big moment came when Kyle was kidnapped. No fleeting pictures of beach or ocean or sky could fight the strength of the dark shadows that seemed to have voice, that seemed to whisper a mocking phrase. *We told you so ...*

It had taken years of counseling to get them under control once more. She'd gone to a counselor trained in Neural Linguistic Programming and found out her Big Sur replacement practice was one of the tools of NLP. She learned to catch the shadows as they were emerging and reduce them to the size of a pea in her mind, then explode the pea into a million minuscule particles—the Pea Big Bang she laughingly called it—and immediately replace it with a full color picture of Big Sur.

Later she added the Grand Canyon and Akaka Falls on the Big Island of Hawaii.

Gradually, oh so gradually, the shadow side of her mind retreated. Running helped, too, as gobs of oxygen worked like a magnificent air hose in her brain.

But now the shadows were back.

We told you so ...

She was startled by a knock at her door.

35

Dylan went over the safety rules he'd learned from his cop friend. They came out a little fuzzy, but he heard them in his friend's voice.

The gun is always loaded.

Don't ever point that gun at anything or anybody you're not willing to shoot.

Keep your finger off the trigger until you intend to shoot.

Keep guns away from children.

I mean it, make sure you have a gun safe.

Aim for the center body mass.

His friend also taught him the proper way to prep and insert the magazine, insisting that Dylan do it right, like a piano teacher drilling a pupil in the scales—you held the gun with your dominant hand and placed the magazine in the magazine well with your non-dominant hand.

He did that now, holding the gun in his right and the mag in his left. He shoved the magazine firmly with his left palm. Then he used his left hand to rack the slide and chamber a round.

He made sure the safety was on.

Now all he needed was something to shoot at.

Or someone.

Could he really do that? Actually shoot to kill?

Guns.

Killing.

He remembered in a flash a moment when Kyle was three. Dylan was watching the news about the war heating up in Afghanistan, and footage from a dusty brown village with soldiers firing furious rounds at an unseen enemy.

Kyle had wandered into the family room and was behind him looking at the set, Dylan alerted to his presence only when Kyle said, "What they doing?"

A simple yet profound question from a preschooler. And Dylan realized at once this was a pivot, a full turn from the innocence of childhood toward a dark window giving a blurry glimpse of a real world to come. How much should he tell his son? This precocious boy who had a way of looking at you when he felt a question was being dodged. He would accept whatever Dylan said because he trusted him, but there was sometimes a squinted eye or furrowed brow before an implicit shrug of shoulders as if to say, *Oh, so that's the way it is. Got it, Dad.*

How should he explain death to Kyle? Real, physical death? Dylan remembered his own introduction to the big sleep, by way of a cartoon and a cat that died and its angelic spirit rising from the body, clad in a white robe playing a harp. He asked his own father about that and his father said he'd explain it later, hoping that Dylan would forget, which he did.

It was four years later when his grandfather died and he learned what real death was.

But there were no cats on TV now, only soldiers with rifles, and Dylan knew this was a question he couldn't dodge.

He knelt so he could be eye-to-eye with his son. That was the default position for a serious moment.

Dylan said, "There are mean people who want to hurt other people, people that we like. Sometimes they even want to hurt us. And sometimes they use guns."

But Kyle's concept of guns was virtually nil. He couldn't recall if Kyle had ever seen a Western. And he knew there had been no gun battles among the Muppets or in Mr. Rogers' Neighborhood.

"Bullets come out of guns," Dylan said, "like rocks. Remember throwing rocks at the beach?"

Kyle nodded, trying to make sense of it.

"But the bullets come fast and can go inside your body and hurt you bad, and sometimes they kill a person ..."

Kill? What did Kyle know of that?

"It makes people's bodies stop working," Dylan said.

That didn't seem to register with Kyle.

"It means they can't walk around ever again. They go to sleep and never wake up."

His son was thinking about it.

"So people that we like have to use guns sometimes to stop the mean people. That's what is happening on TV. Those men are trying to stop mean people from hurting us."

Looking at the Beretta now, held properly, trigger finger on the side of the barrel, Dylan nodded at his remembered words.

Yes, he could do it. He could shoot someone.

And stop the mean people from hurting us.

36

Erin thought it might be Monica.

But the peephole revealed a smiling Anderson Bolt. He was holding a bottle of champagne.

Before the door was fully open, Erin said, "What are you doing here?"

"I think they call this being spontaneous." He held up the bottle and rocked it.

"Andy, this is weird. Especially after the flowers."

"Flowers?"

"Somebody sent me flowers at work."

"I have a rival?"

"Hardly."

"Good! Then let's have one sip of champagne." He pronounced it *shamPAHNya*, like that character Christopher Walken played on SNL a long time ago. "Please?"

"Just one," Erin said. She opened the door and he came in, smelling pleasantly of cologne and the night. But as she closed the door she was suddenly aware of the lights. Too bright, and how did that make her look? Her lipstick! She hadn't applied any since finishing her Panda Express an hour ago. Her hair was probably like wild Malibu grass in a breeze. And she remembered the small zit on the left side of her chin. A zit! At fifty years old! Yeah, buddy, maybe fifty is the new sixteen!

"You'll find champagne glasses in the kitchen cupboard," she said, turning off the hall light. "I'll be right with you."

"Check," Andy said.

As he ambled toward the kitchen, Erin banked the other way, to the front bathroom where she put her makeup on in the morning. She closed the door and looked at her face in the mirror, and fought the urge to cry out, *Look away! I'm hideous!*

The zit was staring back at her with arrogant pride.

She grabbed the Clinique and used the applicator sponge to smother the zit with skin toner. She gave it a quick smooth-over with her little finger. Then the lipstick, Raspberry Glace.

Her hair actually wasn't half bad.

She brushed it anyway.

Then threw all the stuff in a drawer, lest he should use this bathroom.

When she got back to the kitchen he said, "I hope you don't mind Dom Perignon."

"As long as he doesn't mind me," Erin said.

"Dish towel?"

"Behind you."

Andy put the dish towel over the champagne bottle and twisted. The cork came out with a full-bodied *poomp!*

He poured two glasses, put the bottle down and handed her a glass.

"What are we celebrating?" Erin said.

"Us," Andy said.

They clinked and drank.

"Ah," Andy said. "The champagne is crisp and energetic. One can taste the sunny hillside where the grapes are grown."

"You are a connoisseur," Erin said.

"Actually, I have no idea what I'm talking about. But I try to make it sound good."

Erin resisted the urge to say, *Is that what you're doing with me?* Because she was liking the champagne and the company and the distraction from her memories.

"Can we take this somewhere?" Andy said.

"Oh! Of course. Follow me."

She led him to the living room. Thankfully, only one table lamp was on, with low level lighting. She could handle that.

Erin sat on the sofa, positioning herself in the middle. Andy didn't take the hint and sat next to her, hip against hip.

"Does the champagne come with some brakes?" Erin said.

"You want skid marks on your carpet?" Andy said. He'd brought the bottle with him and placed it on the coffee table.

"One glass," Erin said.

"Let's finish, and then decide," Andy said. He lifted his glass to her and sipped.

She mirrored him, and he looked into her eyes with a soft but focused gaze. Erin didn't know whether to melt or laugh. His romancing was not subtle.

"Now," he said, "who is this guy sending you flowers? Should I get out my dueling pistols?"

"Were you born in 1777 or something?"

"Answer the question," he said.

"Don't put me on trial," she said.

"I just want to know."

"We're not"—she almost said *boyfriend and girlfriend* but it sounded silly in her mind—"an item."

He smiled. "I like that. An item. From the shelf at the Love Store."

"Finish your champagne," she said.

Putting his half-filled glass on the coffee table, he sat back on the sofa and crossed his arms.

"Now you're being childish," she said.

"Why can't you tell me about those flowers?" he said. "Were they from your ex-husband?"

"No!"

"They had to come from somebody."

"This is getting personal."

"Of course it is," Andy said. "Don't you want it to be?"

"To be honest, I'm not sure what I want right now."

"Because of what you told me, about your son?"

She nodded.

"Well," he said, reaching for his glass, "I guess this is the part where I'm supposed to say 'I'm here for you.' That seems a bit of a cliché."

"But a nice one," Erin said.

"And now what I'd like to do is kiss you," he said.

"Not yet," Erin said

"Soon, though," he said.

"Not tonight," she said.

"Drat."

"Okay?"

He sighed. "Whatever you say."

"Then cheers," she said.

37

The house Tabitha Mullaney told Dylan to come to was across the 5 freeway from the Bob Hope Airport. It was an old neighborhood tucked up against the Verdugo Hills which, in the daytime, were a brown and scrubby obtrusion surrounded by housing developments. But at night they formed a dark refuge for coyote and snake.

A perfect place for her home to be, Dylan thought, as he followed the instructions given him by Tabitha. He parked exactly as she told him to, at the corner by a DWP box, under the street light which was radiating a dull yellow light.

As Dylan got out of the car the sound of a dog barking in the distance gave off a *Hound of the Baskervilles* vibe. He started thinking Tabitha was running the sound on a loop, through speakers, just for his benefit.

She had set everything up so neatly, why not that?

He popped the trunk of his car and unzipped the soft gun case. He looked around to make sure he was alone, then removed the Beretta lifted the back of his coat and tucked the gun in his waistband. He closed the trunk. Looked around once more.

Took a deep breath and blew it out slowly.

The hound barked again, this time as rapid as Dylan's heartbeat.

Her house was two from the corner, so she said. He checked the number on the front when he got there, barely visible by the light of another street lamp. In the dim, the house looked like any other single-family dwelling. The front window was illuminated, yellowish through soft curtains. Dylan imagined Tabitha sitting there like Madame Defarge, knitting the names of all the people she wanted to destroy.

He was on the sidewalk at the edge of a cement path to the front door. He didn't move, but kept watch, as if he expected her to jump out like a jack-in-the-box, or one of those hands that shoots out of the shadows in a horror movie.

This was crazy.

This was nuts.

This was not Dylan Reeve, normal human being and professional healer. With a freaking gun in his pants?

What if he just walked away now?

Would it be his last chance to find out the truth about his son?

Could he live with the uncertainty of that for the rest of his life? Or had she read him like the proverbial book, the kind with predictable characters and tragic endings?

The door cracked open.

Soft light from inside the house made a silhouette of the figure that appeared in the space.

It was a man.

"Mr. Reeve?" he said.

"Who are you?" Dylan said. He kept his voice soft, as if he might disturb a neighbor or start another dog barking.

"Please come in," the man said.

"Where's Tabitha?"

"She's here."

"Who are you?"

"I'm here to help."

Dylan didn't move. "I don't know you."

"That makes us even, Mr. Reeve. Would you prefer we talk out there?"

"I think I might," Dylan said.

"All right."

The man came out, closing the door behind him. As he approached, Dylan assessed. The man was big, over six feet, barrel-chested, wearing a Hawaiian shirt over khakis and running shoes. His head was round and bald. Tabitha had mentioned having a brother. Maybe this was him.

Dylan watched the man's hands. They seemed relaxed.

Or coiled.

"What is this?" Dylan said.

"Tabitha has asked me to be an intermediary," the man said. His voice was not threatening. It was a car salesman's voice as he showed you the floor model.

"Why would she do that?"

"She knows you're wary."

"What a shock that must be," Dylan said.

"But she has every right to be wary of you as well."

"Are you kidding me?"

"Please come in and let's settle this thing once and for all."

"Who are you?" Dylan said. "What's your name?"

"All will be explained."

Dylan didn't move.

"If I wanted to do you harm," the man said, "I would have done it already. This is about seeing your son again. There are papers to look over."

"Papers?"

The man nodded.

"Are you a lawyer?" Dylan said.

"Thank God no," the man said with a smile. "I used to be a cop. I'm a private investigator now."

The man took out a leatherette card holder and flipped it open, holding it up for Dylan to see. In the thin glow of the street light Dylan could make out PRIVATE INVESTIGATOR across the top of the laminated card. On the left side was a photo that looked like the guy. On the right was a seal of some kind. There were several lines of writing, like on a driver's license.

"Come on inside and let's make this thing legal," the man said.

"May I know your name? I couldn't read it on the card."

"Milton Carbona," he said. "Feel free to call me Milt."

The inside of the house was spare. Nothing on the walls. It was like a place that someone was about to move out of. Or perhaps had never fully moved into. Only a few items of furniture, nothing that matched. The man motioned for him to go into what would have been the living room. The expanse of hardwood floor had a couple of folding chairs and an overturned crate that could have been used as a table. The small lamp providing the only light was by the curtained window and had been placed right on the floor.

"Homey," Dylan said.

"Think of this more as a business office," Carbona said.

"What business is that? Extortion?"

"We don't have to be unpleasant about this, do we?"

"Where is Tabitha?"

"If I'm any judge of women, I think she's making sure she looks good. Entirely for your benefit."

"I just want to get this over with," Dylan said. "Do you know anything about my son?"

"I do," Carbona said. "I know he's alive."

Dylan was filled suddenly with a distant longing, an ache that made his arms tingle and his hands feel weak. Like a man trapped in a collapsed mine, entombed in darkness, sensing the slight flickering of the light of the search-party torches just beyond the rocks. He wanted to cry out.

"Why don't you have a seat?" Carbona said.

Dylan remained standing. "How are you involved?"

"Give me a second." Carbona went to the overturned crate. Dylan could imagine gangsters in an old Warner Bros. movie playing cards on it as they waited out the cops.

Carbona bent over, lifted the crate and reached for something underneath it.

When he stood up again he was holding a revolver.

Pointed at Dylan's chest.

"I'll need your gun," Carbona said.

"What?"

"The heat you're packing, as we in the industry like to say. Lift your hands up for me, please."

"This is ridiculous."

"Mr. Reeve, ridiculous is that you've come here with a gun under your coat. You're an amateur and it's not safe. Hands up, please."

Feeling like a kid caught with a cookie before dinner, Dylan raised his hands. The gesture brought heat to his face—embarrassment, mostly, for being so obvious.

Carbona approached, keeping the gun at chest level, and Dylan was once more quite aware he was no action hero. He wasn't going to slug the PI and take his weapon. He was as helpless as a baby in a high chair.

With his left hand, Carbona reached behind Dylan's shoulder and guided him into a half turn. Then he reached under Dylan's coat and removed his gun.

Holding the stippled gun butt with his thumb and two fingers, Carbona said, "Have a seat."

No use fighting it. Dylan lowered himself into one of the folding chairs. Its cheapness squeaked under his weight.

"Beretta M9," Carbona said, nodding. "Fine weapon. Not quite as reliable as a Glock, in my opinion, but perfectly fine if you know what you're doing."

"Obviously not," Dylan said.

"It's experience, Mr. Reeve. That's all. You're trained in chiropractic, not security."

Carbona gently placed the Beretta on the floor, as if it were a dead fish on a gutting board. Then he put his foot on top of it and with a swift motion sent it skidding across the hardwood floor. It came to rest under the window.

"What are you doing?" Dylan said.

Carbona sat in the other chair, facing Dylan. He rested the revolver on his legs with the barrel pointed off to the side.

"My grandfather was a troubleshooter for the movie studios," Carbona said. "He helped keep people like Robert Mitchum from getting into more trouble than they already did."

"That's really fascinating," Dylan said. "But isn't it about time you told me what this whole setup is for?"

"All will become clear very soon," Carbona said.

"Let's make it clear now," Dylan said.

Carbona cocked his head, seemed to be listening for something. Then he nodded. "Three minutes," he said. "Give or take."

He listened again.

Then Dylan heard it.

Sirens.

Getting closer.

Fast.

38

To his credit, Andy had not tried to kiss her before he left. But he did give her a predictive squint, a promise of more to come. She was good with that. His attentions were not unwelcome.

And he'd left her the champagne. She'd had another glass, got in her PJs, and tried to read a book. An actual, physical, hardcover book. Not that she was against ebooks. She had a Kindle, and an app on her phone. But she'd always liked holding books, ever since her mother introduced her to the wonderful world of Stockton-San Joaquin County public library. The first book she ever checked out on her own was *Charlotte's Web.*

Then here in L.A., when the family was intact, when Kyle turned three, she started taking him to story time every week at the local branch of the L.A. library system. And then would let him pick out books to bring home for her to read to him.

Which was why she checked out books from the library. It was a subtle connection to the memory of her son.

The books she read were not thrillers. She'd enjoyed that genre before Kyle was taken. But after that she found she couldn't take the feelings a thriller engendered. They usually involved someone in great peril and pain at the hands of a very bad villain, and that was just too close to home.

She didn't go for the traditional romance genre, either, though they contained a "happily ever after" ending. That was pure fiction, a denouement she couldn't ever again buy into.

So she went for epic fantasy, finding pleasurable escape in the imaginary worlds and complex plots.

Tonight it was more from Diana Gabaldon.

Erin had just made it through four pages when a thought flashed in her mind and started making noise.

The thought was that Dylan was in some sort of trouble.

39

"Police?" Dylan said.

Carbona nodded.

"Here?"

He nodded again.

"What is this?"

Carbona did not respond.

"I'm going outside," Dylan said, standing.

Carbona stood up, too, pointing the gun at him.

"Where's Tabitha?" Dylan said, just as Carbona's arm made an arc like a boxer's right cross.

Hard steel slammed into Dylan's skull. Fireworks exploded behind his eyes. He was aware of falling, hitting hard floor, his body responding on its own now, seeking to shut itself down to stop the pain, but not able to go all the way.

Not able to move. Not able to speak.

Groaning.

And sounds following like an audible kaleidoscope. Sirens closer. The screech of tires.

Dylan's own head ringing.

Then a retching sound, and Dylan realizing it was from his own throat.

A door slamming open and voices and radio static and feet.

And hands, grabbing him, yanking him to his feet.

More voices.

His arms yanked behind him. The feeling of handcuffs on his wrists.

He was surrounded by cops, touched by strong hands, hearing voices, but they were growing distant, and he went into another world, long ago, seeing the Mickey Mouse balloon from Disneyland when he was four, and his dad tied the string around his wrist. But he wanted to hold it himself so he slipped the string off his wrist and held the balloon and waved it around. Then had to scratch his back and somehow the string got away, and the balloon went up, up, up and he said *Oh no oh no oh no*, and he could only watch, helpless, his grief expanding because Mickey was all alone in the sky, no one to help him. Unmoored.

Dylan was barely aware that he was moving, or that he was being placed in the back of a police patrol SUV.

A million little devils poked his brain with their pitchforks. He wanted to crawl out of his head and leave it on the seat. But he was cuffed.

Arrested?

And now a medic of some sort was talking to him, reaching into a little black bag, touching his face with something wet and stingy.

"Hold still," the medic said.

Dylan almost said something but thought passing out might be a better plan. Just sleep. Wake up and this will all be over. I'll be back in my office with Jaquez Rollins, laughing, and this week will not have happened.

He closed his eyes.

The medic left him.

Dylan heard more voices and the tinny sound of official police chatter over the radio.

40

Dylan didn't answer his phone.

Erin left a voice message, a light one, a "just checking in, no big deal" kind of thing. But she found she wanted to talk to him. Desperately.

Or maybe this was all just what your mind did under stress. What was it her high school English teacher, Mrs. Tomosina, had said? About Keats? *Heard melodies are sweet, but those unheard are sweeter.* That was the quote. Mrs. Tomosina gave a lovely interpretation of the words. But after class Erin had asked if the opposite was also true—that unheard and unsweet melodies are worse?

"You're quite a thinker," Mrs. Tomosina had said, then assigned Erin to write a paper on the subject.

For which she got an A. The thesis was that we tend to make things worse than they are, because our imaginations are boundless and turn pictures of bad into pictures of worse.

The answer, she wrote in the paper, was to give your imagination another direction, like a good book. Mrs. Tomosina had circled that paragraph and written next to it, with her red pen, *Wonderful point!*

So Erin went back to the Gabaldon and tried to get absorbed by it once again.

She gave up after two pages.

Control your thoughts.

Erin laughed, surprising herself. An absurd argument was opening up in her head, like in some Mad Hatter Tea Party.

She shook her head, returned to the book.

Her phone buzzed.

Private number.

She chanced it.

"Yes?"

"Hey, Erin!"

Him.

"Can you hear me?" he said.

"Yes."

"Good. I won't be on long. Just listen. Kyle is safe and sound. You are very close to seeing him."

Dear God, did she dare believe it? Dare hang on to this call? Her body felt like it was on an elevator dropping from the sixtieth floor with no safety cables, just the straight drop, accelerating. Her free hand shot outward in an instinctive attempt to grab something.

"Do you understand?" he said. "How good this is?"

She couldn't form a word.

"All you have to do is wait for my call," he said.

"Call?" Erin said. "What do you call this?"

"Generous," he said. "You'll see."

"I want to see now."

But he was gone.

41

"Do you feel like you can talk?" the detective asked.

"Why am I even here?" Dylan said.

Here was a spare box of a room at the jail in Van Nuys. He was in a chair at a table, and a detective in a short-sleeve shirt and tie, loosened at the collar, sat in the only other chair in the room.

The detective was in his late forties. His demeanor was something between a mortician and a CPA at tax time. He had introduced himself as Detective Warren Smith.

They'd given Dylan a cold pack to hold on the side of his face. Sweet of them.

At least the cuffs were off. Surely they weren't arresting him for some sort of assault on the guy who hit him.

"You're here on suspicion of murder," Smith said.

That word pounded into Dylan's head like six-penny nail. For a second Dylan's sight was bathed in red, as if the small room had been lit by a mad cinematographer from a cheap horror movie.

"Do you understand?" Detective Smith said.

"This is crazy. Where—"

"I need—"

"Who died?"

"—to advise you—"

"Somebody cracked my head open! Wait ... Tabitha?"

"If you want to continue," Detective Smith said, "I must advise you of your rights."

The devils invaded the carnival, fresh pitchforks in hand, poking right behind the eyes.

Dylan slammed the cold pack on the table. "I didn't kill anybody! I got whacked on the side of my head ... did you get him? The guy who did this to me?"

"Do you want to talk about it?"

"Ya think?"

Smith removed something from his pocket, placed it on the table. "This is a digital recording device," he said. "If at any time you want to stop the interview, you just tell me and I'll turn this off."

"Go," Dylan said.

"You have the right to remain silent. Do you understand?"

"Yes."

"Anything you say may be used against you in court. Do you understand?"

"I get all that!"

"You have the right to the presence of a lawyer both before and during questioning. Do you understand?"

"Come on."

"Please answer yes or no."

"Yes!"

"If you want a lawyer but cannot afford to pay for one, a lawyer will be appointed for you free of charge before questioning. Do you understand?"

"Yes. I'm ready. Now you listen. I didn't kill anybody."

Detective Smith said, "I want to make sure you waive your right to have an attorney present."

"Yeah, right. And if I ask for one you'll think I'm guilty."

"We don't operate that way, Mr. Reeve."

"Just doing your job, huh?"

"My job is to find the truth, and to make sure that we don't ask questions unless you voluntarily agree to talk with us. So I'm asking you again if you want to consult an attorney."

"I don't want an attorney. I want you to ..."

"Yes?"

"Just listen to me."

. . .

Smith's expression did not change. "Then let's begin. Your name is Dylan Reeve?"

"Yes."

"Were you personally acquainted with the deceased, Tabitha Mullaney?"

"How did she die?"

"Just answer my questions, sir."

"The guy who hit me, he must have done it."

"What was the nature of your relationship with the deceased?"

"We met through a dating site," Dylan said. "I thought things were going well. Then she turned out to be some sort of ... I don't know what you'd call her, a sociopath. She was trying to ..."

"Take your time, Mr. Reeve. Put it in your own words."

"I don't know if I have the words. Do you know about my son?"

"No, sir."

"He was kidnapped. Fifteen years ago. Never found."

Detective Smith nodded.

"A few nights ago I got a note slipped under my door. It was written in crayon. It said, *Your son is alive.* That's all. I showed it to my wife. My ex-wife. That wasn't a good conversation. It brought up all kinds of bad memories."

Smith waited.

"And then I got another note. This one told me what Kyle's favorite toy had been when he was five. How would somebody know that if they didn't do it?"

"Did you take these notes to the police?"

"I didn't get the chance."

"What does that mean?"

"I went out to dinner with Tabitha that night. I was trying to keep things normal between us. I was beginning to like her. A lot. Then after a very pleasant meal she told me that if I wanted to see my son again I would have to do exactly what she said."

"Naturally, that upset you."

"Ya think? I ... wait, wait."

"Yes?"

"I see what you're doing."

"What am I doing, Mr Reeve?"

"I'm telling you right now I did not kill her. Yes, I was upset. Wouldn't you be? But not enough for murder."

"Please continue, sir."

"She told me not to go to the police. Or anybody else. She said I'd never see him again if I did that."

"And you believed her?"

"I don't know what I believed. I never thought I'd see Kyle again anyway. I've pretty much come to believe that he's dead and his body will never be found. To have this dangled in front of me, it just messed me up. I thought I would give it some time and maybe ..."

"Would you like a drink of water?" Smith said.

Dylan shook his head, which brought a rush of pain. He ignored it. "She said she was going to tell me what I should do. I was to come over to this house and talk to her. When I got there a guy was at the door. He got me inside and—"

"Can you describe this man?"

"Of course," Dylan said. "He talked to me. He was a big guy, big chest and arms, bald. In a Hawaiian shirt. Wait a second, you should know that. He's the one who called the police, who hit me."

Smith said, "I just want to get it all from you. How did this man get you to come inside?"

"He just told me to come in. He said he was the intermediary. That's the word he used."

"And you did? Just like that?"

"I wanted to find out what was going on. When we got inside he pulled a gun on me. It was already there, under a crate."

"A crate?"

"I'm sure you know what I'm talking about. You've been there. How did Tabitha die?"

"Did you have a weapon?" Smith asked.

"You found it, obviously."

"Did you bring it with you?"

"I didn't shoot anybody with it, if that's what you're leading up to."

"Continue," Smith said.

"He had me sit down. He sat down, holding his gun. Next thing I know there are sirens. I got up and he whacked me on the side of the head with the gun. I went down and now here I am. And now here you are. I'm not the criminal here. Somebody else killed her."

Smith was silent. His expression was exactly the same as the first moment Dylan saw him.

Dylan said, "You need to find that guy. His name is ... I can't remember."

"Milton Carbona," Smith said. "We interviewed him."

"Did you arrest him?"

"He's retired from the Los Angeles Police Department."

"So?"

"With an impeccable record. And he says he came to the house at the victim's request, but you got there first. He found you inside, standing over the body of Tabitha Mullaney."

"No—"

"You pulled your gun and that's when he hit you."

"You can't believe that!"

"Why can't I, Mr. Reeve?"

"Because ... it's a setup."

"Mr. Carbona showed us a client agreement he had with Ms. Mullaney."

"For what?"

"She was afraid you were stalking her."

"Come on!"

"And she wanted you and Mr. Carbona to sit down like adults and talk it through."

Dylan leaned back against the metallic chair. There would be no convincing this detective if he bought a story like that. An elaborate noose was being woven by this Carbona and the detective was trying to pull it tight. Forget the presumption of innocence or suspicion of another suspect.

"Interview over," Dylan said. "I want a lawyer."

"You have that right," Detective Smith said. He clicked off the recorder.

"What about my phone call? You still give dangerous criminals a phone call, right?"

"I'll let that pass," Detective Smith said. "Be careful what you say. We'll have a phone brought in."

"I can't use my own phone?"

"You are an arrestee."

"Unbelievable." And it was, truly, as unbelievable as having your child taken away from you in broad daylight at a public park. As unbelievable as having your heart ripped out and pounded with a hammer and shoved back into your chest. Yet that all happened, too.

A few minutes later, a uniformed officer brought in a touchpad phone and plugged it into a jack in the wall.

Detective Smith nodded.

"Can I have some privacy, please?" Dylan said.

"Afraid not," Detective Smith said.

"Don't I have a right to privacy?"

"Only if you talk to your lawyer."

"I want to call my receptionist," Dylan said. "Her number's in my phone."

Smith said, "I understand. I'll just be a moment."

He went out of the interview room. The uniformed officer stayed.

"Having a nice night?" Dylan said.

The officer did not say anything.

"How 'bout those Dodgers?" Dylan said.

The officer raised his finger to his lips.

A minute later Smith came back to the room, holding Dylan's phone.

"What's your receptionist's name?" he asked.

"Paige Howe."

Smith thumbed Dylan's phone.

"You can't do that," Dylan said.

"I can," Smith said. "Here's the number." He read it.

Dylan punched the numbers on the touchpad phone.

Paige answered on the third ring.

"It's me," Dylan said.

"Hiya, boss," Paige said. "It's past your bedtime, isn't it?"

"I've got some bad news. You have something to write with?"

"Yes ..." Her voice was low and tremulous. "What's wrong?"

"I'm under arrest, and—"

"For what?"

"Just listen! And write. I've been arrested for something I didn't do. I'm at the Van Nuys police station. I'm going to be held here. I don't know how long. I'm going to need you to call all clients and cancel the whole week."

"The whole—"

"Please, just listen. I need you to pick up my car. Do you have someone you can call to go get it?"

"Yes, I do, but—"

"There's an extra car key in the right front drawer of my desk. Now write this down." He gave her the address and told her the car was parked around the corner.

"As soon as I sign off, I want you to get hold of Sam Wyant at the law firm of Wyant, Pouler and Ellis. Got that? Tell him where I am and to get down here as soon as he can."

"Yes. Should I tell him what you're charged with?"

"Yeah, tell him. And I don't want you to worry about this, because it's all a big misunderstanding. The charge is murder."

The pause on the other end of the call was as palpable as a gas explosion.

Then Paige said, "Oh my God."

"Call him too," Dylan said.

42

Erin dragged herself into the office the next morning feeling like an extra in *The Walking Dead*. Yumiko was nice enough not to say anything other than, "Let me get you some coffee."

"Just bring me the pods," Erin said. "I'll eat them like potato chips."

Thankfully the next three hours were spent in her admin cubicle facing nothing but a monitor and communicating exclusively with Excel. Companionship was lovingly provided by the Keurig machine in the kitchenette.

But the voice of the man on the phone played the intruder.

Erin fought it off each time by concentrating extra hard on her spreadsheets, or by going over paper files with the meticulousness of an OCD accountant. But the voice fought back, and she knew she would hear it again, and soon, for real.

By eleven she was at least starting to feel less like the Bride of Frankenstein and a little more like a human being.

At 11:15 she took her turn at the reception desk, hoping for as little walk-in traffic as possible. She just wanted to make it to lunch with a minimum of human interaction.

Some receptionist.

Then, at 11:31, the phone system routed her a call for the inquiry line.

"DeForest, this is Erin, how may I help you?"

"You know the B&B Market on Moorpark?"

The voice. He said he would call.

"Did you understand the question, Erin?"

"What do you want?"

"Do you know the B&B?"

"I ... no."

"Erin, please don't do that. Don't lie to me. I wasn't asking. I know you get salads there quite often."

The sense of violation was as real as the heat coming through the reception-area windows.

"Go there," he said. "Be there in fifteen minutes."

"I can't."

"You will go to the pay phone there. I will call you. And remember, I'm here to help you! God, if you only knew. So don't call the cops, because if they show up you won't see your son ever again, and that would be too sad. Okay? Don't be late."

The call cut off.

"Hey." Yumiko's voice made Erin jump. She had completely missed her friend's approach.

Yumiko said, "You okay?"

"I have to go out," Erin said, removing the receptionist ear piece. "Can you cover for me?"

"Sure, but—"

"I'm in a hurry."

"What's this about?"

But Erin had already stood and grabbed her purse. She uttered a terse "Thanks" and headed for the elevators.

She got there the same time as one of the students, a single mom named Sandy McCallister.

"Hi, Erin."

"Oh. Hi." Erin hit the down button.

"I was hoping I'd run into you," Sandy said.

"Oh?"

"I was wondering what I have to do to finish my class next semester. My little girl needs surgery and ..."

The elevator doors opened. Feeling like a complete jerk, Erin stepped in and said, "We have a continuance form online." She hit the button for the parking garage.

"I saw that," Sandy said, "but there's a fee, and I was wondering if that could be waived."

"I'm sorry, Sandy, I'm in a hurry." The doors started to close. "Let's talk when I get back."

On the way down, Erin loathed herself for shining on a student like that. But even more did she loathe that she was a plaything for the voice on the phone.

But what choice was there? The scent of Kyle's clothes was still fresh, bringing with it the faint whiff of hope that she might see him again. It was enough to put all things behind her until she knew for sure if he was still alive.

And that would mean, she knew, the setting aside of some fundamental human niceties.

So be it.

The elevator opened up to the parking garage.

Erin's hand shook as she fumbled in her purse for the car key.

43

What Dylan knew best about Sam Wyant was his right hip. Dylan had been working on it once a month for two years. The best bit of advice Dylan had given to the sixty-year-old attorney was to opt out of the law firm basketball league and take up golf. A suggestion Wyant always rejected with the sentiment, "Too slow a game. I need the juice."

Dylan also learned along the way that Wyant was one of the most successful, and expensive, criminal defense lawyers in Los Angeles. But gratis one day Sam Wyant gave Dylan this advice: "First rule is, don't ever get arrested. Second rules is, don't get arrested. Third rule is, if you do get arrested, keep your big mouth shut and call me."

Well, he'd already blown those commandments. But at least Wyant had come to see him immediately. They were at the station, in the same interview room where Smith had hammered him. Dylan, after a sleepless night in a cell, and with his head still throbbing, felt—and smelled —like a dumpster in back of a fish market.

Sam Wyant, on the other hand, smelled like a freshly scented emperor of Rome.

Wyant was medium height, shaved-head bald, his pate as hard and shiny as a Spartan's shield. The black-rimmed glasses softened his look, adding a monk's piety to the warrior's eyes. But his salt-and-pepper goatee was in fighting trim, and Dylan got the impression that if he touched the fabric of Wyant's three-piece, slate-gray suit, it would feel like iron mail.

All of which was a relief. Dylan needed a fighter on his side, and probably a magician, too. One who could pull street-smart rabbits out of a hat.

Sam Wyant shook Dylan's hand and at the same time placed his leather briefcase on the table.

"I didn't do this," Dylan said, as Wyant sat in the chair opposite him.

"Who hit you?" Wyant said.

"Guy with a gun," Dylan said, touching the puffiness with his index finger.

"They treat you?"

"They gave me this." Dylan showed him the used cold pack they'd handed him before putting him back in lockup. It felt like a dead squirrel in his hand.

"You want another one?" Wyant said.

"I want to get out of here," Dylan said. "This whole thing is crazy. I didn't kill anybody."

"Then let's see where we are," Wyant said. He popped open the briefcase and took out a yellow legal pad and pen. He closed the briefcase and clicked the pen, then scribbled something at the top of the pad.

Dylan said, "Do we need to talk fee?"

"Of course," Wyant said. "But not now. This is an initial consultation, and it costs you nothing. You know that it's confidential, right? Anything you say to me stays with me. I'm like a walking, talking Las Vegas. And you're lucky to have me."

"I always knew you were confident."

"You know vertebrae, I know juries. You crack bones, I try cases. And I win."

Certainly true, that. Sam Wyant rose to prominence around the same time Dylan hung out his shingle in L.A. A star running back for the USC Trojans, Terrell Skyles, a Heisman Trophy frontrunner, had been charged with the rape of a seventeen-year-old high school student. It looked like the end of a promising career, not to mention first-round NFL-draft money. Nor was Skyles the most likable defendant. He had a record of disciplinary problems stretching back to his small-town Texas middle school.

The USC administration distanced itself from Skyles. Dylan

remembered that part vividly. They suspended Skyles without a hearing or any chance to defend himself.

Since the alleged attack took place at a party in Brentwood, the L.A. District Attorney, having learned the lessons of the O. J. Simpson murder trial, ordered that the case be tried in Santa Monica.

Everyone knew what that meant—mostly white jurors.

The alleged victim was white, too.

Which was why Terrell Skyles's management team hired a white lawyer named Sam Wyant.

And in the face of all the negative publicity and the almost nightly denunciations on cable TV, Sam Wyant won an outright acquittal. He did it by breaking down one of the supposed eye witnesses on cross-examination, gaining an admission that the whole thing had been a setup to try to extort money from a rising star.

The press, tail between its legs, had to admit it was a stunning courtroom triumph. "A Perry Mason moment," the *L.A. Daily News* called it. And in an ironic and humorous twist, the *L.A. Weekly* did a follow-up interview with Skyles who, at one point, asked, "Who is Perry Mason?"

From there, Sam Wyant had gone on to represent actors, record company executives, Beverly Hills housewives with prenups, and one Los Angeles County Supervisor caught on video taking a bribe in a hotel room, looking at an open attache case of cash and chirping, "Merry Christmas to me!" Wyant got him off by convincing a jury it was entrapment by overzealous feds who should have been after home-grown terrorists.

So while Dylan was slightly relieved he had Sam Wyant in his corner, he was not taking anything for granted.

Dylan said, "You know me. You know I couldn't do this."

Wyant held his pen between his thumb and forefinger. "I'll tell you what the prosecutor would say. He would say that you were in a romantic relationship with Ms. Tabitha Mullaney and you were at her house where she was found dead. You were surprised by a private investigator who was watching the house because Ms. Mullaney was afraid of you—"

"What!"

"—and oh yes, you pulled a gun on this man."

Dylan was not one for swearing, but he did so now.

Wyant said, "Those words and a couple of bucks will get you a cup of coffee."

"But don't I have to have a motive?"

"Motive is not an element of the crime of murder."

"You're kidding, right?"

"Do I look like I'm kidding? I'll let you know when I'm kidding, and it won't be any time soon. Clear?"

Dylan closed his eyes and absently put the dead cold pack on the side of his face.

"A motive strengthens the case for the prosecution," Sam Wyant said. "The jury can infer a motive."

"Like what?"

Wyant said. "Why don't you tell me how you met."

44

She pulled into the parking lot of the strip mall. B&B Market took up most of one corner. The pay phone was outside the front doors, next to an old *Daily News* newspaper dispenser that was faded and empty.

But as she got out of the car, a guy with long stringy hair, no shirt, and ratty pants went to the phone and shoved in some coins.

Erin looked at her watch. Three minutes until the call would come in.

She hurried to the phone just as the guy was putting in another coin and said, "Can I ask you to wait?"

The guy, holding the phone to his ear, glared at her. His deeply-tanned face and unkempt beard glistened with sweat and the greasy dirtiness of the street dweller. He had a bright red eruption on his left cheek, an infection of some kind. Erin tried not to look at it but it was like trying not to see a red light at a dark intersection.

The man did not use words.

He growled.

Actually growled.

Erin backed up a step, seriously wondering if he might try to bite her.

The guy was probably schizo, the way he acted. Yet he was using the phone just like a normal person would. A mix of sane and insane, right in keeping with this madness about Kyle.

The guy started yelling into the phone. What Erin could pick up between the four-letter words was something about rent, getting kicked out, and threats to remove body parts.

Now Erin didn't know which she feared most—the phone call to come, or an explosion by this crazy man who might want to take out his ire on her.

She ducked into the market.

And was immediately greeted by Julietta, one of the checkers.

"Early today," Julietta said. She was a stocky woman who was always polite and friendly. Erin often contrasted her with the checkers at the bigger market down the street, who didn't seem to care all that much about customer relations.

"Waiting to use the phone," Erin said, nodding her head toward the doors.

"The pay phone?"

Erin nodded.

"You want to use mine?" Julietta said, reaching into her pocket.

"No," Erin said. "I'm expecting somebody to call me."

"Out there?"

"It's a game," Erin said. She'd already revealed too much.

"Like a scavenger hunt?"

"Something like that," Erin said.

"Somebody else on the phone?" Julietta asked.

"Right now, yes."

Julietta took a step to the left so she could look out the front doors. "Oh, that guy."

"You know him?"

Julietta nodded. "Been around here all morning. Comes in the store, goes out. I know he's scared some people."

"Can't you call the police?"

"I did. They said they'd send a car by, but so far, nothing."

Surely, Erin thought, the man would know that a busy signal meant someone else was on the phone. He wouldn't hold it against her.

Right?

Not right. None of this was right. Erin looked down at the rack of impulse-buy items by one of the cash registers. Next to it was a display of tabloids. On one of them appeared unflattering head shots of two Hollywood stars, a former couple now involved in a nasty divorce, with the screaming headline *"I will destroy you!"*

And she suddenly felt the urge to tear that tabloid to shreds, and every copy of it, and make a pile of the papers and set fire to it, as if in some ancient ritual that would purge all the ugliness in the world, or if not the world at least the immediate area surrounding B&B Market.

Through the glass she could see the wild man.

He turned his head and looked directly at her.

And screamed.

45

"She connected with me on a dating site," Dylan said.

Sam Wyant loosened his tie as he sat back, listening.

"I looked at her profile. On the part that talked about sense of humor, she mentioned that she had grown up loving *Saturday Night Live*, especially Eddie Murphy and Joe Piscopo. Well, me too. So I suggested we get together for lunch. Which we did, and I really liked her. We talked on the phone a couple of times after that, and then I asked her to have dinner. So we met at Clearman's, in Pico Rivera, and we were having a great time. Or so I thought. Then after the meal, we were finishing up and she drops this bomb on me."

"Bomb?"

"I have to back up a little. A lot's been happening. The other night I got a note slipped under my door. It was in an envelope and it was written in crayon. It said, *Your son is alive.* My son was kidnapped fifteen years ago. He was never found."

Sam Wyant scribbled something on his legal pad.

"I thought it had to be some sick guy playing a trick on me, and then I got a second note. Same crayon, and this one said that Kyle's favorite play thing as a kid was the Harry Potter Lego set. And that's true. So then after our nice dinner, so to speak, Tabitha looked at me and said if I wanted to see my son again I was to do exactly as she said."

"Wait." Sam Wyant wrote faster. Then put his pen down and folded his hands. "Extortion?"

"She didn't tell me what I had to do."

"She didn't bring up the subject of money?"

"No. She had some fantasy about her and me and Kyle being happy together, but I didn't believe ... I didn't let myself believe Kyle was alive. She said she had proof. A photo. That I was to come to her house to see it. I had to see it."

"You didn't report this to the police?"

"She had it all set up, didn't she?" Dylan said. "She could deny everything. Make me look like the crazy one."

"So you think this woman was in league with someone?"

"Yes," Dylan said. "He has contacted my ex-wife."

"Where does she live, your ex?"

"Here in the Valley."

"I'll want to talk to her." Wyant wrote something, then underlined it twice. Then looked back at Dylan. "You said the victim contacted you through this dating site."

"Right."

"You didn't make the initial contact?"

"No."

"You didn't know her?"

"No."

"Yet she expressed this desire to be with you and your son?"

"That's what she dropped on me, yeah."

"Do you think she was serious about that?"

Dylan hesitated. He went back over Tabitha's demeanor, hearing her voice. How steady it was. How perfectly modulated. And realized he couldn't tell a thing by it.

"I have no idea," Dylan said.

"Because if she was," Wyant said, "she had to be someone from your past. This elaborate entrapment would require a fixation that borders on insanity. Her claim to have your son, or access to your son, could have been a mere device to manipulate you into further action. She would have to be an expert on your life somehow."

Sam Wyant tapped the legal pad a couple of times with the point of his pen.

"Now," Wyant said, "the guy who hit you."

"He said his name was Carbona. The detective who interviewed me, Smith, says he is ex-LAPD. Supposedly with a good record."

"We'll get his records," Wyant said as he wrote.

"He's lying," Dylan said.

"Then I'll shred him like yesterday's newspaper. Speaking of which, let me do the talking to reporters."

"Reporters?"

"Of course. Or what used to be called reporters. Real journalism is as rare as the blue-footed booby."

Sam Wyant picked up the legal pad and put it in his briefcase. He slipped the pen into its holder in the case, then shut and latched it.

"I will represent you, Dylan. But I will need fifty-thousand to get started. If there's a trial, it could reach two to three hundred grand."

Dylan lost breath.

"I know," Wyant said. "I wish it were not so. Believe it or not, I'm giving you a break on my normal fee. If there's a problem with that, I'll be happy to find you an—"

"Can I get a loan on my house?"

"It's done all the time," Wyant said.

"I want you to do this," Dylan said.

"Then I will."

"What about bail?" Dylan said. "Can I get out of here?"

"We'll set a bail hearing right away," Wyant said. "It'll be something substantial."

"How substantial?"

"With your profile, it won't be seven figures—"

"Seven figures!"

"Won't be," Wyant said. "I'll try to get it to five, but most likely it will be six."

"Can I post a bond?"

"Of course."

"What is it, ten percent?"

"Normally. But I do business with a solid bondsman, and if I refer he only charges eight percent."

Dylan rested his forehead on the palm of his right hand. The hand was giving off heat like never before.

"You've got to believe me," Dylan said. "I did not do this."

"I do believe you," Wyant said. "Now we start getting other people to believe you."

46

The crazy guy was still screaming into the phone. Erin looked at her cell. It was eighteen minutes since she'd been instructed to come here.

She stood at the door, looking directly at him. He gestured wildly and she could hear his voice, the F-words flying.

Erin didn't want to get within ten feet of that phone now, even with him off it. She wondered what incurable disease the guy's saliva was spreading all over the mouthpiece.

Which gave her an idea.

She went to the aisle with the care products and picked out a blue travel pack of Handi Wipes. When she got back to Julietta's check stand —the only one open—an old woman was loading a ton of groceries on the belt, at the same time fighting a handful of coupons and complaining to Julietta about the lack of cereal choices.

Just then the wild man walked past the doors on the outside, away from the phone.

"I'll pay for these in a sec," Erin said to Julietta, who gave her a smile and a thumbs-up.

Ripping a couple of wipes from the pack, Erin stepped outside, looking left to see where the crazy guy was. No sign. Maybe he was in the donut shop. She'd better light a candle for that donut shop, she mused.

The phone rang.

Erin picked up with her left hand, with a fresh wipe in her palm, and gave the handset a rub down with a wipe in her right. Still, when she spoke, she held the phone as if it were a radioactive carbon rod.

"You're late," the voice said.

"Couldn't be helped," Erin said.

"I don't like to be kept waiting."

"I told you—"

"You don't tell me anything. I tell you."

"Then tell me," Erin said.

"There is a lot to tell," the voice said.

"Just come out with it, then," Erin said.

"I am going to give you more instructions."

"I don't like this game."

"I told you before I'm very good at games, Erin. I know how you play."

Whatever that meant.

"Are you still there?" said the voice.

"Yes, I'm—"

A scream ripped through her ears. Erin's heart slammed against her chest. She jumped back, hit her head on the edge of the pay phone bay.

It was wild man. And he looked as deadly as a rabid dog, like he wanted to bite her arm and chew flesh.

Operating on pure adrenaline, Erin used the handset as a weapon and cracked him as hard as she could across the nose.

Blood spurted from his nostrils.

He put his hands to his face. Then looked at his blood-stained palms and howled. Erin saw a couple coming toward the store, a young man and woman, maybe mid-twenties, looking, pausing, keeping their distance.

"Call the police!" Erin shouted.

Wild Man's head snapped up at the word. His red-rimmed eyes narrowed at her.

Hunter and prey.

The young man took out his phone.

Erin held the tethered handset like a club. It felt small and ridiculous.

Wild Man jumped at her.

His hands were clawed, glistening red.

Erin crossed her arms, expecting contact.

Instead, something exploded.

It happened a microsecond before Wild Man's hands would have clutched at her face or arms or blouse. And in the next microsecond Erin realized to her horror and strange relief that the something that had exploded was Wild Man's head.

47

Back in the holding cell, Dylan's head throbbed with the beat of merciless and unresolved thoughts. He kept going over and over the events, but they wouldn't mesh or coalesce. They bled into each other in the muddy battlefield of his mind.

At least he had the best criminal lawyer in the city on his side. For a hefty fee, of course. But that didn't matter in the slightest. He would gladly give up everything he had to get out of this, as long as that included finding out if Kyle was really alive.

That was the thought that he knew would drive him crazy.

So he turned his thoughts to Erin. The last couple of times he'd been with her, even with all this going on, he'd felt some of the old feelings. They were ragged, of course, because of the tearing that had happened between them. That rip could perhaps be mended, but never completely covered up. The lines would show.

But what marriage of any length didn't have lines?

While he told himself the decision to divorce had been mutual, the result of a shared inevitability based upon a pain that would not relent, he knew it was more his fault than Erin's. That thought had always been there, but he'd managed to ignore it over the years. Professional activity and playing in a couple of men's leagues—softball and basketball—kept the guilt at bay.

But it was different in a four-by-six cell when all you have to look at are concrete-block walls and a stainless steel toilet.

He was filled with a longing to see Erin, talk to her. To explain all things before the media mangled the truth.

48

First there had been a patrol car and two officers, both men. The older one was named Rodriguez. His partner was Kerr.

Shaking, Erin thanked God for Julietta, who helped her wash off the dead man's blood from her face and arms, and wrapped a beach towel around her spattered blouse. She also brought her hot tea from the coffee bar and sat on the small retaining wall outside with her arm around Erin as the cops asked their questions.

Erin kept her back to the pay phone and the bloody corpse. Two other black-and-whites had arrived, and an officer was putting up crime-scene tape while another directed a small crowd to back away.

Just as Erin was finishing up with Officer Rodriguez, a Channel 7 news van pulled into the strip mall.

Great.

"Can you keep the news away from me?" Erin asked Officer Rodriguez.

"You don't have to talk to them," Rodriguez said. "But they have the right to set up here. You can wait for the detectives inside the store if you like."

"We have an office in the back," Julietta said.

She kept her arm around Erin as she led her to the small manager's office. It smelled like yesterday's coffee. But it was private and away from the swirl outside. It had a desk—moderately messy—a bulletin board, and a squat file cabinet with a Mr. Coffee machine on top.

Erin sat on one of the chairs, her body sending a request to shut down. It was a familiar query, just like at the six-mile mark of a marathon. That's when her body would request a break. Erin's brain chimed in "Do it! There's twenty freaking more miles to go!"

Erin had learned early on that you have to keep putting one foot in front of the other and close off the voices of retreat.

Erin took a couple of deep breaths and made herself sit up straight. The digital clock next to the coffee machine read 12:32.

She took out her phone and called Yumiko.

"I'm going to be late," Erin said.

"What's up?" Yumiko said.

"I can't really talk right now."

"Where are—"

"Cover for me?"

"Sure, but—"

"Thanks."

"Anything I can do?"

"Just keep the place running until I can get—" She stopped at the sight of two LAPD detectives at the office door. "Until I can get out of here."

The lead detective was in his late forties, tall and angular. Murray was his name. His partner, a woman named Stills, was in workout shape. After Murray introduced her, she gave Erin a nod and left the office.

Murray closed the office door.

"How are you feeling?" he asked.

"Terrible," Erin said.

"I understand. Can you talk a little?"

"I suppose I have to."

"It would help us out."

"I'll try."

Murray pulled the other chair from the side of the desk and sat opposite Erin. He had soft brown eyes that gave the impression of having recording devices behind them.

"This is a terrible thing, I know," Murray said. "A man shot right next to you. A lot of blood."

"Yes."

"Did you know this man?"

"Of course not!"

"Then let's start with how you happened to be here."

"What do you mean?"

"Why were you here at the store?"

"I come here often. Mainly at lunch time."

"A little early today then, right?"

Was he trying to trap her? He'd keep up this line of questioning until she told him about the excited-voiced man on the phone? But she'd been warned about involving the cops.

"I sometimes take an early lunch," Erin said.

"You took off from work?" Murray asked.

"Yes."

"Which is where?"

"DeForest."

"Over here on Vineland?"

Erin nodded.

"So you did not know this man who was shot. You told one of the officers that he was about to attack you, correct?"

"Yes."

"Do you know why he would do that?"

"He's obviously crazy," Erin said.

"You didn't do anything to set him off?"

"No! I was just ..."

"Go ahead."

"I was standing at the pay phone," Erin said.

"And why was that?"

"To make a call."

"You don't have a cell phone?"

Stupid! They don't have to trap you. You walk right into the net, with bells on. Weren't you taught never to lie? That lies only end up in disaster.

"I was actually waiting for someone to call me," Erin said.

"Why at a pay phone?"

"Because those were my instructions."

Detective Murray leaned forward, elbows on his knees. "Whose instructions?"

"I don't know. I can't tell you any more than that."

"Why are you following someone's instructions?"

Erin took a long, labored breath. "I can't tell you."

"Why not?"

"Part of the instructions."

Detective Murray sat back a little, considered her, then rested his elbows on his knees once again. His body language was unmistakable. Closing in.

"Mrs. Reeve, this is serious. A man is dead. Murdered. It may have something to do with you and that pay phone and those instructions."

"No, that poor man, it was just a coincidence that he was there."

"And that he was shot?"

"I don't know what to think about that."

"Do you think you might have been the target?"

"I ... don't think so."

"You're going to have to tell us more, Ms. Reeve."

"I can't."

"You don't have a choice. You're a material witness to a murder, and you are now withholding evidence."

"I don't want to do that."

"Then talk to me."

Erin hesitated, heart throbbing.

"We can hold you if need be," Detective Murray said.

"I honestly don't know! I don't know who has called me. I don't know why this man was shot."

"You can't even guess as to a connection?"

She shook her head.

The other detective appeared at the office door and asked Murray to join her.

"Excuse me a moment," Detective Murray said.

"I need to get back to work," Erin said.

"Not yet." He got up and went to the door. The two detectives spoke in low voices.

Erin looked at the walls of the office. It was the size of a jail cell. The detective said they could hold her. Where? In a real jail cell?

And then she noticed something on the other corner of the desk. A paperclip. Unattached. Sitting there as if waiting for someone to use it. Or was it recently discarded? How long had it been there? Was it unnoticed? Was it ... lonely?

That thought brought a flood of emotion crashing inside her. Kyle, at four, had started ascribing feelings to inanimate objects.

She vividly recalled the first time it happened. She had told Kyle he needed to clean up his room, put his toys away in the wooden chest.

She went back to the kitchen to check on the pork shoulder she was cooking in the Crock Pot. A few minutes later Kyle came out holding an empty box. It had held a softball Kyle got as a present from his grandma, Erin's mother.

"Do boxes have feelings?" he said.

Erin put the lid back on the Crock Pot. "What?"

"Do boxes have feelings?"

"Feelings?"

"If I throw it away, will it feel bad?"

His heart. She always knew it was tender, a good heart, something God granted him. It would, she knew, be a heart easily hurt. It had compassion, even for a box!

Erin had both tears and laughter at that moment, dropping to her knees, pulling Kyle to her.

And then she said to him, "No, sweetheart, no. Boxes don't have feelings, but people do. And sometimes people have feelings about their things. That's what this is. You can throw that box away. But you know what? If it did have feelings, it would be very happy that you got a ball out of it. It would be very happy to go now and maybe get made into something else someday."

Kyle smiled then, widely, and handed the box to his mother.

Erin reached over and picked the paperclip off the desk.

And kissed it.

Murray came back and resumed his seat. He was holding a plastic bag, the kind police put evidence in.

He said, "Mrs. Reeve, a few more questions, if you don't mind."

"And if I do mind?" Erin said.

"I need to ask." He didn't say it offensively.

She nodded.

"Your husband is named Dylan Reeve?"

"Ex-husband."

"When was the last time you spoke to him?"

"Why are you asking me this?"

"Please, Mrs. Reeve."

"A couple of days ago."

"Then you don't know where he is now?"

"I assume he's at his office."

Detective Murray shook his head. "He's in jail, Mrs. Reeve. He's being held on suspicion of murder."

"That ... can't be!"

"Did you know he was seeing a woman?"

Erin nodded.

"The woman he was seeing is the victim," Detective Murray said.

Erin fought for voice. "There's no way."

"That's not my concern at the moment, Mrs. Reeve. But you say you did not know the man outside who was shot."

"Right."

"I wonder if you might be able to explain something strange."

Stranger than this?

She waited.

Detective Murray said, "We found this on the victim, in his back pocket."

He held up the plastic bag so she could see what was inside.

It was Dylan's business card.

49

Petrie said, "Change of plans."

Jimmy said, "Where's my money?"

"You'll get your chance."

"Not what I asked."

Jimmy took a pull on the long-neck Bud. His third. Petrie was still nursing his double Jim Beam. Easy and sweet.

The bar was dark and not a lot of people yet. A few spics, which is how Petrie liked it. Among the wetbacks he could enjoy his supremacy. And nobody was going to hassle him, not with Jimmy right there.

"Guy's in jail now," Petrie said. "Murdered some tail he was into."

"No way," Jimmy said.

"Funny how life works out, isn't it?"

"What about this kid?" Jimmy said.

"What do you know about that?"

"Enough that I'm asking where he is."

"You just leave that to me," Petrie said.

"Where is he?" Jimmy said, eyes like blue ice.

"He's nowhere," Petrie said.

Jimmy squinted at him. Took another swig. "What's goin' on?"

"You don't ask that," Petrie said. "I'm paying you, you don't have to know anything but what I tell you to do."

"You ain't paid me yet." Jimmy slapped the bar top. The droopy-eyed barman looked at him. Jimmy pointed at his beer bottle.

The bartender pulled out another Bud and popped the top, set the beer in front of Jimmy.

"I don't like the way you don't tell me things," Jimmy said.

"Haven't I always been good on my word?" Petrie said.

Jimmy frowned.

"You got the job," Petrie said.

"I was supposed to get five grand," Jimmy said. "Up front."

"Why I'm here," Petrie said. "I got good faith money for you. How's about five yards?"

Petrie took out his wallet and pulled out five crisp one-hundred dollar bills. He set them on the bar.

"That's it?" Jimmy said.

"On account," Petrie said.

"How long I gotta wait?"

"I don't know," Petrie said. "I want to let things hang in the wind for a while."

"You really enjoy that kind of stuff, don't you?"

"What?"

"Making people suffer," Jimmy said.

"It's called payback, Jimmy. It's not the same thing. The bigger the payback, the bigger you want 'em to hang. Remember that."

Jimmy took another drink, put the bottle down. He picked up the five bills and tapped them on the bar top, putting them neatly in a row. He folded them once and put them in his shirt pocket.

50

"And you have no idea why your ex-husband's business card would be in the possession of this man?" Detective Murray asked.

Erin stared at the bagged card in the detective's hand. "I ... no ..."

"Here's what I'm dealing with," Detective Murray said. "Your husband is arrested for murder, there's a murder this morning. The connection is you. This victim has a business card with your ex-husband's name on it. You were told to come to this location to receive a call on a pay phone. You are withholding some information from me. There's a picture here that isn't complete. I believe you're the only one who can complete it."

Erin was seeing a picture, too, only it wasn't merely incomplete. It was a funhouse nightmare. Everything was distorted and mad laughter echoed in the background.

"Were you and your ex on good terms?" Detective Murray asked.

"What? Yes. Of course. Wait. What do you mean by that?"

"It's been known to happen."

"Detective," she said, "Dylan would never, ever kill someone."

"Let me remind you, he's been arrested for doing just that."

She shook her head. "There's got to be some other explanation."

"Ms. Reeve, that's often what a wife says."

Emotional exhaustion began to give way to anger. "You are not going to get anywhere with me by being nasty."

"I'm not trying to be, Ms. Reeve. I'm only—"

"Oh, then it's just your manner? Your way of conducting interviews?"

"I try to be professional," he said.

"I think you need work," she said. "Now am I finished here?"

"You certainly can be," Detective Murray said. "But I'll need to follow up. What would be the best time to contact you?"

Erin stood.

"Sixteen years ago," she said.

51

They loaded Dylan on a Sheriff's bus, along with five others from the Van Nuys jail. They said he was being shipped to the jail facility in Castaic. It might as well have been the surface of Mars.

All Dylan knew about Castaic was that it was through the pass that connects the civilization of Los Angeles to the desert and jack rabbits of whatever was past Magic Mountain in Valencia. He couldn't remember the last time he'd been out that far on the 5. He pictured tumbleweeds and dried cow skulls.

And the razor wire of a prison.

Which is exactly what he was, a prisoner. For a murder he had not committed. For a murder that he was set up for.

In what possible universe could this be happening?

He thought of the movie *The Fugitive* with Harrison Ford. One of his favorite movies of all time, in fact. In further fact, he and Erin went to see it before they were married, at a revival theater that charged only one dollar per ticket. In the movie things worked out for Harrison Ford. Tommy Lee Jones, who said he didn't care, turned out to care a lot. And Harrison Ford, against all odds, kept alive on the streets, avoiding the clutches of Jones's crack team of trackers—long enough to find the real murderer.

But that was a movie. This was real life.

And Dylan did not feel like Harrison Ford.

He looked out the barred window of the bus, at the cars passing on the freeway. From the back of a Hyundai, a little boy looked up at the bus, mouth slightly open in wonderment.

A little boy about Kyle's age when he was taken.

Get a good look, son. The world isn't the playground you think it is. I hope you make it in life.

The boy's eyes met his for an instant, then the child turned his head away.

The Hyundai drove on, seeming to take with it his last view of normalcy.

How could he fight this? A man crushes your face and lies, but has an impeccable record as a cop. What a perfect profile for a false witness. Had he been the one to kill Tabitha? If so, why?

Would Sam Wyant be able to find anything out? Dylan wondered just how strongly the lawyer believed him. Oh, he'd give Dylan every benefit of the doubt, but benefits eventually dry up and doubts have a way of calcifying.

And speaking of drying up, Dylan would have to do something about his practice. And Paige.

He had a friend who could probably take a few of his regulars, but how long could that last? There were a thousand-and-one practical things that needed taking care of. Feeding his goldfish. Making sure his bills were paid. Keeping an eye on the security of the house.

He suddenly felt like the bus was one-tenth its actual size. He was inside a metal tube, constricted, looking through the grate that separated two deputies from the prisoners, of which he was one.

"There's too many of them."

The phrase flashed through his mind. It was something Kyle had said, right before his first T-ball at bat.

That day Kyle was nervous. Dylan had to talk him into showing up for the game. T-ball practice had demonstrated that Kyle's skills were not yet as developed as some of the other kids. It took ten minutes of cajoling, but Kyle finally announced he was ready, and put on a brave face.

But when he got to the field and saw the other team warming up, he squeezed Dylan's hand harder.

And when it came time for him to take his first official T-ball swing, Dylan was standing right behind the fenced dugout clapping his hands.

As Kyle walked by, he looked out to the field and back to his father and said, "There's too many of them."

Dylan said, "Just hit the ball and run as fast as you can."

If Kyle's face was any indication, Dylan's advice was as effective as a car horn in rush-hour traffic.

But then the miracle happened. Somehow everything came together in Kyle's swing—force, contact, follow-through—and he smacked the ball up the middle, past second base and into the outfield.

And stood there, watching the ball with a sense of wonder.

Dylan, along with the coaches and other parent spectators, screamed, "Run!"

Which is exactly what Kyle did. He ran. He ran faster than Dylan never seen him run.

Directly to third base.

With the cries of coaches overlapping howls from the stands, Kyle stood on the third-base bag and looked around, wondering what all the commotion was. Finally the boy playing short fielder threw the ball to the second baseman, who seemed to know what he was doing, for he ran all the way to first base and put his foot on the bag.

Then laughter from the stands, and Dylan saw the moment when Kyle realized it was aimed at him. When an umpire told Kyle to return to his bench, he walked fast, head down. A couple of his teammates patted him on the back, but at least one appeared to say something nasty.

Kyle sat heavily on the bench. Dylan could see his shoulders quivering.

After the game, Dylan told Erin he wanted to take Kyle out for ice cream—alone. Erin understood. It was one of those times for a man-to-son talk.

And at 31 Flavors, over a cup of Rocky Road, Dylan told Kyle how proud he was of him. "There were too many of them, you said, but you hit the ball anyway, and you hit it hard, and you ran, just like I told you."

"But I ran the wrong way," Kyle said.

"A lot of us run the wrong way sometimes," Dylan said. "Even grownups like me."

"You do?"

"Sure we do. I'm not talking about baseball. I'm talking about things we do in life. They're called mistakes. But the main thing is that you take your swings. You try, and you run, no matter how many there are out there who want to stop you. That's something you can learn today and keep for the rest of your life. Just keep taking your swings."

"You mean T-ball?"

"Yes. And when you're a little older, I'll tell this to you again about other things in your life. Okay?"

"Okay."

But of course, he never got the chance to tell his son those things again.

And now, here on the bus, there were too many of them. Detectives and deputy sheriffs and an ex-cop trying to put him away and to tear him apart inside.

But then he could almost hear Kyle's child-voice, giving his own advice back to him.

"Take your swings, and run as fast as you can."

52

"You the bone cracker." It was a statement, not a question.

"Chiropractor," Dylan said.

"For the Lakers, right?"

The phrase *news travels fast* came fast to Dylan's mind. It was the day after his first night in the North County Correctional Facility, a sleepless one in the dorm-style cattle room housing other blue-outfitted jailbirds.

Now he was seated at a table with a tray of what they euphemistically referred to as lunch. And this other inmate had decided to join him.

He was thin with slicked-back black hair and dark tats on his neck. One of the tats was in script, something in Spanish. The one word Dylan recognized was *vida*. Life.

The guy was probably around forty years old but the eyes looked older. There were deep-rutted crow's feet at the corners.

"So how come my sister's back keeps goin' out and she keeps goin' to the bone cracker. How come she don't get better?"

A professional consultation in jail? Dylan almost felt relieved. "Every case is different."

"Just like in here, huh?"

Dylan looked down at his food. It consisted of a yellowish glop that resembled mac and cheese, apple slices with browning edges, and a black square that he supposed was some sort of brownie.

His uninvited guest said, "You kill your woman?"

Dylan closed his eyes, trying to wish the guy away.

"Got no secrets here," the guy said. "You do it?"

"No," Dylan said.

"Look me in the eye, tell me you didn't do it."

Now Dylan looked into the man's eyes and was mildly surprised that he wasn't intimidated.

"Why?" Dylan said.

"Cause I'm askin'."

"This some sort of jailhouse test?"

"You don't want no test. Not a pink fish like you. No, no, no, a test is what you don't want."

"I want to be left alone."

"You pick the wrong place for that." The man reached over and took Dylan's brownie.

And said, "Did you do it?"

"No," Dylan said. "I didn't do it. Now give me back my brownie."

"What you say?"

"I'm not afraid of you," Dylan said.

Man, what was he doing? The guy had called him a pink fish, and he knew enough to know it meant easy pickings to the veterans of lockups and prisons and vomit-smelling police benches. He was as likely to get a plastic fork to the eye as he was to get his brownie back. But at that moment, Dylan Reeve did not care.

Or, cared more than he had in fifteen years. Cared about pushing back against life, not letting it run over him like a tank with spiked treads. Not just lying there waiting for the next pass to crunch his guts again.

And then the guy smiled. Nodded. He put the brownie back on Dylan's tray.

"I believe you," he said. "And I don't believe you."

Feeling an odd sense of elation at having his brownie back—his simple, stupid square of sugar and chemicals—Dylan said with added force, "What's that supposed to mean?"

"I believe when you say you didn't do it," the guy said. "I can tell. I seen enough guys to know when they ain't bein' straight up."

"So what don't you believe?"

"That you ain't afraid of me."

"So what's that prove?" Dylan said.

"Proves you got some cashews, man. Tellin' me you ain't afraid when you are. But that can get you jumped, you don't watch out. Or got somebody watchin' out for you."

Dylan said, "You're offering to be my protection."

"You got it."

"In return for what?" Dylan said.

"Your brownie," the guy said with a smile.

"Are you serious?"

"I look like a clown to you?"

"Just take it," Dylan said.

"And one more thing," the guy said.

Here it comes, Dylan thought. The jailhouse service that shall not be named. Or some other humiliating show of subservience. Here it comes, because you're in a nightmare and aren't going to be waking up anytime soon.

But Dylan did summon the guts to look him in the eye again. He didn't know what he'd do when the guy made his demand.. He wondered what it would be like to get in a fight. He'd probably end up losing teeth. Or half an ear.

Then the guy said, "Can you get me an autographed picture of Jaquez Rollins?"

Dylan Reeve started laughing. It came up like bubbling crude, a fierce and hysterical laughter that he knew was pure release, something his body demanded of him, and he didn't fight it. He laughed like a crazy man and couldn't stop, even though he felt the eyes of the other prisoners on him. Tears from the laughter—and the release—streamed down his cheeks. Dylan wiped his eyes and managed to say, "Yes, I can … get you … that picture." And then he laughed some more. He laughed as he grabbed his brownie and put it on the guy's tray.

53

Alone in her condo at noon on a Wednesday made Erin feel like she was sick.

And maybe, in a very real sense, she was. Having a man's head blown off when he's about to grab you was not to be found under any heading marked *Normal.*

Yumiko had been nice enough to cover for Erin for another day. But Erin could hear in Yumiko's voice on the phone how anxious she was to know what was going on. Erin didn't want to go into it, told Yumiko she'd come in tomorrow and they'd talk. It was exactly the wrong thing to say, for it fired up Yumiko's determination to get Erin to spill all beans. Erin had to quickly thank her again and disconnect.

She needed this silence.

She wasn't hungry. Her stomach felt like it was sloshing around in a bowl of grease. She finally decided to sip some chardonnay. *A little wine for thy stomach,* her mother had been fond of saying before taking her medicinal nip of sherry at night. Maybe Mom and the Bible knew whereof they spoke.

Erin poured the wine and walked it to the living room. She sat on the sofa, took a deep breath, and a small sip. The chard was cool and crisp on her tongue. She tried to think of the time she and Dylan had gone to the Hollywood Bowl together a few weeks after they'd started dating. It was one of the great evenings of her life. Dylan had prepared the picnic himself—red grapes and Edam cheese to start, seared ahi tuna for the main, mini-cheesecakes for dessert.

And a bottle of California chardonnay. It could have been a bottle of tap water, as far as Erin was concerned, because she was in love.

But the memory wouldn't stay. It was blasted out by the bloody remains of the man at the pay phone.

And by a strange, incongruous image trying to assert itself—of Dylan Reeve, her Dylan, sitting in a jail cell accused of murder.

It was time to find out more.

She picked up her phone.

"Dr. Reeve's office."

"Paige? It's Erin."

"Then you've heard."

"How on earth can this be happening?"

It was an absurd question, because the same could be asked of her own situation. But she didn't have time for her thoughts to catch up with her doubts or her inability to make sense of it all.

"He has a lawyer," Paige said. "He's in jail now. I just can't believe this."

"I can't either," Erin said. "There is no way Dylan would kill anyone."

"I was questioned by a detective. I didn't like it one bit. But what I gather is it looks pretty bad."

"I want to go see him. Do you know where he is?"

"No. They were supposed to take him to another jail. But I haven't heard yet where."

"Will you call me as soon as you know anything?"

"Of course."

Pause. Then Paige said, "Are you doing all right?"

"Sometime I'll fill you in," Erin said. "Thanks for all your support for Dylan."

Erin went out to the balcony and sat in one of the chairs. The sun bleached North Hollywood and Studio City and the air was fairly clear for the Valley. Yet she found it hard to breathe deeply. Her chest was tight and her lungs were like fists.

Her phone buzzed, no source number showing. But she knew it was him. She'd been expecting it. And was thinking maybe he would give up information that might help the LAPD track him down.

She took the call but said nothing.

His voice said, "Did you like what I did?"

She remained silent.

"I think you do. I know you do. You were standing right there. I shot him in the head. Do you know not many people could have made that shot?"

Finally, she found voice. She kept it steady, hoping to draw him out. "Why did you do that? What are you trying to prove?"

"I *am* trying to prove something. To you. I want you to see how good I am. I know that you teach your pathetic little students competency in irrelevant little matters like accounting and statistics. None of that means anything. Not in the grand scale. I am much more than that. So I want you to tell me just how good a shot I am."

"Why did you shoot him?"

"I was protecting you."

"No. You set him up. You put my ex-husband's card in his pocket, didn't you?"

"Well done! I am really happy that you think that. It just means I am so right about you."

"You don't know anything about me."

"Oh, but I do. And it's all good."

"None of this is good," Erin said.

"What about your son? I am doing all this to prove to you that I can give you what you want."

"You want to torture me. You're enjoying this."

"I tell you I am not. I want your respect. I don't want you to be scared of me. In fact, I think it's about time you and I met face-to-face."

"No," Erin said. "Never."

"Never say never," he said. "I am going to set it up."

"I don't think so."

"I'll spring it on you, as a surprise. A loving surprise."

"No! You will not—"

The call dropped.

54

On Thursday morning they bussed Dylan and several other prisoners to the courthouse in San Fernando. They were herded into one big holding cell where they sat on benches like third-string football players, waiting to be told they were cut from the team.

A little after nine o'clock, a couple of deputy sheriffs herded Dylan and half a dozen others through a door that led into a courtroom. They were told to sit in the jury box.

Sam Wyant was in the courtroom, looking regal in a three-piece suit. He was chatting with the bailiff as Dylan took his place in the box. He said something that made the bailiff smile.

Working the room, Dylan thought. That's why he gets the big bucks.

Sam walked over to the jury box and motioned for Dylan to stand.

"They treating you okay?" Wyant asked.

"I'm eating like a king," Dylan said. "What do I do now?"

"The judge will call our case. You stand up and say nothing until the judge asks how you plead."

"When can I get out on bail?"

"I'll get us a hearing."

"A hearing?"

"On bail."

"Why not right now?"

Sam Wyant shook his head. "Doesn't work that way for a felony. One step at a time."

"Make it two steps," Dylan said.

Sam Wyant patted him on the arm.

The judge's name was Alex Avakian. He looked fiftyish, with black hair and deep complexion. He handled a few matters, including one chewing out of a seemingly clueless defense counsel, then called Dylan's case.

Sam Wyant stood like a potentate greeting a fellow ruler. Dylan stood as instructed.

"Good morning, your honor. Sam Wyant for the defendant, Dylan Reeve. We will waive a reading of the complaint and statement of rights and are ready to enter a plea."

"Very well," the judge said. He looked at Dylan. "Mr. Reeve, has counsel explained to you what's happening this morning?"

"Yes, your honor," Dylan said.

"You understand the charge against you is murder under California Penal Code section 187?"

"Yes."

"And how do you plead?"

"Not guilty."

Judge Avakian looked at his computer monitor "We will set this matter for preliminary hearing on . . . March twenty-seven at nine a.m. How's that work?"

The prosecutor, a sharply dressed woman who looked fresh out of law school, said, "Fine for the People."

Sam Wyant said, "I'll be returning from Puerto Vallarta that day, your honor."

"Oh? A little fishing?"

"I have a house there," Wyant said.

"A little tequila drinking?"

"A lot, I'm hoping."

"Well, we can kick this to the twenty-eighth if the People are open."

"I'd rather go to Puerto Vallarta," the prosecutor said.

"I'll take that as a yes," the judge said. "The twenty-eighth it is, nine o'clock."

Dylan looked at the players and thought, how can they be so congenial? When a man was standing before them being set up for murder?

Sam Wyant said, "May we be heard on the issue of bail?"

"Have the People received notice?" the judge said.

"We have not," said the prosecutor.

Judge Avakian looked at his monitor again. "Bail hearing Monday at ten o'clock?"

"All right for the People," the prosecutor said.

"All right for the defense," Sam Wyant said.

Not all right for me, Dylan thought. Two more days in jail. Not all right.

55

And so there was running.

It was how she escaped, the sensation of movement and street and her body trying to reach a limit. Something to look forward to. It brought a forgetfulness, a way to become one with legs and pavement and lungs, so that nothing was interfering, no sadnesses dragging her down. Running put her inside a bubble of breath and motion, the rhythm of heart and feet.

She ran in the twilight. Even though she was on the busy strip of asphalt that joined North Hollywood and Studio City, even though she was slightly aware of the looks of admiration—*There goes an older woman running, looking lean, good for her!*—she made herself think of oceans and sunlight and laughing children on the beach. It was a way to keep other pictures out of her consciousness.

She ran easily but with just the right amount of push to make her body work, for that is what she wanted—the rush of adrenaline and sweat.

She turned down Burbank Boulevard and was happy to see there was another runner coming her way. A younger version of herself, in fact. A ponytailed woman in a tank top with an armband holding an MP3 player and earbuds. When they passed each other they gave the runner's nod, a sign of approval, and it made Erin feel like she was a part of an exclusive sorority of running women, showing the world what they were made of.

She had a favorite course that took her through a residential neighborhood. Here there were retirees watering lawns and young couples pushing baby carriages or walking dogs. She always gave a smile and gentle wave. They always waved back. If only life could be this way all the time! What was it Sam Cooke sang? *What a wonderful world it would be.*

But then her mind would betray her, and she would think it's not a wonderful world, not even close. And that would make her push some more, run harder, make her lungs burn for oxygen.

To forget.

As she made her way down a familiar lane, street lights coming on and a few cars returning home, she sensed that a light behind her was not quite right.

It was an instinct born of hundreds of these runs. She looked over her shoulder and saw a car—dark blue of some kind, with headlights on—cruising slowly, matching her pace.

Perhaps the car was being cautious about a runner on the street. She had on her reflective-mesh running vest, and her New Balance shoes with giant Ns that were almost mirrors.

This wasn't a busy nor particularly narrow street. No reason the car couldn't go easily past her and on its merry way.

But it didn't.

For forty yards or so it kept itself at exactly the same distance.

Erin banked to the sidewalk. She didn't like running on concrete, especially on these L.A. sidewalks where tree roots often pushed up sections that could lead to nasty trip-and-falls.

A quick look at the car.

It was speeding up.

She took a sharp turn at the corner.

The headlights followed.

And flashed brights at her.

She never brought her cell phone when she ran. She never wanted to be one of those who was tied to her phone all the time, like the students at DeForest who all had neck problems from looking down. Or she laughingly supposed.

She wasn't laughing now.

The car suddenly burned rubber and came up fast, passed her. It had darkened windows. She couldn't see inside. The car screeched to stop at the curb, ten yards in front of her.

Erin turned and sprinted back the way she'd come.

And heard the roar of the car, the squeal of tires.

Get back to the main drag. Burbank Boulevard. To people.

The headlights hit her again.

56

Dylan Reeve, county inmate booking #4684921, lay on his back on a bottom bunk, looking at the underside of the upper. Not like the movies. Not Jimmy Cagney or Bogart. No escape plans. No Tim Robbins tunnel from *Shawshank Redemption*. Nobody rooting for you. No one calling the governor to get you a pardon.

Instead, you're in a jail cell with a clammy coldness on your skin, feeling the prickles as if they were a permanent rash. You felt this before, yes, that time, you were twelve and Dad called you to come sit with him in the study.

Mom was at the hospital, but hospitals were where they made you better. They had doctors and nurses and machines and medicine, and it would be all right.

Dad sat you down and put his hands on your shoulders, something he hadn't done before. He wasn't crying but his eyes were wet. That's when you got scared, when the coldness hit your skin.

"Listen, champ," Dad said, "you and I, we've got to get ready for something, okay? It won't be easy, okay?"

You knew it then, you knew Mom wouldn't be coming home. The frozen pinpricks up and down your arms.

"Can't they help her?" you said, your voice squeaky.

"They're going to try, but it's a rare form. It's not something they know that much about. And ..."

Dad paused to catch a breath, but he never finished the sentence.

You felt that sense of powerlessness, and then loss, even though you would see her for a few weeks yet, see her weak and thin and helpless. Hating it and crying when you were alone.

Getting behind in school.

Giving up.

Until you figured out you had to go on.

Well now you have that same choice, don't you?

It starts in your mind, man. Only you can decide. Only you can do it.

57

"Are you insane?" Erin let the anger flow like Gatorade. Her body was amped from the running. She had no desire to be calm.

"Wait a second," Andy said.

He was standing by his stupid, frosted-window car just off Burbank. It had taken her a moment to recognize his voice.

"No, you wait a second," Erin said. "What are you following me like that for?"

"I was coming over to show you my new car," he said. "So I'm driving and I see you running. I thought it would make a nice surprise."

"So you follow me and flash your lights?"

"I was obviously trying to get your attention."

"It didn't occur to you I might think you some kind of crazy person?"

"I'm innocent, I tells ya."

"Don't make light of this. I've had some bad things happen to me in the last couple of days."

Andy took a step toward her, arms out.

Erin stepped back and gestured for him to stop right there.

Andy said, "That's another reason I was coming over. Yumiko told me what happened. It was on the news. I wanted to see you and see what I could do for you."

"Next time just call and leave a message and wait for me to get back to you, how does that sound?"

"Of course. But I do want to help you."

"You best stay out of this. It's in the hands of the police."

"I can at least be with you. Be a support."

"Andy, you're a nice guy—"

"Uh-oh."

"No, listen. I mean it. But it's just not going to work out between us. Especially not right now."

"I don't think you really mean that."

"I don't care what you think. I'm telling you."

Andy folded his arms. "I'm not going to give up on us."

"There is no *us,*" Erin said. "I'm telling you to give it up. I don't need a persistent suitor-slash-stalker at the moment, if you don't mind."

Andy's face hardened. "Thank you so much for calling me a stalker."

He spun around and went to the driver's side of the car.

"Andy ..."

Saying nothing, he got in and slammed the door. A second later he gunned the car away from the curb.

58

"Come over here," Petrie said.

The kid didn't come.

"You hear me?" Petrie said.

The kid held the broom close to his body and looked at the floor. At times like this he never looked Petrie in the eye. He was standing by the wall near the concession stand.

"You don't come over here you know what's gonna happen." Petrie said.

Slowly, keeping eyes down, and holding the broom like a security blanket, the kid shambled over and stood in front of Petrie.

"I got another complaint about the bathroom," Petrie said. "You know how I like the bathrooms. Right?"

The kid didn't answer. His eyes were still cast down.

"Right?"

The kid gave one nod.

"That's better," Petrie said. He put his arm around the kid's neck, pulled the kid's head to his chest. "You know I'm the only one can help you, right?"

Nod.

"Always have, always will," Petrie said. "You've just got to remember to do exactly what I say all the time. Right?"

Nod.

"Good, good." Petrie kissed the top of the kid's head. "Now go do the front bathrooms, and remember how I told you to make them so clean you could eat off the floors? Go on. Show me what you can do."

59

Erin woke on Saturday morning as if emerging from a dream. For a few seconds her room, her bed, the ceiling—even the light—seemed unfamiliar. She could have been anywhere, from a motel in some backwater town to the rabbit hole in *Alice in Wonderland*.

When she finally came to herself, she felt a residue of anger from Andy's stupid stunt coating her thoughts. She got out of bed and made a beeline for the coffee machine.

Twenty minutes later she was making plans for the day, which included a drive out to visit Dylan. Why they had him all the way out in Castaic was a mystery to her. But then again nothing about the past ten days was making any sense.

A little after ten she got a call from Detective Murray.

"Just wanted to let you know," he said, "that the victim was a homeless man who apparently went by the name Hacksaw. He stayed mostly under the freeway overpass on Tujunga. There are others down there, not all that reliable or helpful. Would your ex-husband have known anyone by that name?"

"I have no idea. I can ask."

"I would appreciate that. Maybe we can talk again soon."

"Sure," Erin said, ending the call abruptly. And then thought, *Hacksaw? Whatever happened to Bill or Fred?*

60

Dylan wanted to reach through the Plexiglas and hold Erin's hand. He might as well have been in Siberia with a phone hookup.

"I can't believe you're in jail," Erin said into the handset.

Dylan said, "You know I didn't do this."

"Of course not. Not for a second. I can't stand that you're in here."

"I'll get out on bail. I've got a good lawyer. An expensive one, but good."

Erin closed her eyes, took a breath.

"What about you?" Dylan said. "How are you getting along?"

"Dylan, something really strange and horrible has happened."

"More than this?"

"Let me tell you. I can't make sense of it. That man called me, the one who wrote the notes. He knows where I work, my habits. He told me to go to the little market I go to sometimes, to wait for a phone call at the public phone. A man was there, a crazy looking man, like someone on drugs. Or off them. He was using the phone and screaming. When he finally got off I went to the phone to wait, and he came back and jumped at me."

Dylan squeezed the handset.

"But just then," Erin said, "he was shot."

"Shot!"

"Right next to me. It was awful."

"Who shot him?"

"I don't know! The police say it was a rifle shot. It hit him in ..."

"It's okay, Erin, take your time"

She took a deep breath and wiped her eyes with her free hand. "It got him in the head. The police came and a detective talked to me. I told him everything but then he showed me something they took out of the dead man's pocket. Dylan, it was your business card."

"How ... who was this man?"

"He was some homeless man who called himself Hacksaw."

"Hacksaw?"

"I know. Crazy, right? Dylan, what is going on?"

Dylan shook his head. "We are both being played for some reason."

"Do you think they know where Kyle is?"

"If this was really about Kyle, they'd have given us proof and asked for money."

"But they knew about Harry Potter."

"Information they could have gotten somehow."

Erin was silent for a long moment. Even after ten years apart, Dylan could read her face. She'd always had a transparency about her. It was one of the things he loved about Erin when they'd started dating. In her were no hidden chambers, no dank closets obscured behind false fronts.

Once, during those first awful weeks after Kyle was taken, Erin tried to put on a steel mask, a look of coping and confidence. He loved her for that, too, even as the mask melted into hot tears almost as soon as it appeared. They'd been at a restaurant, trying to eat like normal people, knowing they'd never be normal again. The food was largely uneaten. And as Dylan attempted to make conversation he saw the mask, saw the effort. Erin said something, the first strong and hopeful utterance since the taking, and he was surprised and pleased. He reached for her hand then. It was cold to the touch. He wrapped his fingers around hers and squeezed softly. The steel mask lasted another second and then was gone.

Now Dylan wanted to take her hand again. He wanted it more than anything at this very moment. He put his own hand on the Plexiglas, fingers spread, trying to send heat through to her.

Erin put her palm on the glass, meeting his.

"We'll get through this," she said.

He saw the steel in her look, only this time it was natural on her, softer somehow on the features, yet stronger, too, as if it had been part of her all along.

Dylan nodded.

Simultaneously, they put their hands down. As if a vow had been taken and a sacred commitment made.

61

Driving home from the jail Erin decided to stop for the most amount of comfort food with the least amount of thought. A Jack-in-the-Box was the ticket. She told herself she'd make up for this indulgence with an evening run.

She ordered a bacon cheeseburger, curly fries, and a Coke, took her tray to a table by the window that gave her a lovely view of the Taco Bell across the road.

She'd forgotten how good a bacon burger was. That first bite was love in Paris in the spring. Of course she knew it would soon be sitting in her stomach like a cinderblock. After all the healthy eating she'd done in the last ten years, this indulgence would carry its own punishment.

But the journey over the tongue was worth it. The curly fries were more bits of transient heaven, and the pure Coke—not diet, not that Zero stuff—was the king of soft drinks.

One of the female servers, who couldn't have been more than twenty, dressed in her crisp uniform and wearing a customer-relations smile, placed a slice of cheesecake on Erin's table.

"Oh," Erin said, "I didn't order—"

"Your boyfriend wanted to surprise you," the server said. "He's a sweetie, by the way."

"You got the wrong girl," Erin said lightly.

"And," the server said, as if she hadn't heard, "he said to give you this."

She handed Erin a large, square envelope. Hallmark size. The moment Erin touched it, a dread realization gripped her. She looked past the girl at the rest of the dining area. It was almost full. Families, couples, a group of retirees sipping inexpensive coffee.

And in the farthest corner from where Erin sat, a man in sunglasses and a baseball cap pulled low.

It was a Cubs hat. A big red letter C with a white outline, on blue.

Erin's stomach tightened and she let out an audible gasp.

The Cubs. Kyle's team.

The man was looking directly at her, leaning back comfortably in his booth, smiling.

"Enjoy!" the server said, and off she went, leaving no sight buffer between Erin and the man.

She was cold and hot at the same time. It was like the air conditioning in the place had fallen ten degrees in one second. Yet her insides burned like a fever.

Mr. Cub made a gesture with his hands—opening a book.

He wanted her to read what was in the envelope.

For a long moment she didn't move, trying to make sense of what was happening. Obviously, he had followed her to the jail and then to this place where she sought a little food comfort. He was violating her, toying with her. He wanted her frightened. He loved it.

When she got her hands moving again, she dropped the envelope on the table. It hit the edge and fell to the ground. Involuntarily, she looked at the man and he wagged his finger at her—no, no, no.

Her eruption of anger at that patronizing gesture almost had her leaping up and running at him, over tables and retirees both. But she knew he would be prepared for anything. And was dangerous.

She met his shades with a stare of defiance.

He shook his head slowly, then made the same gesture that she should read what was now on the floor.

She hesitated, then bent down and picked up the envelope.

It was not sealed.

She pulled out a folded piece of paper, opened it.

It had a juvenile scrawl, in black felt-tip marker.

Mom, I want to see you again.

62

"How'd the visit go?" Rodriguez asked.

Emilio Rodriguez was the name of the brownie-loving inmate who wanted the autographed picture of Jaquez Rollins.

And, increasingly, it looked like, Dylan's meal companion.

Today's lunch was a sumptuous fare of forest-green meat mixed with off-white rice, baked beans, two blocks of what appeared to be corn-bread, a slice of something with powdered sugar on it, and a cup of red liquid described as a "vitamin beverage."

"You want my cornbread?" Dylan asked.

"No, man, it's all yours."

"Thanks."

"I mean it," Rodriguez said. "I know you saw your lady."

He really did seem sincere. But Dylan was not going to trust him — or anybody else—very far.

Dylan said, "It's hard to see someone on the other side of the window and you can't be with them."

"Three ways to look at it, man."

"Only three?"

"First way is the glass is half full. Second way is the glass is half empty."

"The third?"

"Third way is, we're the ones in the glass, bein' watched."

"That's cheery."

"They're watchin' to see if they can break you."

"We are in jail."

"Don't matter. Long as I got three hots and a cot, I'm good. Can't break my spirit. Which is what's happening to you."

"Is that right?"

"See it in your face. You ain't somebody knows the inside of a place like this. You're a first-time killer. You got to fight back."

"Yeah? How?"

"You just wait."

"Wait?"

"Wait."

"Thanks for the great advice," Dylan said.

Rodriguez smiled. "Always open for business. And yeah, if you don't want that cornbread ..."

63

Mom, I want to see you again.

Erin stared at the writing, blurred now by brimming tears.

It couldn't be.

She closed her eyes and felt the squeezed-out tears falling. She put her head in her palm. The stressors of the past week had played havoc with her brain. She knew she wasn't thinking straight. But something had to be done now.

Opening her eyes she looked past the tears and at the vague whiteness of the table top. For a moment she was lost in a vastness of white, like being stranded on an ice floe in some arctic wasteland. It both frightened her and exhilarated her. And then she knew what she would do.

She gave herself another second, breathing in and out. She was going to approach him and shove the note in his face. Put up or shut up. She wanted to see Kyle and if he tried anything ... well, they would just see, wouldn't they?

Ready or not, here I come.

She raised her head and looked back at the man.

He wasn't there.

Standing, she scanned the parking lot through the window.

He was out there, running and jumping in a black car.

Erin grabbed her phone and started for the exit.

And plowed into an elderly woman holding a tray.

The tray flew out of the woman's hands. The woman squealed and dropped to the floor with a sickening thud.

Erin stopped.

The man in the black car was tearing out of the lot.

Erin knelt and looked at the woman, whose face was a wince. Pitiful little sounds came out of her mouth.

"I am *so sorry*," Erin said, making a move to help the woman up.

"Don't touch her!" A severe-looking man with gray hair and wire-rim glasses stood over them. "I'm a doctor. Get out of the way."

64

On Monday morning, Dylan was shipped by bus with a load of other inmates to the courthouse in San Fernando. They put him in the lockup with some other prisoners. A couple of them were chatty, but not in a let's-have-a-party style. More like the walking dead talking about what it once felt like to be alive.

At 9:35 a deputy sheriff called Dylan's name and escorted him down a corridor and through the backdoor of a courtroom. He told Dylan to sit in the jury box and wait for his attorney to announce his readiness.

Another arraignment was happening, a sad-looking woman sitting at counsel table with an equally sad-looking female lawyer. Both of them seemed defeated already.

Sam Wyant was sitting in the front row of the gallery whispering to what look like another lawyer. They were both smiling.

The sad woman lawyer was now asking that her client be released without bail. The judge, according to the name sign, was LaToya Hartwell. She looked cool, calm, professional. Dylan would have liked to see a little milk of human kindness on her face. But apparently it wasn't there this morning.

The judge said, "Bail is set at five-thousand dollars, cash or bond."

The sad client sobbed.

Dylan looked out at the people sitting in the courtroom. It looked like family members supporters. He had told Paige to stay at the office and watch things as best she could.

He wondered how many people were here just to watch a show. He had heard that retirees and others who have time on their hands liked to come to court and watch the human drama. Terrific. He was part of some great soap opera. The viewers would look at him now, seated there, wondering what awful thing he had done.

Then, for some reason, he looked at the far corner of the courtroom. The place farthest from where he himself sat. In the last seat in the last row was a guy in sunglasses and a baseball hat.

A Cubs hat.

Something crawled inside Dylan's chest. Something with claws.

He told himself a Cubs hat wasn't a strange sight, especially since they won the series in '16. The curse had been removed. But the sight of a Cubs hat always gave him a twinge, for obvious reasons.

He heard his name called and turned toward the judge.

"Ready to be heard on bail?" she said.

The deputy DA, a skinny guy in a gray suit, looked like he was the captain of a high school debating team. He stood at his counsel table and said, "Your honor, the People would request defendant be remanded to custody. We've learned that he has significant connections with people of some wealth and celebrity. We don't want him leaving the country."

"Who are these people you speak of, Mr. Garrett?" the judge asked.

"We'd rather not say on the record," DDA Garrett said.

Judge Hartwell nodded. "Then I'd rather not consider it as a factor."

"All right," said Garrett. "It's certain members of the Los Angeles Lakers."

"And so what? Are they going to dribble him out of the country?"

"He has the support of the team, especially one of the star players."

"Mr. Garrett," said the judge, "I find this an odd argument. Are you a Golden State Warriors fan by any chance?"

A wave of laughter rose up from the gallery.

"Mr. Wyant?" the judge said.

Sam Wyant stood. "Your honor, Mr. Reeve is no flight risk or danger to the community. He has an impeccable record, never been arrested, never been ticketed, even for jaywalking."

"Mr. Wyant, this is an arraignment court, not a trial court. While I appreciate the rhetoric, being an old trial lawyer myself, let's keep this to the issue of what the bail schedule says."

"Quite right, your honor. It's sometimes hard for me to step into a courtroom and not think I'm in front of a jury. Call it the old warhorse syndrome."

Charm offensive, Dylan thought.

He looked again at the man in the Cubs hat. He seemed to be watching the proceedings with casual interest. It was impossible to see his eyes, of course, but his head was in the general direction of Dylan's lawyer.

"If I may, your honor, this is not a case, nor is it a case with compelling evidence. There is one witness, whose credibility has not been tested. In view of the fact that Mr. Reeve is an honored member of the community, with a professional practice that requires his attention, I would ask the court to consider bail be set at fifty thousand."

Garrett stood, a scornful smile on his face. "We might as well just let him go with lovely parting gifts."

"Make an argument, Mr. Garrett," the judge said.

"This is a murder," Garrett said. "Brutal. The victim was hit with blunt force then smothered. Mr. Reeve had a semi-automatic pistol with him at the scene. The violence of the crime demands a bail that the community will not find inadequate. Fifty thousand is inadequate."

"The purpose of bail is to ensure the personal attendance of the defendant at all times when his or her attendance may be lawfully required," the judge said. "It's not to send messages. For that, try Twitter."

"Your honor—"

"Bail is set at three hundred thousand dollars, cash or bond," said the judge. "Mr. Reeve, you will not travel outside the county of Los Angeles, will not have contact with any witness or potential witness, and you may not possess firearms. What happened to the gun Mr. Garret mentioned?"

"Your honor," Sam Wyant said, "Mr. Reeve's gun is in the possession of the police."

"Any other weapons, Mr. Reeve?"

"Yes," Dylan said. "One."

Sam Wyant looked at him with unwelcome surprise.

"What kind?" the judge said.

"It's a Derringer."

"A Derringer? That's the little thing riverboat gamblers used to carry around, right?"

"Um, yes."

"But up close it can do some damage."

Dylan nodded.

"Where is that weapon now?"

"I keep it in a gun safe."

"At your home?"

"Yes, your honor."

"Any other firearms?"

"No, your honor."

"All right. I will give you twenty-four hours after your release to turn that Derringer over to Mr. Wyant. Is that clear?"

"Yes," Dylan said.

"Anything else from counsel?"

The two lawyers answered in the negative.

"Next case," the judge said.

Sam Wyant said he would begin the arrangements with Sonny's Bail Bond, and that in a few hours, Dylan would be out of custody.

Dylan wondered what Rodriguez would do for his extra dessert.

65

At lunchtime, Erin drove out to the Henry Mayo hospital in Newhall. It was a bit of a trek, but she wanted to check in on Abigail Strickland, the eighty-five-year-old woman she'd bashed into at Jack-in-the-Box.

She got a visitor's tag at the front desk then went to the gift shop and bought a multi-colored bouquet of flowers.

When she got to the room she saw the woman in the first bed of a duo, with a curtain dividing the two beds.

A man sat by the bed. He had glasses and a brush haircut and wore a short-sleeved white shirt.

They both turned their heads at her presence.

"Hi," Erin said. "I hope I'm not disturbing ..."

"And you would be?" the man said.

"The over-anxious pile driver," Abigail Strickland said. Despite discoloration on the right side of her face, her eyes gave a little twinkle.

Erin went with the vibe and smiled. "You are so right, and I am so sorry. I brought these."

She held up the flowers.

"Wait a minute," the man said, rising from his chair. "Who invited you here?"

"Oh, stop it, Milton," Abigail Strickland said. "This is my son. He's a little protective."

"Somebody has to be," he said.

"Take the flowers and do something nice with them," Abigail said.

"I just wanted to apologize again and make sure everything is all right," Erin said.

"Not all right," Milton said. "You could be sued, you know."

"Milton," Abigail said.

"Yes, Mom?"

"Be quiet. No one is going to sue anybody. Go ask the nurse to put those in water."

"I'm just looking out for her," Milton said as he walked by Erin, taking the flowers from her with a firm swipe.

"He's always been a worrywart," Abigail Strickland said.

"I understand completely," Erin said. "Again, I am so sorry."

"Nothing of it."

Abigail raised her left hand for Erin to take. Which she did. It felt dry and delicate.

"I was watching you, you know," Abigail said. "At the Jack-in-the-Box."

"You were?"

"You seemed troubled."

"Well, kind of."

"Have you taken it to the Lord in prayer?"

"I light candles sometimes."

The woman squeezed Erin's hand in a surprisingly firm way. "Let me tell you a little something. The two best prayers are 'Help me, help me, help me' and 'Thank you, thank you, thank you.' Not hard to remember, is it?"

"I think I can remember that much."

Abigail Strickland's eyes were earnest. "You do that, young lady. What is your name anyways?"

"Erin."

"Just one other thing, Erin."

"Yes?"

Abigail Strickland said, "Don't go jumping around like a jack-in-the-box at the Jack-in-the-Box, all right?"

66

Dylan Reeve was a free man.

For the moment, at least.

Outside the courthouse in the afternoon sun he felt like he was in some science-fiction story from an old pulp magazine, about an astronaut being taken to another world, one that mirrored his own yet was foreign to him. Where the people resembled humans but were only copies. He would soon realize this and start screaming in horror as the life forms closed in on him.

He didn't scream at Sam Wyant's driver, though. While Wyant stayed at the courthouse to attend to another matter, the young man named Pete Parris drove Wyant's silver Cadillac CTS-V with Dylan in the back like an important client.

Which he was, for a whopping big price tag.

They had a pleasant conversation about the Dodgers and the Lakers and then Pete dropped the info that he was an actor working on a screenplay.

"I'm shocked," Dylan said.

Pete Parris took the rest of the ride to give him the scene-by-scene breakdown of a movie about a super intelligent chimpanzee who is trained as a hit man. "Sort of *John Wick* meets *Planet of the Apes*," he said. "But with a heart."

And just as KiKi the chimp kills the evil scientist who made him and finds security and understanding with a UCLA anthropology grad student—"I hope Jennifer Lawrence is available!"—they pulled up in front of Dylan's home.

"Thanks for the ride," Dylan said. "And good luck with the movies."

"Look for me on *The Tonight Show!*" Pete Parris said, and drove off.

Dylan stood for a moment looking at his house. It was only a temporary abode now. Heck, it could actually be taken away. He had to collateralize it to get the bond and would have to do more of the same to pay his lawyer.

And there was no guarantee the truth would come out.

Ever.

At least his car was in the driveway. Good, reliable Paige.

He went inside and knew immediately his house had been searched. One thing Dylan had always been was neat. About appearance, about his things. He'd become obsessive about it after Kyle's kidnapping. One of his coping mechanisms, Dr. Reimer said. Complete control over his immediate surroundings because he was powerless to bring his son back.

His shrink had even suggested he be purposely sloppy for a while. Dylan tried it. He took out some books from the shelf and left them around the house. That night he couldn't sleep. He got up at 3:37 and put all the books back, and made sure their spines were even on the shelf.

But here was a home that had been tossed. Furniture moved, cushions on the floor, throw-rug rolled up and dropped in a corner.

Fury rising, Dylan went through each room of the house, finding drawers out and clothes on bed and floor. Even his medicine cabinet had been given the once over.

His computer. Somebody had been at it. The keyboard was slanted about thirty degrees.

At least they didn't take it, but it felt like a violation anyway.

And then he thought, What if it wasn't the police?

One way to find out. He fired up the computer and opened the security camera app. He brought up the home screen which showed the four camera-view angles. Gadge Garner had shown him how to watch the pictures in fast motion. Which delivered nothing but a fast-motion cat pooping in his side yard, the mailman, and a nicely dressed woman dropping what turned out to be a real estate flyer. Dylan had tossed it in the waste basket.

Basically a whole lot of nothing.

Until the cops arrived. Detective Smith and his partner and two uniformed officers. They went around the whole perimeter. Then disappeared.

Because they went in the house.

Dylan sped ahead.

And whipped past a guy taking pictures of his home.

Dylan stopped the video and replayed it. The guy was tall and lean, wearing his hair short. Looked around thirty-five. He'd come up to the door and knocked. Then stepped back and took pictures of Dylan's front porch. He was using what look like an expensive camera. He wore a camera case looped over his shoulder. The time stamp was two days ago, in the morning.

The sense of intrusion was overwhelming. Yes, it was all over the local news about the popular chiropractor accused of murder. Social media meant people in France and China would hear about it. He knew there was a Facebook group dedicated to civic issues in his part of Whittier. They loved to talk about the crime. Now he would be subject to what in the old days would be called small-town gossip.

Bringing looky-loos to take pictures of his home. The place where the killer lives!

A visceral feeling of real homicidal intent came over him. He wondered if he could really do it, kill the guy who was playing him and Erin, and then wondered why he even wondered. It was the law of the jungle now.

But he would need to play it cool as far as the cops and the law were concerned. They were watching.

He remembered the Derringer.

He took it out of the safe and brought it to the kitchen. He got a large plastic bag and put the gun inside. He put a twist tie on the bag. Just like peanut butter and jelly.

He'd made an appointment to drop the gun off at Sam Wyant's downtown office. Since the cops had his cell phone, Dylan used his landline, the one he had thankfully not cancelled, and called Erin. He asked if he could drop by her place when she got home from work.

She seemed happy to say yes.

67

Erin opened the door, and at the same time they took a step toward each other, and embraced.

"I am so glad you're out of that jail," Erin said.

"You're not nervous being around a hardened criminal?" Dylan said.

"No jokes."

"Laugh or die," Dylan said. "Remember we used to say that when we first got married?"

They walked into the late-afternoon light of the living room.

"I like that you get so much sun in here," Dylan said.

"In the morning it's direct," Erin said. "In the afternoon it reflects off the buildings at Universal. At sunset everything is orange."

"So you get real light and fake light."

"It's hot, whatever it is," she said. "I need to get better glass on the sliding door."

He smiled at that. It reminded him of the home they'd bought when Kyle was two. How they sat down together that night over glasses of wine and made plans for improvements. They'd had the place painted, got a new front door. They were talking about putting on an addition for the new baby they'd planned on having ...

Dylan's smile faded. He looked out the window. He was barely aware of lowering himself to the sofa.

"I need to show you something," Erin said. She went to the dining room table and got something, came back, handed it to Dylan.

It was a note.

Mom, I want to see you again.

"Where'd this come from?" Dylan said.

"From him," Erin said, sitting beside him. "He must have followed me, out to the jail, to the Jack-in-the-Box where I stopped. Dylan, he was wearing a Cubs hat."

Dylan tensed. "I saw him, too. In the courtroom."

"I hate this!" Erin said.

As if it were as natural as breathing, Dylan put his arm around Erin's shoulder and pulled her close. She let him, and he was astonished by the letting, as if a gift of incredible worth had been handed to him with no strings attached.

After a long moment, Dylan said, "Remember that time we rented the beach house in Ventura?"

"I'll never forget it," Erin said.

"Kyle was three."

"He'd just turned three."

"He started talking a blue streak around then," Dylan said. "Like somebody threw a switch."

"He loved to talk," Erin said. "Just like his father."

"And I went out and did some body surfing, the two of you were watching me, and when I came back to the sand he was excited, he said, 'Daddy, you swam inside the water!' "

"I remember that," Erin said.

"And then when we were walking home, on that little street—"

"Shelburn Lane."

"And Kyle ran a little bit ahead and ducked behind one of those cinder block walls those houses have."

"And he hid."

"From us," Dylan said. "Of course, when he shouted, 'Find me!' it made our task a little easier."

"But you kept saying, 'Where's Kyle? Where is he?' "

"When I came around the wall, he was standing there with his eyes closed, completely still, as if that made him invisible. So I waited. I waited for him to open his eyes. And when he did and saw me, he didn't run away, he just laughed and laughed and jumped up and down. Like he didn't know what to do next. Hidden? Found? I see him there, Erin,

frozen, eyes closed. And I wait for him to open his eyes, but he doesn't
..."

A fist in his throat blocked off the words. He closed his eyes.

"I got some advice today," Erin said. "From a little old lady who looked like she knows."

"What little old lady?"

"Just someone I bumped into."

"Oh?"

"She said the two best prayers are 'Help me, help me, help me' and 'Thank you, thank you, thank you.' "

"Works for me," Dylan said. "So why don't we run right at this guy?"

Erin sat up. "Meaning what?"

"No more giving in, letting him make all the calls."

"I like it," Erin said.

Dylan smiled. "Can you take the day off tomorrow?"

"I think so."

"Because I have an idea."

68

Dylan picked up Erin the next morning at ten. They headed for the underpass on Tujunga where the Hollywood and Ventura freeways crossed.

Driving there now was like visiting a side street in an undeveloped country. Tenants and boxes and overstuffed shopping carts made up a village of the damned. Los Angeles was experiencing an influx of homeless due to weather and California's legalization of marijuana.

Dylan pulled the car to a stop on Riverside Drive.

"You sure you want to do this?" Dylan said.

"We've come this far," Erin said.

"You can wait here in the car if you like."

"Not on your life. We're in this together."

He reached for her hand and squeezed it once. And without another word they got out of the car.

They approached the encampment slowly. No way Dylan was going to charge right into the heart of the assembled and makeshift homes. It would be like trespassing.

On the corner just before the underpass, as cars whizzed by above, Dylan stopped and looked into the gray of the shadowy world. Not much movement. He could make out one large body inert on the ground, presumably sleeping, though death would not be a shock here.

Further on, a woman was screaming epithets. A shirtless man whose ribs were visible even from where Dylan and Erin stood, walked over to the woman and said something. She continued her tirade. The man waved his arms. The woman ignored the gestures and turned her back to him and went on with the harangue.

The shirtless man followed her, stepped around in front of her, then hit her in the mouth with his fist. She stumbled backward and fell on her rear end. She didn't say anything else. She put her head in her hands. The man helped her to her feet and put his arms around her.

A voice behind them said, "Married life."

Dylan turned. A young man stood there, also shirtless, and leaner than good health would call for. His hair was long and stringy and his jeans sagged on his hips.

He had no shoes.

"You live here?" Dylan asked, and immediately felt foolish, like he was referring to some suburban development with fences and yards. But of course, for these people, it was something like that after all.

Stringy Hair smiled. He was missing at least four teeth. The ones that were left were brownish. "You reporters?"

"No."

"You're not cops.

"No. Just looking for some information."

"How come?" Stringy Hair said.

"It's about a man who was shot about a week ago. He lived down here. Called himself Hacksaw."

Stringy Hair shrugged.

"Did you know him?" Dylan said.

"You got some money?" Stringy Hair said.

"A little."

He shook his head. "Someone such as you is likely to have quite a bit." The guy spoke with good enunciation, as if educated in the art of rhetoric.

"We're trying to find out who Hacksaw was dealing with, somebody who drove a black car."

"It's going to cost you."

"Do you know?"

"Payment, please." Stringy Hair smiled again. The rotting pylons of his teeth pushed against dried, cracked lips.

Dylan pulled out his wallet and turned slightly, so Stringy Hair couldn't see the contents. He pulled out a five-dollar bill. He closed his wallet and turned and stuck out the five. Stringy Hair took it and said, "It needs a mate."

"I gave you some money," Dylan said. "Now your turn."

"This is worth at least a twenty."

"No way," Dylan said

Stringy Hair put the five in his pocket and looked at Dylan as if challenging him to get it back.

Erin said, "How come you're here?"

"Huh?" Stringy Hair said.

"Here," Erin said. "On the street."

"You should know," he said, and it seemed to Dylan there was some sort of secret connection going on between this guy and Erin. She had an instinct about her. She could connect with people.

"Drugs?" Erin said.

"What else would it be?" Stringy Hair said.

"You have a mother?" Erin said.

Stringy Hair said, "Kicked me out."

"You deserved to be kicked out, didn't you?" Erin said.

He looked at her without expression.

"Right?" Erin said.

"So?"

"Give him the twenty," Erin said to Dylan.

With a sense of wonder and dread, Dylan fished a twenty out of his wallet and handed it over.

"Now tell us what you know," Erin said.

Stringy Hair said, "Not me."

"We had a deal!" Erin said.

"I'll take you to the guy who can tell you."

"Jerome."

"Whu ... ?"

"Jerome, wake up."

Stringy Hair was talking to a snoozing fat man sitting in a folding chair that was almost entirely hidden by his girth.

"Whatchou want?" Jerome said. His heavy eyelids moved achingly upward.

"Who was that guy with Hacksaw?" Stringy Hair said.

The skin around Jerome's cheeks moved. His eyes changed from slits to circles.

"How come?" Jerome said.

"Good people here," Stringy Hair said.

"Ain't no good people," Jerome said.

"They want to find out who killed Hacksaw."

Jerome gave Dylan and Erin a slow scan.

"Dead and done," Jerome said.

"Be friendly," Stringy Hair said.

"Too hot to be friendly." Jerome laced his fingers over his stomach. "Got any money?"

"Not as much as I used to," Dylan said.

"What's that mean?"

Erin said, "Come on. Let's go. Nothing here."

Dylan looked at her, asking with his eyes what she was doing. She took his arm and started to walk him away.

"Hold up," Jerome said. "Let's see what you got."

Erin reached in her back pocket and pulled something out. Dylan was surprised to see a couple of folded bills in her hand.

Jerome held his hand out to take it. Erin shook her head. "First you tell us what we want to know."

"All depends on what you want to know," Jerome said.

"The name of the man who picked up Hacksaw in a black car."

"Yeah," Jerome said. "That's something I know."

"Let's have it," Erin said.

"What you got in your hands?"

"You can find out," Erin said.

Jerome thought about it. Then said, "Frozo."

"Frozo?" Erin said.

" 'Swhat I said. Frozo."

"What kind of name is that?" Stringy Hair said.

"I don't make 'em up," Jerome said. "That's what he called him. Frozo. Like yogurt or somethin'." He reached out and snatched the bills from Erin's hand. Counted it.

"Six bucks?" he said. "That's all?"

"You wanted to see what I had," Erin said. "And that's it."

Jerome leaned forward in a strained attempt to get up. The look on his face was not friendly. Stringy Hair put a hand on Jerome's shoulder and kept him down.

Over his shoulder, Stringy Hair said, "You better go now."

Dylan took Erin's hand and started walking.

Erin looked back at Stringy Hair and said, "Call your mother."

From somewhere close a booming voice shouted curses that echoed underneath the freeway.

69

"What exactly were you doing back there?" Dylan said as they drove away.

"Negotiating," Erin said. "Start to walk away. Let the other side call you back."

"How did you happen to have money in your pocket?"

"I always carry a few dollars in my back pocket. Emergencies. "

"Isn't that what you used to do in high school?" Dylan said.

"You remember," Erin said.

"Yeah," Dylan said. "I remember everything about you."

They drove in silence as Dylan got on the freeway heading toward downtown.

He said, "Frozo? That's not a real name. What were we expecting? A Social Security number and photo?"

Erin said, "Hacksaw and Frozo. Sounds like a vaudeville act."

"You still make me smile," Dylan said.

"I'm glad," Erin said.

"You know I didn't kill that woman."

"Of course you didn't."

"I liked her. But she didn't compare to you."

"Maybe we better not say anything like that right now. We're like soldiers on the battlefield, liable to say things we'll want to take back later."

"I'm not going to take it back," Dylan said. "I'm glad you're with me right now."

"One more thing then," Erin said, "in the interest of full disclosure."

"That sounds ominous."

"I went on my first date since the divorce the other night. One of the students asked me out."

"You've got my attention," Dylan said.

Erin said, "He's young enough to be my ... younger brother. I don't know what he sees in me."

"I do," Dylan said.

70

Dylan's house in Whittier was quaint, inviting. Reminded Erin of Dylan in high school. He always dressed sharp, but never pretentious. He wasn't into the *Who cares?* look so many of the kids were. Ripped jeans and Ts were all the rage the year they met. Rebellion was popular. That's why everybody looked the same.

"How about some fresh coffee?" Dylan said.

"Sounds good," Erin said. She followed him into the kitchen.

"I can't remember the last time I made coffee for two," Dylan said as he positioned the coffee maker on the counter.

"It's like riding a bike." Erin looked around, thinking it would be a nice space to cook something big. She hadn't cooked for two in a long time, either.

Dylan got a bag of coffee from the refrigerator, Seattle's Best, and started to scoop.

"Remember those *Thin Man* movies we used to watch?" Dylan said.

"William Powell and Myrna Loy," Erin said.

"Let's call ourselves Nick and Nora."

"Then we can't drink coffee," Erin said. "They had martinis in every scene."

"You're right," Dylan said. "I'm not about to test that theory."

When the coffee was ready Dylan poured two cups in black ceramic mugs and they went to his office and sat at the computer.

"Let's see what we can dig up about Frozo," Dylan said, typing the word into Google.

Erin read the top result, something about a character named Frozo the Renowned.

"It looks like some gaming thing," Dylan said.

"That would make sense," Erin said. "He told me he was very good at games."

"Looks like a game called World of Warcraft. Role playing. I have no idea what that world is like."

"So suppose he is a gamer," Erin said. "That only makes him one of two hundred million, right?"

"Wait a second," Dylan said. "There's an ice cream store called Frozo Mama in Canada."

"That's got to be it," Erin said.

Dylan smiled. "Your delivery is still perfect."

"I wish we could laugh again, the old way."

"We will."

Someone knocked at the door.

"Excuse me," Dylan said, and got up to answer. She heard the door open and an old man's voice said, "My boy, my boy. I know this is not true, what they are saying!"

"Come in," Dylan said. A moment later Dylan returned to the office with a rail-thin old man smelling of tobacco.

Dylan said, "Erin, this is my neighbor Cesar Biggins."

"Hello," Erin said, standing.

"At your service," Cesar said, bowing with a flourish, his arm extended to the side.

"Cesar was a clown for Ringling Brothers," Dylan said.

"How cool," Erin said.

"Maybe he knows a clown named Frozo," Dylan said.

Cesar said, "How's that?"

"It's a crazy name, isn't it?" Dylan said.

"Say it again."

"Frozo."

"There was such a clown," Cesar said.

"You're kidding," Dylan said. "I've heard of Bozo."

Cesar shook his head. "This was not a happy clown. It was from a very disturbing motion picture, made a long time ago. I hope you have never seen it."

"What movie?" Dylan said.

"It is called *Freaks*. It is about sideshow unfortunates, and they were real, used in the movie. Had a clown in it. His name was spelled, I believe, P-H-R-O-S-O. Phroso."

"It's easy enough to find out," Dylan said. He came back to the computer. As Cesar and Erin looked over his shoulders, he Googled *Freaks IMDB* and got to the movie database.

"Here it is," he said. "*Freaks*. 1932. Directed by Tod Browning."

He scrolled down.

"Yes! An actor named Wallace Ford played Phroso."

"It is a very sad picture," Cesar said. "I saw it when we played San Francisco. One of the other clowns told me about it. I had nightmares."

"Do you think it means anything?" Erin said.

"What are you two looking for?" Cesar said.

Dylan said, "Remember I asked if you'd seen anyone suspicious around here? Well, a man using this name is suspicious. Why would he use this name?"

Cesar shrugged.

"What's the synopsis of the movie?" Erin asked.

Dylan read the screen. "A circus' beautiful trapeze artist agrees to marry the leader of side-show performers, but his deformed friends discover she is only marrying him for his inheritance."

"It's much sadder than that," Cesar said. "I knew many of these types of performers over the years."

Erin said, "Maybe he thinks of us as freaks."

"That could be," Dylan said. "I want to run this by a man named Gadge Garner."

"Who's that?" Erin said.

"Security guy," Dylan said.

"Life used to be so simple," Cesar Biggins said. "I could solve most problems with seltzer and a large rubber mallet."

"Whatever works," Dylan said.

"Something has to," Erin said.

71

On Wednesday Erin came early to the office. One way to fight back against uncertainty was to work. Be normal. Don't give Phroso the satisfaction of interrupting her daily life. She would make herself work. Life was going to go on. *Keep calm and carry on.* That's what her English-born grandmother used to say. And she had seen the lights of the Blitz.

I *can* carry on.

I *will.*

She got a coffee from the Keurig in the kitchenette. That brought thoughts of yesterday, being with Dylan, how good it felt. For a moment she held that feeling with a kind of terrified longing.

Then got to her workstation in a hurry.

She was alone in the building as far as she knew. On her computer she called up the scheduling program and began to look at next semester's assignment blocs. Things were falling into place since DeForest had replaced one of the more troublesome profs, one Moffat, with a fellow named Carr, a retired accountant who reminded Erin of the angel from *It's a Wonderful Life.*

As she began typing Carr's name into a cell she got an IM alert at the top of the screen. She didn't have it set up to see the message. That way she could decide if she wanted to keep working or not.

But since things looked smooth she went ahead and popped over to see who had contacted her.

It was anonymous.

The message was: *I'm jealous.*

Erin jumped from her chair, knocking her desk and spilling coffee all over the neatly stacked papers and folders.

With a yelp she ran back to the kitchenette, feeling an invisible hand around her throat. She grabbed the whole paper towel roll off the holder, ran back to her desk and did as much cleanup as she could.

Another IM: *You still there?*

She was almost outside her body, watching herself. But she had the presence of mind to capture a screen shot. Then she typed:

I'm still here, Phroso.

No instant reply. She could almost sense his disquiet. The longer the pause, the better. It was only a little something, but worth it.

A full minute went by. It felt oh so good.

Then the next message: *This will cost you.*

She took another screen shot.

And that was the last she heard from him.

Just before nine, Yumiko filled in the middle of Erin's cubicle entrance, preventing any escape.

"So?" Yumiko said.

"So?" Erin said.

"Yesterday!"

"What about it?"

"Were you with him?"

"Who?"

Hands on hips, Yumiko said, "You know!"

"Are you talking about Andy?"

"Who else?"

"No."

"No *what*?"

"I wasn't with Andy. And I'm not going to be."

Yumiko overplayed a chin-drop. "You broke up?"

"We were never together."

"You better have a good reason for letting that one go."

"Yumiko, you better get to the front desk."

"I've got thirty seconds. Talk fast."

"Can this wait till later, please?"

"Until ten-thirty," Yumiko said. "Then I want to hear about this sad ending."

Poor choice of words, Erin thought.

She dove back into the morning's current project, preparing an email blast to former students. There was a certain gratification in being assigned that task, as opposed to one of the millennials in the office. The one who'd handled it before her, a nice enough young woman fresh out of community college, had trouble with spelling and basic grammar. She'd sent out one big mailing about the new real estate class with the subject line: LOCATON LOCATON LOCATOIN.

It was a wonder to everyone how the young woman could have two consecutive typos of the same vintage, then a third word with the right letters in the wrong places.

The young woman was let go, but for several weeks the staff at DeForest had spoken to each other in a slow incantation: "Locaton. Locaton. Locatoin!" As if it would raise the dead or turn a politician into a newt.

Erin loved the creative part of it, the copywriting. Getting into a flow state was easy here as she tested phrases and possible headers.

In fact, she was so into it that she almost shrieked at the sight of Yumiko, ashen-faced, staring at her.

72

"We'll hear what you have to say," Sam Wyant said. "But I'm ready to advise my client not to answer any questions if I deem them inappropriate."

"I would expect no less, counselor," Detective Warren Smith said.

The three were sitting in the conference room of Sam Wyant's law office in the 400 South Hope building. Sunlight streamed through the massive windows and reflected off the polished maple conference table that took up most of the room.

Smith had called Wyant to set up this meeting because of what he'd cryptically called "new information."

"Now," Wyant said, "tell us why we are here."

"I want to know exactly what your relationship with Tabitha Mullaney was, especially as it concerns your lost son."

"Don't answer that," Wyant said. "You said you have new information."

"Fair enough," Smith said. "Your client says that the victim claimed to have his son."

"And that I could see him," Dylan said.

Smith said, "We searched her residence. We did not find any evidence relating to your lost child."

"What about this guy she was working with?" Dylan said.

"The one you say sent you notes?" Detective Smith said.

"He *did* send me notes."

"We did not find anything linking her with anyone, but we also did not find a phone."

"There you go!" Dylan said. "Whoever killed her took her phone."

Detective Smith said nothing.

"You don't think I have it, do you?" Dylan said. "You searched my house."

"Do you have her phone?"

"No."

"But you did get a voice message from her, correct?" Smith said.

"That's enough," Sam Wyant said.

"Let's listen," Smith said, and pulled a small recorder from his pocket. He placed it on the table and pushed a button.

Tabitha's voice came through:

Dearest, I need you to know that I forgive you. I'm not hurt, except for a bruise on my arm. You don't know your own strength, maybe. I know you've got some demons in your past and that maybe they come out like this. I don't want this to break us up. One of the things people do when they love each other is work through things, you know? I'm willing, if you are. I'm willing ...

Smith stopped the message. "Heard enough?"

"What is this?" Sam Wyant said.

"It was a voice message from the victim to Mr. Reeve," Detective Smith said. "We'd like an explanation."

"Say nothing," Wyant said. "And this time listen to me."

Dylan kept his mouth shut.

"You're never going to get that into evidence," Wyant said.

"We searched your client's phone incident to lawful arrest," Smith said.

"Maybe you haven't heard of a little case called *Riley v. California.*" Wyant snapped off the name of the case like it was firecracker in his mouth. "Unanimous decision of the United States Supreme Court. Year of our Lord 2014. No searching of cell phones incident to arrest."

Detective Smith gave a half smile. "Not going to introduce it, counselor. Just wanted you to hear it, and have your client tell us why he hurt her."

"She's lying," Dylan said.

"She's dead," Detective Smith said.

"So is your case," Wyant said. "We're done here, detective. Thanks for stopping by."

73

In the DeForest kitchenette, Yumiko sat with Erin at one of the two small eating tables, holding her hand. The warmth of it helped stave off the numbness overtaking Erin's body.

Anderson Bolt, dead.

Murdered.

An LAPD detective named Steve Hogan had called the school, talked to Yumiko. He gave few details, but did say it happened in Andy's apartment last night and that the cause of death was a "sharp force injury" to the neck. And that he'd want to ask some questions of people who knew him. He left his name and number.

"Why don't you go home now?" Yumiko said. "I can cover."

Erin shook her head. "I'm going to stay. I'm going to work. I'm not going to let him stop me. In fact, let me call that detective right now."

Yumiko retrieved the Sticky Note with the number and brought it back to Erin.

"You sure you want to do this now?" Yumiko asked.

"I'm sure. Go on up front. I'm fine."

After a reassuring pat, Yumiko left the kitchenette.

Erin input the number.

"This is Hogan."

"This is Erin Reeve."

"Ah, thanks for calling. Have you got time to talk?"

"A little. I'm at work."

"I understand. Quickly, then. Were you in a relationship with Mr. Bolt?"

"No. Well ..."

"Yes?"

"He wanted to. We went out once. He wanted it more than I did."

"Was he at your home a week ago?"

She felt suddenly like a child at the cookie jar busted by her mother. "How do you know this?"

"It was on his calendar, so I—"

"He came over with a bottle of champagne. I wasn't expecting him."

"Even though he had it marked as an appointment?"

"He planned it. I didn't."

"Would you know of anyone, maybe there at the school, who might want to do him harm?"

"Not at the school, no."

"Or anyone else?"

"Do you know about the messages I've been getting?" Erin said.

"No," Detective Hogan said.

"Or about the man who was shot when I was standing next to him at a pay phone?"

Pause, then the detective said, "I think we need to schedule a time to talk more fully. What would be a good time?"

Erin wanted to say, *There will never be a good time, ever again.*

Instead, she said, "Would after work be okay?"

74

In Sam Wyant's conference room, Dylan sipped a cappuccino made to order by legal assistant and screenwriting wannabe Pete Parris. If the kid didn't sell his script he could always get a gig at Starbucks.

Wyant, coatless now that the detective was gone, nevertheless looked like he was wearing a uniform. Dylan could not spot a single wrinkle on his powder-blue shirt, or one out-of-place dimple on his maroon tie. When he sipped from an Evian bottle, the water seemed respectful and compliant.

"We need to discuss a few matters," Wyant said.

"Only a few?" Dylan said.

"The ones that count. How are you getting along?"

"I haven't freaked out for twelve or so hours."

Wyant smiled, nodded. "Let's keep that record going. You've seen the news?"

Dylan shook his head.

"You're a big local story," Sam Wyant said.

"Just like O.J.," Dylan said.

"Not that big. And thank God for that. I'm preparing a press statement. Want to have a look at it?"

"Why don't you paraphrase it for me."

"Basically going to say we are prepared to defend your innocence to the full extent, and all that. That you are a member of the community in high standing, the case against you is weak—"

"Is it weak?"

"It all comes down to this Carbona guy."

"You mean the bald-faced liar?"

"He claims he was working for Ms. Mullaney."

"Doing what?"

"Protecting her."

"From what?"

"From you."

"Right," Dylan said. "The freaking serial killer."

Sam put his elbows on the conference table and laced his fingers together. "I'm going to tell you something. I don't want you to get upset, because I don't believe it for a second."

"Do tell."

"Carbona is prepared to state that the victim told him you threatened her, that when she refused to have sex with you, you told her she'd be sorry."

Dylan almost ripped the arms off Sam Wyant's fancy conference-room chair. He shot to his feet and circled around the back of the chair. And then cursed like he never had in his life.

"I understand," Sam Wyant said.

"Isn't that hearsay or something, what she said?"

"There's an exception to the hearsay rule," Wyant said, "when a witness is unavailable. In this case, because she's dead. The prosecution will argue that it is relevant to her state of mind when she hired the guy."

"So what are you going to do to discredit him?"

"Sit down, Dylan."

"I asked you a question!"

"I think you'd better sit down and calm yourself."

"You're talking like a doctor telling me I've got six months to live."

"Have a seat."

Dylan sat down.

"Of course, Dylan, I have people who will dig into every inch of this man's prior history. We'll look at his past record, we will find anything we can, any disciplinary action, anything to cast doubt on his credibility. We will absolutely find something. Okay?"

Dylan shrugged.

Wyant said, "We need to talk about options."

"Meaning what?"

"Going to trial is like going to war," Wyant said. "And the general who anticipates the most contingencies is going to be the one to gain the victory."

"What contingencies?"

"Let's suppose for a moment that we can't find anything to impeach the testimony of this witness. Let's suppose, in fact, that he is lying."

"No supposing about it. I told you he is."

"Of course. It's just lawyer talk."

"I hate lawyer talk," Dylan said.

Sam Wyant smiled. "Most people do. Now, if his testimony comes in without an issue, it's going to be his word against yours. They have some supporting testimony. They have the waitress at the restaurant who observed you in a state of being upset."

"Yeah, because she just told me she had my son!"

"Nobody heard that," Sam Wyant said. "Nobody but you."

"Meaning?"

"We may have to put you on the stand."

"Do it then!"

"But I've got to tell you, that is virtually always a bad idea."

"Sure, if the person is guilty. But I'm not."

"This prosecutor is good. I've seen him on cross. He could get Gandhi to admit he's packing a gun."

"I don't think that's funny."

"No, you're right. There's nothing funny about this. Which is why we should consider another option."

When Wyant didn't immediately say anything, Dylan felt cold all over.

"As in?" Dylan said.

"We have to consider the possibility of a plea."

"No way!"

"Now hear me out," Sam Wyant said. "I have to discuss every option with you."

"Not this one. I didn't do it! What kind of deal is that?"

"It's a deal that could be the difference between twenty-five years to life, or three years for manslaughter."

"That's my choice?"

"For purposes of discussion."

"I don't want to discuss it."

"And I don't want to see you get prison for life. This is a high profile case now. We also have to consider that we have a sympathetic victim and a grieving mother."

"This is getting better and better."

"I'm sorry, Dylan. I tend to be direct. No bedside manner."

"Forget it," Dylan said. "I guess I have to hear it. So you're saying that if we go to trial on this, and lose, I could be put away for the rest of my life?"

"I've not lost a criminal case in ten years."

"But it could happen."

Wyant nodded. "In all fairness, I've not gone to trial without a strong hand."

"I'll take the stand," Dylan said. "I won't fold. And my ex-wife will testify. She'll talk about the threats she's been getting, how it ties in to what I'm saying."

Wyant said, "Of course we'll go there. I just could not in good conscience keep you from seeing the whole picture."

"I've seen it," Dylan said. "And it stinks." He looked at the shelf of law books that covered one wall. Leather-bound antiquities. He could imagine a California earthquake happening right now, and getting buried under those heavy, lifeless tomes.

"Meanwhile, sit tight," Wyant said. "Keep a low profile. Get in touch with your ex-wife and let's set up a meeting."

"What about my phone?"

"Obviously they're keeping it."

"Can they do that?"

"Short answer, yes. For the moment. But they can't use the evidence, so I'll subpoena it and get it back." He picked up the handset on his land line and pressed two keys. "Pete? Bring us in a disposable phone, will you? Thanks."

Wyant hung up. "On the house. Pre-paid."

"You can afford it."

Sam Wyant nodded.

A moment later Pete Parris entered with a phone. At Wyant's nod, he handed it to Dylan.

"That's enough for today," Wyant said. "Pete, will you show our client out?"

"I know the way," Dylan said. He stood and shook Wyant's hand, then Pete's.

He left the conference room and made his way down the hall, past a couple of work stations with young associates tapping away. As he passed through the door that brought him back into the reception area, all thought of lying witnesses left him with a jolt.

He was face-to-face with the guy who had been taking pictures of his house.

75

"Who are you?" Dylan said, stepping right up to the guy's face.

The guy had the same camera case around his shoulder. He was dressed in a faded red T-shirt and jeans. He didn't look shocked or threatened by Dylan's confrontational question.

"I'm a reporter, Mr. Reeve."

"What paper?"

"Blog."

The receptionist was watching the whole thing. She was young and dressed for serious business. She said, "Shall I call Mr. Wyant?"

"Yes," the reporter said.

"No," Dylan said. "You're leaving."

"You don't tell me where to go," the guy said.

"Oh, I'll tell you where you can go all right," Dylan said.

"Ha, ha. I'll quote you."

"That a threat?" Dylan said.

"Mr. Reeve, I'm just doing my job."

"Shall I call security?" the receptionist said.

"Good idea," Dylan said.

"You don't want to do that," the reporter said. "You need friends in the press."

"I have no idea who you are."

"Let's talk."

"I don't want to talk. Especially to somebody who came sneaking pictures at my house."

He shook his head. "I wasn't sneaking. I was right out there for all to see. I knocked on your door."

"You knew I was in jail."

"All I knew is you weren't home. I just wanted some pics for the profile."

"What profile?"

"It depends."

"On what?"

"Whether I'm writing about the heart of a grieving ex-boyfriend, or the twisted mind of a killer."

"Now I know you're a reporter," Dylan said.

"Tell me your story."

"Did you follow me here?"

The reporter shook his head. "It's serendipity. I think that's the word."

"A real reporter would know what word to use," Dylan said.

"Ha, ha. Another good one. I came here to talk to your lawyer and, serendipity, here you are."

The receptionist said, "You need to make an appointment to talk to Mr. Wyant, and there's no guarantee he will talk to you."

"He'll talk to me," the reporter said. "I know he likes publicity." He took a card from his back pocket and handed it to Dylan. "I also have a deal with the *Times*."

"I'm supposed to believe that?"

"There's an editor you can call. Want to?"

"Not interested," Dylan said.

"I'd love a comment from you," the guy said. His name, according to the card, was Stephen Brett.

"I don't know you or your blog," Dylan said.

"You will," Brett said. "I'm all over this, like nobody else. I can be on your side."

"The truth is on my side."

"Mr. Reeve?" the receptionist said.

He looked at her. She was shaking her head.

Dylan said, "I'm really not supposed to talk. If you can get through to my lawyer, have at it." Dylan started for the door, stopped. "And don't come snooping around my house again."

"Now who is threatening who?" Brett said.

"Whom," Dylan said.

"Ha, ha," Brett said.

76

It was just after six-thirty when the two detectives—a man and a woman —arrived at Erin's condo. She met them at the front door of the complex. The man, in his fifties, introduced himself as Detective Steve Hogan, and his partner as Sharon Peralta. Peralta looked around forty.

They were dressed in business casual, and wore their detective shields on their belts. Hogan might have played football at one time, but his face was friendly. Peralta seemed more businesslike and wore no wedding ring.

Erin showed them up to her condo and felt obligated to ask if they'd like anything to drink. Both declined, which was a relief. The sooner this was over the better.

They sat in the living room, with Peralta taking notes in a small notebook as Hogan took the lead.

Hogan said, "We're waiting for a call from Detective Murray, who's handling that homicide you witnessed at the market. How you doing about that?"

"I'll tell you something strange," Erin said. "That's not the worst thing that's happened to me lately."

"I understand, Ms. Reeve. We just need to ask a few questions about the victim, Mr. Bolt. How close were you with him?"

"Not that close," Erin said. "As I told you, I wasn't dating Andy. But he was a nice guy. He had a lot ..."

The detective waited.

"He had a lot going for him," Erin said.

"I wanted to ask, do you think these two murders are related? The man at the store, and Mr. Bolt?"

"Definitely. A man has been stalking me, on the phone, and by computer. He claims to have my son, who was kidnapped fifteen years ago. He uses a strange name. Phroso."

Detective Peralta said, "Can you spell that for me, please?"

"P-H-R-O-S-O," Erin said. "It's from an obscure old movie, we think."

"We?" Hogan said.

"My ex-husband and his neighbor, who is a retired circus clown. Do we have to go into that?"

Hogan said, "Let's back this up a little bit. To the homeless man who was shot while you were at a pay phone. Why were you at that phone?"

"Because this guy I'm telling you about told me to go there to receive a message."

"What was the message?"

"I never got it, because of the killing. He contacted me later though."

"How?"

"He called my phone."

"What did he say?"

"He wanted to know what I thought of his work, which meant the shot that killed that man. Who went by the name of Hacksaw, by the way."

Hogan said, "You know this how?"

"My husband and I did some digging."

"Does Detective Murray know this?"

"At this point I'm not keeping track, okay?" Erin rubbed her temples. "This morning I was working at my station when Phroso messaged me on my computer."

"What did the message say?"

"It said he was jealous."

"Of who?"

"I figure it was Andy. I called him by his name. He didn't know that I knew it. He said I was going to pay for that."

"Did he say how?"

Erin shook her head. "That was the last message he sent."

Hogan paused. Peralta scribbled some notes.

Then, with a slight change of tone, Hogan said, "What did you know about Anderson Bolt, I mean his personal life?"

"Not very much," Erin said. "We only had one lunch date. He did come over to my condo with champagne and was working hard at being very charming. Oh yes, and the other night I was out running and he came up behind me in his car."

"He was following you?"

"Sort of. He saw me, I guess, and wanted to surprise me."

"And you didn't like that."

"No, of course not. I ..." Erin stopped herself. Both Hogan and Peralta said nothing. They just watched her.

Erin said, "You're not suggesting I'm a suspect, are you?"

"Not suggesting anything, Ms. Reeve. Just asking questions."

Erin stood. "I have to think about this."

"Certainly," Hogan said, also standing. "If you have nothing more to add about Mr. Bolt, we can leave it at that for now." He removed the card from his shirt pocket and handed it to Erin. It was an LAPD card with Steve Hogan on it and a contact number.

"If you think of anything later, please call me," he said.

"I will," Erin said.

Peralta closed her notebook. Erin showed them to the door.

"I'm sorry I couldn't be more helpful," Erin said. She reached for the doorknob but never found it.

Detective Sharon Peralta put her body between Erin and the door.

Detective Steve Hogan put his hand over Erin's mouth and slammed her into the wall.

77

Dylan looked at the clock on the wall and was surprised to see it was close to seven. He was sitting in the downtown L.A. library. He'd walked from Wyant's office, only a five-minute hoof down Grand. It was almost as if his feet had taken him there by their own volition and for his own good.

He often visited the library when dark clouds rolled into his mind. He'd pick a subject at random and find the shelf of books and take a few to a chair and read. He found that a couple of hours of immersion helped stave off the rain of despair. And besides that, he could learn something.

So after Wyant's, he came to the library and saw a flyer on the front desk extolling a photo exhibit of Riverside, a contiguous county to L.A. It emphasized something called the Perris Indian School which was opened there in 1903. That was enough to get Dylan down to the history floor and several volumes relating to Riverside. He pulled a couple of volumes and checked the indexes and found one that mentioned the school.

He took it to a chair and read about a man named Frank Miller who campaigned to have the school moved to Riverside. His argument was that Perris did not have an adequate water supply for the school, but what he really wanted was tourist business for his hotel. He thought people might drop by the school to have a look at "real, live Indians."

And what do you know, they did.

Dylan took a few more spins around Riverside, and now that it was seven he decided to walk back to his office to fetch his car.

He walked down to Olive Street and turned right, past the Biltmore Hotel and Pershing Square, barely noting the asphalt river of cars and busses and pedestrians.

He cut over on 9th, to the Ralphs Market. He was hungry and for some reason his stomach was calling for their in-house fried chicken. Warm, crispy, greasy, friendly. And he could wash it all down with a cold beer.

At the deli counter he asked for a couple of thighs. This wasn't anything to write home about, but he felt immensely grateful. He was, for the moment, free. He could eat what he wanted to eat, drink what he wanted to drink. He'd been a jailbird for only a few days, but that was enough to give him a greater appreciation of free air.

He wondered what Rodriguez was getting tonight. Would he get a brownie?

Dylan picked up a six pack of Corona and a bag of peanut M&Ms on impulse at the checkout line. He was ready to par-tay.

He didn't expect Paige to still be at the office, but she was.

"Hi, boss," she said.

Dylan loved hearing that from her. The way she said it, with an uplift. At twenty-five, Paige Sargent was different from so many of her contemporaries. She kept her hair its natural color—ash blonde—and liked hard work. She wasn't wedded to her phone, spoke in complete sentences, and treated every client with cheerful respect.

"You should be home already," Dylan said.

"Just juggling some things," Paige said. "How'd it go with your lawyer?"

"Oh, an adventure in fine living. Want a beer?"

He put the grocery bag on the reception-window sill and took out the six-pack of Corona.

"Planning a big night?" Paige said.

"How many cancellations have I had?"

Paige paused. "Four today."

"Then let's have four beers," Dylan said.

"You're not really?"

Dylan shook his head. "I'm not going down that lane. But money is going to be tight around here for a while."

Paige nodded.

Dylan said, "I don't know how long—"

"It's okay," Paige said.

"I can't ask you."

"I'll let you know," Paige said. "What's that smell?"

"Oh. Chicken. From that palace of fine cuisine, Ralphs."

"You spared no expense?"

"Care to join me?" Dylan said.

"I wouldn't miss it," Paige said.

78

They ate chicken off paper plates, and drank their Coronas from the bottle. When it was only bones left, Paige said, "Boss, I wish I could do more."

"You're doing more than enough," Dylan said. "Has Mrs. Nussbaum given you an earful?"

With a smile, Paige said, "She did, but it was all on your side. It was all, *Those lying Cossacks! Trying to railroad him!*"

"Cossacks?"

"I didn't press her on it. But she said she'd go down to the police station and give them a piece of her mind if they didn't let you go."

"I hope you were able to dissuade her."

"Mrs. Nussbaum?"

"I see your point." He lifted his nearly drained Corona bottle and Paige did the same. They clinked.

"Do I have any appointments the rest of the week?" Dylan said.

"Two on Friday morning," Paige said. "I was going to call and cancel for you. You want to see them?"

Dylan nodded. "Let's just hope they don't keep up on the news. Why don't you take the day off tomorrow?"

"I don't need to," Paige said.

"Maybe go to the beach with that boyfriend of yours."

Paige looked at the bones on her paper plate, and quietly said, "I think not."

"What happened?"

"I had to give him a spurn notice," she said.

"A what?"

"We broke up."

Dylan smiled.

"Boss?"

"Hm?"

"Maybe I can help."

"Help?"

"Be another set of ears," she said.

"I don't want to put any of this on you," Dylan said.

"It's for the team," she said.

He trusted her completely. No problem there. And maybe hearing the information again, and running it through her, would open up some sort of crack he hadn't seen before.

So he gave her the latest, up to the strange name Phroso and its connection with a film called *Freaks.*

"I've heard of that one," Paige said.

"Have you seen it?"

She shook her head. "My little brother is a film nerd. Sixteen and he's seen everything. He told me about that movie. He tried to make me watch it even, but I didn't."

In an offhand way, Dylan said, "Maybe he can figure out why this guy would use that name."

"I'll ask him," Paige said. "It couldn't hurt."

Just before leaving the office, Paige did something she hadn't done in the year she'd been working for Dylan Reeve.

She hugged him.

Alone in the office, Dylan popped another Corona and thought of his first years at U. C. Davis, where he had come to appreciate suds. He and his roommate had a saying that one beer was not enough, two was just right ... and three was not enough. There were times when he'd pushed past to four or five and ended up in the oval office, as they say. He couldn't remember the last time he'd had more than two beers in close proximity.

Tonight he'd stick with two.

He thought about the reporter, took out his card. He used the desktop in the reception area to get to the guy's blog.

And read it, with increasing clenching of jaw.

Hey crime buds, your beat reporter was on the move today. Guess where he showed up? If you said the office of the mayor of Los Angeles, you'd be thinking straight, but that wouldn't be it. Somebody more famous than the mayor. The guy you've seen on TV doing his lawyer thing. That legend in his own mind, Sam Wyant.

I hear he's really a pussycat in person, but I didn't get to find out. I was there to get a comment on the big murder case he's handling, the one involving the L.A. Lakers favorite joint mechanic, Dr. Dylan Reeve.

But because I'm always on the move, things happen. We crack reporters call this serendipity (good word, isn't it?).

I walk into the reception area of Sam Wyant's office, and who should I see? None other than the miscreant doc himself.

It's criminal how lucky I am.

The good doctor looked a little nonplussed (another good word) that I was there, asking him for a comment. And then I was unceremoniously asked to leave without a single comment from lawyer Wyant.

Take that as you will. No protestation of innocence. No concern for the dead woman.

But Dr. Reeve was unwilling to give me his side of the story. That IS a fact. You may do with it what you will.

Your intrepid reporter will stay on the job.

Dylan finished his Corona with an angry chug.

And opened another.

79

The first flicker of consciousness had to fight through wet sandbags. Erin was aware only of the thickness of her thoughts, nothing coherent, her head lolling around on her neck. Darkness ... no, something flashing, but where? She wanted to go back to sleep.

No. No. No.

Fight.

Sitting. She was in a chair. She felt the chair arms, tried to move her own, but they moved only an inch.

She moved them again. Heard jangling.

Handcuffs?

Police.

Detectives, in her condo.

The last thing she remembered.

She took a deep breath and willed her eyes to open wide.

The light was in front of her. Some kind of flickering.

It was a movie!

A black and white movie ... a silent movie.

She heard the *wicka wicka wicka* of a movie projector somewhere behind her.

She tried to turn around, then realized her waist and legs were manacled, too.

And she had a desperate need to pee.

The movie. Wait. It seemed familiar. A woman approaching a man in a mask who was sitting at an organ, playing.

The Phantom of the Opera. That was it. Everybody had seen that bit.

But why here?

And now the woman was reaching for the mask, hesitating, reaching again and ...off!

And that face! That horrible face!

Why was she being forced to watch this?

The movie stopped. The projector sound ceased.

For a moment she was in total darkness.

Then lights came on, filled the room. She squinted at the sudden assault on her pupils.

A voice behind her said, "That is one of the great moments in movie history!"

It was him.

The excited voice.

She turned her head as much as she could, but couldn't see directly behind her.

The room was large, with white walls.

"And you've seen it in a beautiful sixteen millimeter print. As clean as the original audience would have seen it."

There were three chairs to her left, and three to her right. She was in the middle of a row of theater seats.

"Did you know," the voice said, "that they had to have ambulances ready outside the theaters showing this movie? At the sight of the phantom many people fainted. Some just could not take it."

Her mouth was dry and in her nostrils a medicine smell. Was that what knocked her out so completely?

"Lon Chaney was the greatest actor of all time," the voice said. "Bar none! Nobody could evoke such feeling just with his face. No words were needed. You're horrified, and then you cry."

"Why ..."—every word an effort— "... am I here?"

"God, you're going to love it here. I want you to be comfortable. I've got this place tricked out like a luxury hotel, if you like rooms made out of cement."

He laughed at that. Too loudly. The laughter bounced off the walls.

"This used to be a bomb shelter," he said. "The theater was built in the fifties, back when there was this big thing called the Red Scare. Americans thought the Russians were going to bomb them into oblivion, so it was a big deal for a while to build bomb shelters. A lot of movie theaters, especially in the Midwest, did that. The owner of this theater did it right. He was a Christian, sorry to say. He wanted to be ready for the Russians and the Tribulation. So here it is. When I bought the place, it was closed up. Had been since the earthquake of '94. You doing okay?"

She wanted to see his face, wanted to spit in it.

"I have to ... go to the bathroom," she said.

"I thought you might. No worries. The bathrooms in my theater are clean. That's one of the things people like about this place. Clean bathrooms. I have a half-wit who does the cleaning. I'd like you to meet him."

"Let me go," Erin said.

"To the bathroom? Or in general?"

She was getting her brain back, her equilibrium. Reasoning power, like a cold car engine struggling to turn over, started to churn.

"You want me to go all over your nice seat?" Erin said.

"Good answer. I like that about you. Always did."

Always?

She heard soft footsteps behind her.

He said, "Now don't be afraid of what I'm about to do. This is just a precaution to keep you from doing something unwise. This won't take a second."

Something looped around her head and tightened on her neck.

"Is that too tight?" he said.

She wanted to reach for it but her hands were immobilized.

He pulled the noose tighter.

"Don't fight me, please," he said.

She complied. She had to let him control her. Her bladder could not wait.

"You just let me guide you," he said. "Believe me when I tell you it's going to be all right. Everything. It will become clear to you. And the bathrooms are clean. I promise. Please don't mind the blindfold when I put it on you. It's just a precaution. Everything needs to unfold in a very specific way. Just let me guide you. Trust me. You really can, you know."

80

Three times in his life Dylan had a dream so vivid and real that he woke up sweating and thinking he could never show his face in public again. It was the same dream, with only a few minor differences.

He had the dream first in college when he was preparing for an oral history exam. He'd fallen behind in his studies and was cramming for three nights straight, kept alive by Mountain Dew and Pizza Hut. The night before the exam he fell into a deep sleep and dreamed he woke up in a New York hotel room seven hours before his exam in California. The dream cut to him running through the airport, getting the last seat on a plane heading to San Francisco. He got off the plane and jumped into a taxi and told the driver he would get a big tip if he could get him to Davis in half an hour. The driver was Arnold Schwarzenegger.

Somehow, Arnold got him to the university and right up to the lecture hall. The dream cut to Dylan bursting through the doors and running down to the front of a packed classroom.

That's when he felt the air conditioning on the most sensitive part of his body. The entire classroom gasped and began to laugh.

Completely naked, Dylan stood for a moment like an inert skeleton in an anatomy class, then looked around desperately for something to cover himself with. The only thing available was an empty paper cup the professor had on the lectern. He grabbed the cup and held it where Adam wore his fig leaf, and started to shuffle toward the exit.

That's when he woke up.

He next had the dream shortly after he received his chiropractic license. Only this time he was speaking to a convention of fellow chiropractors on the issue of vertebrate reconstruction. He woke up in the same hotel room in New York and this time flew to Las Vegas. The taxi driver was still Arnold Schwarzenegger.

The result was the same. Auditorium, air conditioning, laughter. The paper cup this time was from Starbucks.

The last time he had the dream was the night before he was slated to speak to some high school basketball coaches about common sports injuries. In the dream, that turned into the entire Los Angeles Lakers and Clippers teams meeting at Staples Center. New York hotel room, flight to Los Angeles, taxi. Only this time the taxi driver was Magic Johnson.

Crowd. Nakedness. Paper cup.

That same feeling of being exposed and helpless was what he felt now looking at the blog. He was an internet story. He was presumed guilty. They were probably reading about him in China now.

And there was nothing he could do about it.

Using the burner phone, he called Erin to let her know what was happening. But it went to voicemail. He left a short message for her to give him a call back.

He hoped she was hanging in there. And in a way, hoped that he could somehow bring her through this nightmare into the soft, warm light of a lasting morning.

After all these years ... because when they first got married and honeymooned in Sonoma, they'd awakened that first glorious day and looked out their inn window, at a vineyard-covered hillside, his arm around Erin in her soft, white bathrobe, and he'd said, "My life has one purpose now. Your happiness."

And happy they were, especially those first precious years, when it was all newness and passion, and when Kyle arrived a different kind of newness and a deeper love for each other. The evenings they would spend on the bed, just talking, the baby between them in his onesie, until he fell asleep and they gently put him in his bassinet.

He'd wanted to guarantee Erin's happiness, always. Even during the dark years, and in the aftermath of their split.

Now, staring at the computer screen and the reporter's blog, the demon GUILT came at him again, teeth bared.

Because he hadn't made her happy after all.

81

He'd let her use the bathroom but kept the noose thing around her neck. He warned her about taking off the blindfold. It was everything she could do not to rip it off and look at his face. But he said she'd never see Kyle again if she tried it, and she believed him.

She had to tap the stall walls and kick porcelain before she knew where she was. She felt the noose loosen a bit.

"You can turn around now," he said.

"Close the door," she said.

"I can't do that, but I'll turn my back."

Nature made its final demand and she pulled down her pants and lowered herself into the humiliating position.

"You know who you remind me of, Erin?"

She didn't care. And said nothing.

"Claudette Colbert," he said. "In *It Happened One Night.* You know the one, with Clark Gable. Have you seen it?"

She had.

She stayed silent.

"It is *so* good! Always packs the house when we play it. It has that famous scene, where Clark Gable pretends he knows everything about hitchhiking, it's so funny, and he tries to stop some cars with his thumb, but none of them stop. Then Claudette tells him—"

Dear God, can't this man stop talking?

"—give me a chance, and Clark Gable laughs at her, but then she goes to the side of the road and as a car comes by she pulls up her skirt and gives the car a view of her very delicious leg. Screech! The guy hits the brakes. It is so funny!"

Pause.

Relief.

"Are you finished yet?" the man said.

"Are you still turned around?" Erin said.

"Come wash your hands."

The noose got tight again.

He guided her to the sink.

"Let me turn the water on for you," he said.

She heard the shushing of water.

"The soap dispenser is right next to it," he said.

She found the soap and washed.

When she was done, he put a paper towel in her hands.

"He wasn't right for you," he said.

Her body began to vibrate, from her feet to her legs to her chest. Nerve piling on nerve.

"What?" she said.

"That Andy guy," he said. "I've dealt with his kind all my life. Slick smilers. Empty suits. Worthless people. You know who would have played him in a movie? Edward Arnold. The world is better off without him, believe me. We need more real people. We need more Lon Chaneys."

"So you killed him? You monster—"

"No! That's what they always said about Chaney! But I am going to explain all to you, and you'll come to respect me."

"I'll never respect you," she said.

"Maybe respect isn't the right word. More like be in awe of. I have waited a long time for you to be in awe of me. And I don't want you to worry. Let's go back and sit down."

She felt the pull of the noose. A dog, she was. But she wasn't going to let him master her.

When she was in the seat again he said, "Don't you see how awesome it was that I could kill a man attacking you at a phone booth? That I set it all up? That I had him carry your ex's business card just to mess with the police?"

"Monster ..."

"I did him a favor! His mind was riddled with drugs. He used to work for me. Now he doesn't have to wonder where his next meal's coming from."

Erin twisted in her seat.

"I know you're dying to rip my mask off, so to speak. Just like Mary Philbin does to Lon Chaney. A woman just has to know. And you will! Just not yet."

He took her right arm and attached the cuff to it.

"Is that necessary?" she said.

"Be patient, Erin. You're not in any danger. No one's going to hurt you. There's a point to all this."

Left arm, shackled.

"That's enough," she said.

"You're right," he said. "When the time comes, you'll be completely free to move around. Now, are you hungry?"

Erin didn't answer.

He said, "How would you like to have one of the most delicious culinary experiences of your life? I know you would."

"No."

"Ah, not so fast. I'm talking about one of the supreme pleasures. Maybe the second best. What do you think?"

She didn't think anything, except that in this unreal dungeon maybe some old-fashioned movie justice could get done. Somehow.

"You are in such good shape," he said. "A man should be able to compliment a woman on her figure, don't you agree?"

Erin gripped the ends of the armrests.

"Women who let themselves go have no appeal for me," he said. "You have great appeal. You kept it. Now, while I get you some food, I'll give you a little hint. This is not the first time you and I have been together."

What?

A moment later he took the blindfold off her. The room was dark.

Then the projector sound started again, and on the wall in front of her the movie, *The Phantom of the Opera*, started again. Just after the unmasking. The Phantom and his horrible face, he was pointing, pointing at the girl, who was shrinking back in horror.

Erin heard a door open.

And close.

82

Dylan woke up with a headache, which he attributed to the extra beer he'd drunk at the office. He made the coffee strong and sat with a cup and his laptop in his living room.

He looked at the crime blog again and noticed that the post had garnered fifteen comments.

He didn't want to look.

He looked.

The first one said:

The guy did it. Doctors always do. Ever see The Fugitive?

This was followed by a reply:

The Fugitive was INNOCENT, genius.

The first commenter replied to the reply:

It was also a movie, numnutz. This is real life.

And the comeback:

Great logic there, Aristotle.

A lengthier comment followed:

You can't read anything into an accused not wanting to talk to the press, Steve. It's prolly the first thing his lawyer told him, don't talk. Even the innocent shouldn't talk, because things can be misconstrued and then used against him in court.

That comment actually gave Dylan a sense of relief. In the mad swirl of internet and social media, a rough justice could sometimes work its way through the noise.

Dylan turned to answering some emails—two from clients, one from his freshman-year Davis roommate, and one from his older brother who lived in a rural part of North Carolina. Robert Reeve had "dropped out" of city and professional life after taking acid with his girlfriend the night of Y2K. Robert's email was the only one that did not reflect any knowledge of Dylan's legal trouble. Dylan decided to keep it that way. Robert had a happy life with his soybeans, peanuts, hogs, and raised consciousness.

Two cups of coffee later, with his stomach growling under the acid wash, Dylan made some scrambled eggs and sourdough toast, and listened to the local smooth jazz station via iHeartRadio.

After breakfast he called Erin and again got voicemail. He didn't leave a message this time, but a sense of unease began to work its way through his thoughts.

He called DeForest. Erin usually got to the office early, around 8:15 or so if he remembered correctly. But it was not her voice who answered the main line.

Dylan said, "Has Erin Reeve come in yet?"

"No, not yet, can I—"

"This is Dylan Reeve, her ex-husband."

"Hello! I'm her friend, Yumiko. I can take a message for you."

"It's important that I talk to her."

"Of course. What number is best to reach you?"

"Can you at least tell me the last time you talked to her?"

Silence.

"Please," Dylan said "I know about the man she was seeing, that he's dead. I really need to reach her."

"Um, Mr. Reeve, I'm sorry, but can you tell me something to verify who you are?"

"I'm telling you who I am!"

He realized how stupid that sounded the moment he said it. This woman was only doing what was right. He gave her his number and once again urged the importance of Erin's getting in touch with him.

He said, "Please. I'm sorry. I ... just tell her to call Dylan. She has my number."

"I'll tell her the moment she comes in," Yumiko said.

83

She refused to watch the horrid movie. He wanted her to. That was why he had her secured to a stupid theater seat.

She closed her eyes.

The guy said they'd been together before.

Was he a former DeForest student? There had been so many over the years, mostly in passing. A few she'd had one-on-one conferences with. But of those she couldn't recall anyone giving off a creep vibe.

Of course, a real, practiced sociopath wouldn't send out those signals. Quite the opposite.

Could he have been from further back? Before she married Dylan?

There'd been a ten-year span between high school and marriage. She'd had only one serious relationship in that time. Tyson Starr was a car salesman and very successful at it. What he really wanted to do was start his own business and he had several ideas. When one of them turned out to be internet porn, Erin immediately ended the relationship. Tyson tried for a week to get her back, sending flowers every day. But the bloom was off that rose.

She didn't hear from Tyson Starr for six months. Then one day he showed up at her apartment looking totally different. His head was shaved and he had an earring. He'd pumped himself up with weights and asked if he could come in.

Erin said no, but he pushed his way inside and told her he just wanted to talk. He told her he was a different guy now. That he'd "found himself." He was on the ground floor of a new multi-level marketing company, hawking vitamins and herbs, and was starting to bring in the big bucks, so now wouldn't she like to get back together with him?

Erin said no, and politely asked him to go, and no, she did not want a free starter pack of Energy-Wham supplements. Before he left he put out his hand and she took it. He pulled her to him and tried to kiss her. She turned her head away.

The last thing he said was, "I'm a goal-type person. I usually get what I want."

"No sale here," Erin said as firmly as possible.

She hadn't heard from him since.

When at last she looked again at the wall, the movie was heading toward a climax. The Phantom being chased by a mob with torches. They trapped him by the river. The Phantom reached into his coat and came out holding something, threatening the crowd with it. They stop for a moment.

Then the Phantom laughs! He opens his hand to reveal ... nothing.

The crowd closes in on him, finishes him off, then throws him in the river.

Finis.

The lights came on, making Erin squint.

The projector noise stopped.

"No one deserves that," the voice said.

"How much longer is this going to go on?" Erin said.

"It's time for your meal."

Turning, she tried to get a look at him.

She caught a glimpse of someone in a hoodie. A blue hoodie obscuring his face. Like a mask. Like the Phantom.

"Not just yet," he said, moving directly behind her. "First, we eat.

"I'm not hungry."

But she was.

The sound of a door slamming open echoed through the room.

A voice, not his, shouted, "I want my money!"

Her captor screamed his answer. *"Get out!"*

"Give me all of it!"

"Get out of here!"

"Who is that?"

"Get out!"

"You didn't say anything about a woman!"

She heard a scuffling sound, body against body.

"Don't touch me!" the new voice said.

Her captor cursed at top volume.

Then the sound of a thump, deep and resonant, and something falling to the floor.

Then silence, except for heavy breathing.

A man with a buzz cut and tattoos on his arms came into her line of sight. He had some sort of pistol in his right hand.

His voice was a low growl. "Who are you?"

Erin, breathless now, looked at the gun, then at this man's eyes and then ...

Oh, dear God.

His nose.

"What's wrong with you?" he said.

With what seemed like her last ounce of strength Erin said, "Your mother!"

84

A little after nine, and Dylan still hadn't heard from Erin. He thought about driving to the DeForest campus.

He had no place he needed to be.

He wanted to be with Erin.

His phone buzzed. Dylan grabbed, hoping it was Erin.

It was Paige.

"Boss, I've got my little brother with me at the office. Can he talk to you?"

"Your brother?"

"About the movies," she said. "He's kind of anxious to tell you something."

"Put him on," Dylan said.

"His name's Josh."

A moment later a high-pitched and speedy voice said, "Hi, Dr. Reeve!"

"Hi, Josh."

"My sister's told me all about it, and it's like a mystery, a film noir!"

"I wish it were only a movie," Dylan said.

"We can figure this thing," Josh said.

"What do you mean?"

"About Phroso. I don't think it has anything to do with *Freaks*."

Dylan said, "No?"

"Uh-uh."

"So what do you think?"

"*Freaks* isn't the only movie with a Phroso," Josh said.

Dylan's hands started to tingle, the way they did when he was a kid about to get on a roller-coaster.

Josh said, "There's another movie with a Phroso in it, and I think that's the one this jerk is using, because of your son."

Now Dylan sat up straight. "What movie?"

"You know much about Lon Chaney?" Josh said.

"A little. He was the Phantom of the Opera, right?"

"Yeah. And *The Hunchback of Notre Dame* and a whole bunch of others. They called him the man of a thousand faces. He usually played these tragic guys, bodies all mangled, or just him all emotional and dark. Always an outsider. So maybe that's how this guy thinks of himself."

"You said you think there's a connection to my son."

"This is so cool! No, wait, I'm sorry, I didn't mean that."

"I know," Dylan said.

In the background, Dylan heard Paige say, "Calm down, Josh."

"I just mean," Josh said, "when I thought about it, it made sense."

"Please tell me."

"There's this movie Chaney made where he played a magician by the name of Phroso. He had a wife who was part of his act. He loved her. But she was messing with another man. Phroso confronts this guy backstage and there's a fight. The man knocks Phroso over a railing and he falls and breaks his back, and he's turned into a paraplegic."

"You've seen this movie?"

"Yes! Lionel Barrymore plays the other man, by the way."

Dylan said nothing.

"Anyway," Josh said, "I've seen everything Chaney did that's still around. Most of his stuff is lost. So anyway, here's what happens. Phroso has to get around on one of those rolly things, you know, moving himself with his hands and rolling down the street. He hears his wife has come back to town and is in a church, waiting for him. He wheels to the church, drags himself in, and finds her dead. It's not clear why, but right next to her body is a baby girl, who she had with this other guy, see, who is now off in Africa to get ivory. So Phroso plots his revenge. He brings the baby to Africa and put her in a ... my sister doesn't like me to say it."

In the background, Paige said, "You can say *whorehouse*, Josh."

"Whorehouse," Josh said. "In Zanzibar. That's the name of the movie. *West of Zanzibar.*"

"That's it?" Dylan said.

"No way! That's just the opening. We cut to a bunch of years later. For all that time Phroso has been using his old magic tricks to fool the local natives into thinking he's this powerful guy. And then he starts stealing ivory from this man who he's followed to Africa."

"The man who fathered the child?"

"Lionel Barrymore."

"Okay," Dylan said, wanting to get to the point.

"So Lionel Barrymore comes to confront him, and then recognizes him as Phroso. Then Phroso calls for the girl to be brought to them, and she's grown up now, but since she was raised in a ... you know, she is what she is."

"Does this movie end?" Dylan said.

"This is the best part! I mean ... sorry, this is what happens. So Phroso makes a big deal out of showing the girl to Lionel Barrymore, and finally says 'See! This is your daughter! I've had my revenge!' "

The inklings of a scenario, so base and bizarre it was almost beyond comprehension, began to form in Dylan's mind.

Josh said, "Lionel Barrymore sits and puts his head in his hands, and starts shaking. Phroso has this wicked smile, see, enjoying the moment, the moment he's been waiting for for eighteen years. But then ... Phroso sees that Barrymore is not crying, but laughing! Laughing hysterically. And then he tells Phroso that the girl is not his daughter at all, but Phroso's! His wife was pregnant when she left Phroso, and she never ran off with Barrymore after all. Phroso has done these evil things to his own daughter!"

Dylan realized he'd been holding his breath for several seconds. He let it out with a gush.

"See where I'm going with this?" Josh said.

Dylan said, "But that's so ... fantastic. That some guy would kidnap my son and raise him to be something bad?"

"Kind of," Josh said.

Pressing his thumb to the middle of his forehead, Dylan said, "Thanks for that run down, Josh."

"I hope I didn't upset you. It's just that my sister said—"

"Not at all," Dylan said. "I just need to think about it."

What he needed was to get off the phone and figure out a way not to believe this could have happened.

85

Was it him? Or was it her impassioned imagination, desperate to make it so?

"My mom's dead," the tattooed man said.

"Harry Potter," Erin said. "You loved Harry Potter, and Legos ..."

"I gotta clean this up. Good luck."

He stepped around behind her.

"Wait!" Erin said.

She heard a grunting, something being dragged, a door closing.

"Please!"

Nothing.

It was him!

Wasn't it?

But he looked so ... what was the word? Hardened. And yet there was something in the way he'd said "Good luck." Not ice cold.

Or was it all in her tired mind, awash in stress and about to shut down?

She wouldn't let it. She would push past the wall, that part of the marathon that happened to her around the twenty-one mile mark. Every part of her screaming to quit, take sweet rest. That was when it was pure will to keep going, ignore the voice and the beckoning shade of a booth serving cold water and orange slices.

When Kyle was two she'd noted a fundamental decency in him. They say babies come out with a personality stamped on them. The art of parenting was taking what was there and nurturing it, channeling it toward full and wholesome humanity.

Her Kyle had been sensitive. Not the weak kind of sensitive. It was an empathetic kind. She'd seen it one day in the park, Kyle playing in the sand, and a little girl had joined him. The mother introduced herself to Erin as they watched their kids in spontaneous play.

The girl was building something out of sticks and an overturned plastic pail. Kyle was picking up fistfuls of sand and watching it trickle out like an hourglass.

As Erin listened to the mother talk about the conundrum of child care and the working parent, Erin saw a motion out of the corner of her eye.

Two boys, maybe seven or eight, one chasing the other, ran past Kyle and his new friend. One of them accidentally kicked the girl's sculpture. Down came the handiwork. And out came the girl's tears.

"Uh-oh," Erin said.

The mother looked over and got up to see what the matter was. Erin followed.

When they got there Kyle was petting the girl's hair.

It was the most innocent, honest, sympathetic reaction she'd ever seen in one so young. He wanted to comfort the little girl, but not having the words he had only the action of a toddler who had been born—stamped—with a natural tendency toward compassion.

Maybe, just maybe, this madman hadn't been able to carve that out of him.

But what *had* he done?

Time was the enemy now. A tortuous enemy. She had to do *something*.

But cuffed to a theater seat, what chance did she have to get out of the restraints?

None, if you don't try.

That's what her friend Linda had told her when the idea of running marathons first floated across her mind. Actually, put there by Linda herself, a runner of longstanding.

But a marathon? Twenty-six miles, non-stop?

"You'll never know if you don't try," Linda had said.

And at that point in her life, in her grief, in her long twilight of mourning, she decided to try.

The handcuffs on her wrists were connected to the iron under the arm rests. She didn't know anything about theater seat construction. Maybe he'd fashioned his own.

When she pressed on the floor with her feet, there was the slightest amount of give in the three connected seats. Like a clunky and ill-designed rocking chair. The middle joints moved ever so slightly. She didn't know what you called it, but where the bolt connected a joint of some kind, that was where the seat moved.

If she had a battering ram and was free of her shackles, and could ram the center seat as hard as she could, she might be able to dislodge or at least loosen the joints.

And if unicorns lived in lollipop forests, she could have some candy.

All she had were her legs. They had muscle mass, they had some force. Maybe in a hundred years of constant pressure she could get joints to break.

She put her feet flat on the ground in front of her and gave one hard push with her heels, at the same time pressing her back against the chair.

And moved the set one whole inch.

Clearly, the unicorns were a more realistic option than this.

But the effort had produced a shot of endorphins.

She thrust again, only this time rammed her back against the seat. And again.

And again.

Eight times.

Then, spent, like she'd sprinted to a finish, she stopped to catch her breath.

Was it her imagination, fueled by wishful thinking, that told her she'd moved the chairs a little further than before?

Who cared? She was going to keep on doing it until physically unable. And then somehow she was going to figure out how to do more of it even then.

Erin Reeve, human battering ram.

86

It only took ten minutes after he got off the phone with Josh for Dylan to realize he'd go nuts thinking about this alone.

He called Gadge Garner's number and left a message.

He looked at his phone, hoping Erin would call.

He wished he had a dog.

He poured himself more coffee. Then poured it out before drinking it. The jitters he did not need.

Gadge Garner called him back.

"Can we meet?" Dylan asked.

Garner said. "When?"

"Yesterday."

"For that I'll have to move some things around."

"ASAP. And I'll pay for your time."

A short pause.

Garner said, "I can change an appointment and be at your place at two o'clock. Will that do?"

"I guess it'll have to."

"Sounds serious."

"It is."

"I'll be there at one," Garner said.

And he was.

Speaking quickly, it took Dylan fifteen minutes to lay out all that had happened. Gadge Garner took it in, then asked for a blank piece of paper and a pen. He put the paper on the coffee table between them.

Garner said, "So we have two people in on this, which makes it both more dangerous and more open to solution."

"Explain that," Dylan said.

"The nature of a conspiracy, and the reason it's a crime in and of itself, is that two or more minds that get together to do harm generate an evil that is greater than its individual parts. But it also increases the chances of a reveal. Each part has a weakness. We've just got to find them."

"How do you do that?"

Garner tapped his head, then his heart. "Think and feel. Get into their heads, but also their motives."

Dylan nodded.

Garner turned the blank sheet of paper to landscape and drew a stick figure in the upper left quadrant. In the upper right quadrant he drew another stick figure, then put a dress on it and long hair.

"Not politically correct," Garner said, "but for our purposes this is a man and a woman. The guy calls himself Phroso. Why the phony name?"

Dylan said, "To hide."

"That's the obvious answer. What else?"

"To fool people."

Garner nodded. "What else?"

Dylan thought a moment, then shook his head.

"To send a message," Garner said. "To play a game."

"Phroso told Erin he was good at games."

"And Tabitha. She told you something about her name."

"She claimed it was because her mother liked that old TV show called *Bewitched*."

"And who was she bewitching?"

"Me."

Gadge Garner drew a crude broomstick under the woman figure. "This woman thought she could cast a spell on you, and she did, right?"

"Big time."

"Sociopathy 101."

"Is there a 201?"

"Yeah, it's the transition class into psychopathy. How to make plans, intricate, and bring them off. Pass that class and you can move on to 301."

"I'm afraid to ask."

"Sadism. Pleasure, often sexual, in the pain of others. Which brings us to our fella."

Garner drew a circle around the guy stick figure.

"Mr. Phroso," Garner said. "He was probably born a sadist. And capable of kidnapping a child and doing what that movie was about."

"But what about Tabitha?"

"I'm thinking that Phroso and Tabitha were working you together. Then they had a falling out, and that was the end for our gal."

He put a large X over the female drawing.

"Now we have two other dead bodies," Garner said. In the lower left of the page he drew a horizontal stick figure, with little x's for eyes and a sad mouth. He did the same on the lower right.

"These two are connected to your wife," Garner said. "This guy is the wild man at the pay phone who got shot by a long-range rifle. This other guy is the man your wife was dating."

"She said she wasn't, technically," Dylan said, feeling it was important to make that distinction. "He was pursuing her."

"And now he's dead. Why this poor fella? Because of the romance element. Phroso didn't like it. I think he's obsessed with Erin, and has been for a long time. Can you think of anybody in her past who might fit this profile?"

Dylan shook his head.

"Think harder," Garner said

Erin woke up, covered in sweat.

How long had she been out?

She was still in the seat, still constrained. Every muscle in her body ached. Her neck was in a vice.

Must have passed out.

Trying to get the seat to move, yes, that was it.

She pushed with her feet and her thighs burned.

And there was no progress.

All that effort, and she must have passed out.

Despair had claws, and they were dug into her insides, ripping.

Help me, help me, help me.

She heard the door open.

"Let's go back fifteen years," Gadge Garner said. "Is there anyone you can think of among your friends who was into movies?"

Dylan thought about it. "There was one couple, Tap and Chuck Loessing."

"Tap?"

"A nickname. Her real name was Pat. We used to go to the movies with them. Chuck and I liked the summer action movies. But to pay for our sins we had to go to chick flicks."

"They were good friends?"

"Very good. But they moved to North Carolina before Kyle was taken."

"Go back a little further then," Garner said.

"Before Erin and I were married I went to see some movies with a high school friend of mine, Marcus. He actually went into the film business, or tried to."

"Tried?"

"As a screenwriter. I still hear from him on my birthday."

"High school, huh? Anybody else from those days?"

"I was more into sports in high school, so I ..."

"What is it?"

Dylan stood and walked a few paces, lost in a memory.

"What've you got?" Garner said.

"I'm just remembering a guy in high school. He ran a film club. A weird kid ..."

"Go on."

Dylan spun around. He was short of breath. His eyes met Garner's. Garner said, "Spill it. Now."

As if from a distance, Dylan said, "He showed silent movies. One of them was *The Hunchback of Notre Dame.*"

"That's a Lon Chaney!"

"He's also a kid I cold-cocked because I caught him putting his hands on Erin's breast. That got us both suspended, and he never came back."

"Keep going with this."

Dylan ran his hand over his head, trying to coax out the thoughts. "Everybody called him Weezer. As near as I can remember, he didn't have many friends. He ate lunch with the outsiders, you know what I mean?"

"Do you remember his real name?"

"Petrie."

"You have your high school yearbooks?"

"There," Dylan said, pointing to the photos of the juniors. The picture in the yearbook showed a thin-faced, unsmiling boy in a T-shirt, his dark hair uncombed. His eyes reflected aggression, as if he wanted to spit at the photographer. The caption was: *Thomas J. Petrie.*

"How long after high school did you marry Erin?" Garner asked.

"It was ten years. I ran into her one day and we started talking, then dated."

"And Kyle came along when?"

"One year after we were married."

"And he was five when he was kidnapped?"

"Yes."

"There's a whole lot that could have happened in between," Garner said. "Any other pictures of him in here?"

"There was a club." Dylan flipped the pages, got to the clubs section of the yearbook. He found it. "Physics Club."

He pointed at the photo of four students—three boys, one girl— posing in front of a white board covered with math equations. The names were underneath the photo: *Tom Petrie, Terri Boyce, Derek Leake, Jerrod Forman.*

"Fun looking bunch," Garner said.

"So what can you find out about Petrie?" Dylan asked.

Garner made a typing motion with his fingers. "I'll work my magic."

89

"This wasn't the way I had it planned," he said. "But I can adjust."

"It was him," Erin said. "It was Kyle."

"Of course it was. Did you think I was lying to you?"

He was behind her still. She had no idea how much time had passed.

"He hit you," Erin said.

"Jimmy has a temper," he said. "He's gonna pay for that."

"What do you mean?" She was amazed at how powerful her mother's protection instinct flamed inside her now.

"I've got such a headache. He almost sent me to the moon."

"Where is Kyle?" Erin said.

"Jimmy."

"No."

"He'll be around later," Petrie said.

"Later? What do you—?"

"Keep your voice down, will you? My head is cracking."

"Tell me who you are, why you've done this. What do you want from me?"

"You know what?" he said. "I think the time is right."

And then he came around into her line of sight, and sat down in the seat next to her.

His face was angular—sharp lines and tight skin. Rat-like. His eyes were a deep brown, alert and penetrating, eyes made for peeping through bedroom windows at night. His close-cropped black hair had sprinkles of gray in it. Dressed in a clean white shirt and dress slacks, he looked like he was interviewing for a job.

"Hello, Erin," he said.

"Do I ... know you?"

He nodded. "We went to high school together. For a time, at least."

She shook her head, trying to envision his face younger. But nothing clicked.

"I once made a humble attempt to let you know how I felt about you," he said. "But you took it the wrong way, and your boyfriend at the time, with your help, got me kicked out of school."

With a rush of memory, it all came back.

"Weezer," she said.

His jaw clenched. "Don't ever use that name with me, understand?"

Erin said nothing.

He took a handful of her hair and gently pulled her head back.

"Do you understand?"

"Whatever," she said.

He let her go, and smiled. "I'll accept that, because I'm that way. You will call me Tom."

"Thomas Jefferson Petrie," she said.

"At your service."

"How did you ... what is all this?"

"I'm going to tell you. The whole story. It isn't any good without you knowing the whole story. But first we have to arrange the players."

He held something up. A phone.

Her phone.

"I'm giving your ex a call," he said. "I want him to know that you're safe and sound, and that your son is really alive. You have one line to speak, and this is the line: Dylan, it's true. That's all. Think you can remember it?"

"What is this leading to?"

"That's not the correct answer. The correct answer is, yes, I can remember it. Here's the thing, if you don't say that line your son is going to die and you will be kept alive, knowing you'll never see him again. So I think you see the importance of this. Right?"

She paused, then made herself nod.

"Okay," Thomas Jefferson Petrie said. "Here we go."

He thumbed the phone and put it to his ear.

90

Erin was calling. Dylan grabbed it.

"Erin, where are you?"

"Hello, pal."

A man's voice?

"Who is this?" Dylan said, and the moment he said it, knew who it was.

"Erin is fine, just fine," the voice said. "But she won't be unless you do exactly what I tell you. Is there anybody with you right now?"

Dylan hesitated.

The voice said, "I'll take that as a yes. You have one chance at this. If you bring anybody in, you will never see your son or your ex-wife again. I'm arranging a reunion."

Dylan was tempted to throw the name at him—Petrie. But he was too gripped with cold and furious dread to try it.

"It's going to happen tonight," the voice said. "You'll all get together. But only on my terms. Don't talk. And don't try anything high tech, like triangulating this phone. I am always one step ahead of you. And just to prove it, I want you to hear from the woman herself. She's going to tell you whether I have your son and can deliver him to you. Are you ready, pal?"

Looking over at Garner, who was listening intently, Dylan said nothing. He turned his back and walked toward his front window.

"I need to hear you say yes," the voice said.

"Yes," Dylan said, trying to make it sound innocuous.

"All right," the voice said. "Here's your ex-wife."

A couple of seconds later, Dylan heard Erin say, "Dylan, it's true."

Then the voice again. "There you have it. Now for the benefit of anybody who's there, say, I'm glad to hear it."

No way around it. Dylan said, "I'm glad to hear it."

"At six o'clock I want you to be at the 7-Eleven on Newhall Ranch Road in Santa Clarita. Don't miss it. Park and get out of your car and stand under the blue handicapped parking sign. You'll hear from me. And it won't be from this phone. Which is my way of telling you not to get cute. Bye, pal."

The call cut.

Dylan looked at the phone like it was a foreign object.

"Anything important?" Gadge Garner said.

"Nothing that can't wait," Dylan said. He tossed the phone a couple of inches in the air, caught it, put it in his pocket.

Garner said, "Your nonchalance is a tell."

"Excuse me?"

"It means you're not telling me something."

Dylan said, "You don't have to know everything."

"It's something bad," Garner said.

"Look, thanks. For everything."

"That's sounds like the old brush."

"Please! Enough."

"It was Petrie."

"Don't."

"He wants you to meet him."

"Stop."

"Don't do it."

"I don't have a choice."

Garner said, "He told you to go to a place and wait, didn't he?"

"I don't want to go into it."

"He's got all the leverage," Garner said.

"You don't have to tell me that," Dylan said.

"I'll follow you."

"No."

"Don't do this alone."

"I have to."

Garner looked at him a long moment, as if he were gauging Dylan's resoluteness. Dylan didn't have to fake it.

"All right, then listen," Garner said. "I doubt I'll be able to track you. He'll use burner phones himself to contact you, and when you get to the place he's going to get you out of your car and into another vehicle."

Dylan looked at the clock. 3:27. Considering commuter traffic, he needed to get going.

"He will take your phone and either chuck it or randomize it."

"What's that?"

"Attach it to a random car. Has he asked you to meet him at a place with a lot of in-and-out traffic flow, like a convenience store?"

"You're very good," Dylan said.

"I know that," Garner said. "So is he. You know what this could lead to, right?"

"I may not make it."

"You don't need to do this."

"Yes, I do," Dylan said. "I failed my son once. I'm not going to fail my wife. I couldn't live with myself if I didn't try."

"Wait one second," Garner said, and charged out of the room.

My wife.

That's how he'd said it. That's how he'd meant it.

And about the dying, too. He was amazed at how ready he was if it came to that.

A minute later Garner came back in the room holding something in his hand.

"This is a knife," Garner said, opening up a triangular blade on a curved handle. "Cops like it. It's quick, easy, close-quarters. Pistol grip. Don't stab with it. Slice and dice and gut. Do crisscross with it."

Garner demonstrated by whipping his hand in an X pattern through the air.

"No mercy," he said. He closed the blade, knelt, pulled up Dylan's pant leg and slipped the knife into his sock.

"Really?" Dylan said.

"Really," Garner said.

"Won't he pat me down or something?"

"This spot an amateur usually misses," Gadge Garner said. "And what's the worst thing that can happen? He takes it. That'll just make him feel even more superior. Which is what you want. Keep him that way as long as possible. And if there's any way you can contact me, do it."

"Where will you be?"

"Right here," Garner said. "I've still got some work to do."

91

Petrie said, "I wanted your ex to be here. I was going to give you the whole story together. Now I have to do it another way. But we'll have plenty of time to work this all out. Years."

"Never," Erin said.

"Ever hear about Stockholm Syndrome? It's what I used on your boy. Masterful. It works, it really does. I should get a certificate or something."

The cuffs on her wrists jangled, and Erin realized it was not because she had intentionally moved. Her limbs were shuddering on their own.

"So just to let you know, we'll have years together, and you will come to appreciate all this." He sat again in the seat next to her. "The massive amounts of money I've made because I'm smarter than anyone else, especially those buffoons in the meth trade. That was years ago, but the money is fully laundered and at my disposal. I can buy and sell people, Erin. Never thought I'd be able to do that, did you?"

How much of this was a lie? How could she ever tell?

And yet he did have her son!

"Plus, I'll show you a lot of great movies! The silent ones are the best. Garbo and John Gilbert. The chemistry. We'll have that, you wait and see."

He leaned his face so close to hers that she could smell his breath. It had a strange acrid odor tinged with wintergreen. Like acid mixed with the scent of a forest. Poison and freshness.

"You have to eat," Petrie said.

Erin turned her head away from him to avoid the smell.

"One of the things I do very well," he said, "and one of the things—of which there are many—that will earn your trust and yes, even love and devotion, is my cooking. I am a killer cook, if you'll pardon the phrase. So I am going to make you an honest-to-goodness Caesar salad. Absolutely to die for—oops, again you'll pardon the expression. Sound good?"

Erin fought to keep her breath steady. "What are you going to do to my husband?"

"Ex-husband," he said.

"For God's sake, tell me what this is leading to."

"Never for God's sake. She doesn't exist."

"I don't find you funny or clever or the least interesting."

"You will, I promise," he said. "But first the salad. You will love it. You won't be able to help it. And the freshness of it will be the start of my promise to you, to make your life a pleasure, as long as we both shall live."

92

The late afternoon traffic on the 605 was thicker than usual. According to his Google Maps app, it would take him an hour and fifty-eight minutes to get to the 7-Eleven.

If nothing changed, which of course it always did in L.A. Accidents waiting to happen. Millennials testing the limits of texting. Road ragers puffing their chests and blaring their horns. Distracted realtors closing deals on phones. And the standard buzzed drivers who would tell the cops they only had "a couple of beers."

Dylan tried to keep from too much emotion as he drove. He put on the local oldies station. He actually wanted the distraction of the commercials.

Frankie Valli was workin' his way back to a girl he called Babe, with a burnin' love inside.

The clock on the dash read 3:57.

No time for slow-downs, which were completely out of his control.

Dylan heard himself say something.

"Help me, help me, help me."

93

Petrie had wheeled in a serving cart, as if he were a waiter at a high end restaurant. He placed it in front of her. It had a couple of wooden bowls on top, one of them filled with lettuce. There were wooden salad forks, too, and several small serving bowls with ingredients of some kind, and a couple of bottles. One of them was Worcestershire sauce.

He rubbed his hands together as he spoke. "Now, there are very few places anymore that make a real Caesar. Did you know it was invented in Tijuana? By a guy named Caesar? Yeah, funny, isn't it? Most people think it was named after Julius. That idiot Paul Newman has a wreath on his head on the label of his awful dressing. I'm glad he's dead. Fake Caesar dressing drives me nuts."

You're already there, Erin thought.

"What you need is fresh, crisp romaine, but you don't want to bruise it. You have to cut it up, but it must be done carefully."

"I don't care. Please don't talk anymore."

"No, you'll love this! Now, you need a wooden bowl to mix the dressing. If you use glass or steel, the flavors won't meld properly. What I'm going to do is put in freshly minced garlic, finely sliced anchovies, some dry mustard ... there."

She tried to concentrate on something, anything that wasn't him. She found herself picturing Kyle at four in his bedroom, in his PJs, just as she was about to sing to him.

"I take half a lemon and squeeze it through a linen napkin, so we don't get any seeds. Good."

Long years ago ...

"And a *coddled* egg yolk. That's what most people miss. They use a raw egg yolk or, worse, no yolk at all. Well, the yolk is on them! So here we go."

He took an egg from a small bowl and cracked it, then poured between the halves a couple of times. Then he plopped the yolk in the salad bowl.

"A little mixing."

He began to mix it with a fork. It made a *shook shook shook* sound in the wooden bowl

"Anchovies," he said, picking up a small bowl. "Without anchovies, it is not a Caesar, I don't care what they say."

He finished putting in the fish and then began the fork work again. And without a change in tone or cadence, said, "My dad killed himself. Shot himself. Took a gun and put it to his head in the dining room and blew his brains out."

Shook shook shook ...

"Didn't leave a note, didn't say goodbye. He was beaten down by life. Actually, by the people in his life. He worked as an accountant in a construction firm. Big development guys. That put him around a lot of these big macho movers and idiot hard hats who have no hope in life but the next paycheck and round of beers at the sports bar."

Shook shook shook ...

"I was a kid, but I saw it. I saw what a guy said to him and how it affected him. It didn't help when my mom started sleeping with one of the foremen on a job site. I saw that too. My dad didn't do anything about it. He just figured ... well I don't know what that loser figured. Except in his mind and in his little body he accepted the role of victim."

He stopped.

"I need you to know all this, Erin."

She didn't want to engage him in any way. But it was hard not to with him standing right there.

"It's important to me," he said. "And so is this part. Virgin olive oil by sight. That's the artistic part. Not too much or too little."

He poured in the olive oil from a bottle.

"And now Worcestershire."

He dashed some in.

"And I like a dash of hot sauce. Most people use Tabasco, but I've found Tapatio to be a better mix with the acids. It doesn't compete, it complements. Like you and me."

The acids in her stomach reacted to his words. If she'd had any food in her, she would have thrown it up.

94

Dylan crawled through Pasadena. Traffic had definitely slowed.

It was 4:55 p.m. when he passed Lake Avenue. The flow was at about ten miles an hour, not a good sign. But when he followed the 210 heading north, his speed inexplicably picked up. This was the main artery from Pasadena to Santa Clarita, where homes were more afford-able. A good thing for young families but a monstrosity on a freeway system that was never built for massive commuting.

Still, if speeds kept at this level, Dylan estimated he could make it to the appointed spot with ten or so minutes to spare.

A minute later, car taillights blended into a blood-red stoppage.

Now he was crawling at a stop-and-start pace.

That could only mean one thing—an accident.

And, indeed, he saw the flashing lights of an emergency vehicle in the distance.

Unbelievable.

No, too believable. L.A. was once again a living and driving cliché, a virtual parking lot on the freeway system.

Nothing you can do.

One hour to get there.

Not at this rate.

It didn't help that on the oldies station Ricky Nelson was singing about a poor little fool.

He turned it off.

A Lexus cut in front of him, as Lexi were wont to do in L.A. It almost clipped him.

Can't let that happen!

The shadows of twilight were turning into the curtains of night.

He found himself biting the insides of his cheeks. Just like he used to when he was a kid and felt powerless to influence his world.

The flashing lights got closer, and from the movement of the cars Dylan could tell there was at least one lane closed. His only solace then was belief in the physics of urban traffic—just after the accident, things would greatly speed up.

When he reached the accident scene he saw a downed motorcycle crushed up against the median. A Toyota SUV was sitting in the number one lane, almost sideways. A CHP vehicle was parked in front of the mess, along with a red Fire Department medical van, and two patrol officers were assisting two medics with a gurney.

Whoever was on the gurney was completely covered, including the head, with a black blanket.

A movie director couldn't have larded on more symbolism. Dylan almost laughed at the way Los Angeles could imitate art. But the laugh got stuck in his throat.

95

With a set of wooden salad servers, Petrie tossed the Caesar in the large wooden bowl.

"Not too harsh with the romaine," he said. "Just enough to show it who's boss."

He paused, picked up another small bowl, and sprinkled on what looked like grated cheese.

"You must use fresh Romano," he said. "Parmesan is too salty."

He started tossing again.

"Finally, and this is crucial, the croutons. Don't use store-bought. Make your own. Choose a bread that has strength to it, not sandwich bread. Personally, I like a good, solid baguette."

He picked up a bowl of browned bread squares and added them to the salad, saying, "Baked to perfection with an olive oil drizzle, a little fresh garlic, and just a touch of oregano."

One more round of tossing, then: "And there you have it, Erin. You have witnessed the perfect Caesar. Now to taste it."

"I'm not eating," she said.

"You won't be able to help yourself," he said.

He took two white plates from the lower shelf of the serving cart and put them on top. He filled them with salad.

"You don't remember this, I'm sure, but you smiled at me one day in English class. You need to know how much that meant to me. I know you weren't one of the real popular girls, because I had a total knowledge of the class system at our school. You didn't know about the inherent beauty you had. But I did. Excuse me."

He wheeled the serving cart to the side and went behind her again.

Erin stared at the salad. She wanted to kick it over.

A moment later Petrie returned, pushing a table on wheels, with a white linen tablecloth covering it. On top were two elegant place settings, minus plates, complete with two wine glasses. In the middle of the table were a candle, illuminated, and a silver bucket with a bottle of wine in it.

Petrie rolled the table in front of Erin and removed the wine bottle from the bucket.

"A nice, crisp chardonnay," he said. "The best pairing."

He picked up a corkscrew and began to twist it into the cork.

"I wasn't exactly a chick magnet in school," he said. "But I wanted to be friends with you. You didn't want to be friends with me. You weren't real mean about it, but I tried to talk to you once at lunch, I was so shaking when I did. Do you remember?"

Erin shook her head.

"I came up to you and my hands were sweaty and my voice was shaking, you were sitting there with someone on your left hand side, I came up on the right hand side, and you didn't notice me at first."

Petrie pulled out the cork and twisted it off the corkscrew. He sniffed the cork, then placed it on the edge of the table. He put the corkscrew down next to the silver bucket.

As he poured wine into the two wine glasses, he said, "It was hard for me to breathe. And when you finally did look at me, you didn't smile this time. You looked at me like, what was I doing there? And do you know what I said to you? I said, 'What are you having for lunch?' Real smooth, right?"

He stepped around the table and unshackled Erin's right hand. His hands were cold from the wine bottle. He picked up one of the glasses of wine and held it out for Erin.

"No, thank you," she said.

"You must," he said.

Erin said nothing.

With a shrug, Petrie put the glass back on the table. He got the two plates of salad and served them, then pulled up a folding chair and sat opposite Erin.

And smiled at her. Just another nice dinner with a potential lover.

As he picked up his fork, he said, "Your reaction was to look at your friend, I don't even know who it was because I was so fixated on you, but then your friend started to laugh and you started to laugh and I turned away and walked fast and went around to where those big trash cans were behind the cafeteria and I threw up. It just so happened that one of those brainless football players saw me and started calling people over to look. 'Look at Weezer, look at what he's doing with his lunch.' Oh, I'm sorry, that's not a pleasant thing to bring up at dinner. Go on, taste a little bit of heaven."

Erin didn't move. The garlic smell was making her nauseous.

"We are under a bit of a time constraint," he said. "I have a very important appointment coming up. Would you like to hear about it?"

96

It was eight minutes past six when he pulled into the parking lot of the 7-Eleven. There were three cars in the lot, and a dull red and green light issued from the store window.

No one was milling around outside.

Dylan got out and went to the handicap sign, which was right where it was supposed to be. He looked around, almost expecting some cop to come up and write him a ticket or asking him what he was up to. He held his phone in his palm.

The night air was hot and dry, no surprise in Santa Clarita. God had never intended for civilization to be here. This was where snakes and Gila monsters had made their homes for a million years or more.

Why wasn't he getting a call?

He looked around, wondering—no, knowing—that he was being watched. Somehow, somebody had eyeballs on him.

Another minute ticked by, and still no contact.

Maybe this whole thing was to humiliate him. There would be no call. No, not until he drove all the way back to Whittier and the call would come in then, castigating him, mocking him.

The insides of his cheeks were getting raw.

A movement to his right. Dylan turned and saw a man just outside the doors of the 7-Eleven, coming toward him. The guy did not walk so much as he lumbered. In the dying light he looked to Dylan like a

Hispanic male who could have been an offensive lineman for the UCLA football team.

Dylan got ready, watching the big man's eyes.

Which looked down at a phone in his massive hands as he approached.

Then he looked up, at Dylan.

And smiled. Nodded his head. Then looked back at his phone as he walked by. He went to a black Acura, got in, pulled out of the parking lot.

Dylan's mouth was dry.

Behind him a man's voice said, "Hiya, sport."

Almost jumping into the wall, Dylan turned.

Carbona, the lying witness against him, smiled.

"Easy does it," Carbona said. "You're almost home with your wife and kid."

For a moment, Dylan couldn't speak. What was there to say? What was there to do?

"Unless you want to turn around and go back," Carbona said.

"Where are they?" Dylan said.

"Not far," Carbona said. "But I don't want to be followed. Phone please."

Dylan didn't move.

"You'll get it back," Carbona said.

"You expect me to believe that?"

"I don't have any incentive here. You want to leave now, go ahead. You'll never see your son again. I don't know about your wife."

Dylan shook his head and dropped his phone on the ground.

"That's not a good attitude," Carbona said. "Step around the corner now."

Has to be played out. Dylan took a few steps to the other side of the 7-Eleven, watching as Carbona picked up his phone.

"Down there," Carbona said, nodding toward a black sedan, the only car parked on that side.

They walked halfway toward it.

Someone got out of the car. A woman. She wore shades and a jacket, and a dark blue hat with LAPD on the front.

"My partner," Carbona said. "Please turn toward the wall."

"Come on," Dylan said.

"Please."

Dylan didn't move.

"Detective Peralta?" Carbona said.

The woman in the LAPD hat pulled a gun from under her jacket.

"Assume the position," Carbona said. "I just love saying that." He pushed Dylan in the back and smashed him up against the side of the building.

And started patting him down. All over. Chest, arms, stomach, sides, legs.

Ankles.

"What have we here?" Carbona said. He reached into Dylan's sock and removed the knife.

"Look at that, will you?" Carbona said. "A real nasty, this one."

Dylan still faced the wall. Dirt and sand smell assaulted his nose.

"Tracker chip right in the handle," Carbona said. "Professional. Somebody wants to know where we are."

"That's disappointing," the woman said.

Dylan whipped his head around as she was taking off her sunglasses.

"Hello, darling," Tabitha Mullaney said.

97

"I took good care of your boy," Petrie said.

He was sitting back now, legs crossed, sipping his wine. "We lived for a time in the mountains, away from people. There was a long period of adjustment, naturally, but you know what? Children are so resilient. He was only five years' worth of clay, still moist and malleable. I began to shape him."

Head pounding, Erin said, "Please stop!"

"I can't stop now," he said. "You need to know everything. Jimmy doesn't know about any of this, if that's any comfort to you. I was the one who wrote the note that said 'Mom, I want to see you again.' I think that was a bit cruel, honestly, and I'm sorry for it. But you had to know who is in control. Part of that is stripping away mental resistance. You'll know what I mean soon enough."

He took a sip of wine and nodded approvingly.

"You're going to live a good long time," he said. "We are going to be very happy together. It will take several years, but it will happen. I know how to make it happen. The good news for you is that I have a tender side, and I'm changing up my plans just a bit. I was going to have you watch something, but now I don't think that's a good idea."

He paused and looked at her as if waiting for her to talk.

She didn't.

"Don't you want to know what I'm referring to?"

She kept her head still.

"In just a little while your ex-husband is going to know that his own son is still alive and that his dear boy is going to be the one to kill him. After that, I'll bring his body here for you to see. And then I'll put Jimmy out of his misery so you and I have only each other. The circle will be complete."

That did it. With what was left of her strength she swept her free hand across the table and knocked the salad to the floor. A guttural animal sound issued from her as she pulled against the cuff on her left wrist.

Petrie stood, setting his wine glass on the table. "That's good, Erin. You need to get it all out. That's part of the healing. Your reclamation will be a wonderful thing, trust me."

With a force he had not shown to this point, he grabbed her arm and put the cuff back on her wrist.

"You just have to," he said. "You really don't have a choice."

He went behind her. "Now, since you've turned down one of the great eating experiences, I'm going to make it up to you. I should be back just about the time it ends. Enjoy!"

The lights went out. The sound of a projector started up. The big, white wall lit up.

Carl Laemmle
presents
Victor Hugo's Classic
The Hunchback of Notre Dame
with
Lon Chaney
A Universal Production

"No, no!" Erin said. "Turn it off!"

A door slammed closed.

98

Sitting in the back of the car, mouth duct taped and hands zip-tied behind him, Dylan could only look with astonishment at the woman he was supposed to have murdered.

She was sitting next to him, holding the gun, and smiling in a warm and understanding way. Which made the whole thing all the more bizarre.

"I know, dear," she said. "I'm going to tell you."

"Why?" Carbona said, driving into the desert night. Dylan was certain they were on Pearblossom Highway, the strip of two-lane blacktop that traverses miles of Joshua trees, jackrabbits, and desolation.

Nothing good happened out here.

Except it was a good place to dispose of a body.

"He deserves it," Tabitha said.

"There's no point," Carbona said.

"I can't stand to think he'll never know, even if it's just for a little while."

"Make it short," Carbona said.

In a soft, almost loving voice she said to Dylan, "I really liked you, you know. From way back. But you were way out of my league. At the time, at least."

What was she talking about?

"High school," she said. "Remember Physics Club? T. J. Petrie, Derek Leake, Jerrod Forman, and me?"

Her? No. It was Terri. Terri Boyce.

"Yep, it's me," she said. "Terri."

She looked nothing like Terri.

"I had a little makeover," she said with seeming pride. "Pretty good, isn't it?"

If it was true, it was masterful. The Terri Boyce he knew in high school was skinny, had dark hair, and frankly didn't seem to care what she looked like. Tabitha Mullaney was fully figured and coiffed. From what he could remember, the voice was different, too. Terri's had been high pitched. Tabitha's was deeper and more modulated.

"You probably don't remember this," she said, "being Mr. Football and all, but I once asked you to the vice versa dance. I called you. I was almost wetting my pants I was so nervous. You said you already'd been asked. Then I found out Erin Peterson asked you the next day. That hurt, my friend. That hurt."

It came back. Her trembling voice on the phone. His little deception.

"I missed a week of school," she said. "I was so sick. But you know what? You actually did me a favor. Yeah, you did. That was the week I made the decision to grow strong. It changed my life, actually."

"Really?" Carbona said.

"Absolutely," Tabitha-Terri said. "You like the product?"

"I like it," Carbona said.

She said, "So T. J. and I kept in touch, and when it came time to make some real money, when ice was hot so to speak, we were a good team."

"Better when I came along," Carbona said.

"In lots of ways," Terri said with a lilt. To Dylan she said, "So I would have probably gotten to you for free, but T. J. is paying us both in big, non-traceable dollars. And we're going to go away for a long time. Aren't we, hon?"

"You bet," Carbona said. "Where there's nice beaches and no questions."

Terri said, "You're probably wondering about the woman the police found dead."

"You don't have to go into that," Carbona said.

"But I do," Terri said. "He's got to be thinking about that. And I want him to know how good we are."

"He won't be thinking about anything soon enough."

"Then let me finish," she said.

99

Erin only looked at the wall when she couldn't stand keeping her eyes closed any longer.

She did that now, and the movie was showing a scene where the hunchback—the poor, deformed innocent—was being whipped as he was chained to a platform that rotated slowly, round and round in the public square.

The people of the streets of Paris laughing and mocking him.

Why did they make this movie anyway? Why did Victor Hugo write it? She'd never read the novel, and was only passing familiar with the story. The hunchback rang the bells at Notre Dame cathedral, and through some misunderstanding or other gets this flogging. He calls out for water and a beautiful gypsy named Esmeralda gives it to him. And then everybody dies.

Or something cheery like that.

Erin did not need the novel or movie to teach her about the capacity for humans to do evil.

She tried pushing against the theater seats again. But her strength was almost completely gone. Her arms were numb.

A public flogging would be preferable to this. Because then she would be let go.

And could save Dylan.

Oh, Dylan.

100

"Her name really is, or I guess I should say was, Tabitha Mullaney," Terri Boyce said. "Lonely woman. That's why T. J. picked her. He likes his playthings. He likes the ones that won't be missed. Unless it's Erin, of course."

Dylan made a sound that ran up against the duct tape and died.

"Easy there," Carbona said.

"He's all right," Terri said. "So it was a perfect set up for me to get to you, and for you to get into trouble, and for us to accelerate the rate of change. Remember your physics? The rate of change is directly proportional to the amount of force applied, right? Oh, right. You were too busy chasing footballs and cheerleaders."

Carbona made a turn off the highway onto a dirt road. Dylan followed the beam of the headlights illuminating sagebrush and sand before dying in a distant darkness.

"It's almost over," Terri said. "You're going to see your son."

"That's enough," Carbona said. "T. J. wants to explain it."

The zip ties were cutting into Dylan's wrists.

"I just wanted him to know," Terri said. "In these last few minutes, I just wanted him to know."

They drove in silence for what seemed like ten minutes, Dylan trying to keep his heart in his chest.

Then the car made another turn.

After a series of bumps Dylan saw ahead what was waiting for him.

A pickup truck.

And someone standing outside it. Average height, wearing a hoodie. Another person was inside behind the wheel.

The car slowed. Gravel crunched.

The car stopped.

Carbona got out and walked over to the guy outside the truck.

"What we could've been," Terri Boyce said, as if she meant to comfort him.

Dylan tried to burn a hole in her with his eyes.

She looked away.

With his hands behind him there was no way he could take the gun from her.

His moment was going to come. It had to.

Carbona returned and opened the rear door. He unbuckled Dylan's seatbelt, then grabbed him by the shirt and pulled him out. He walked him like a string puppet into the pool of light provided by the sedan, midway between the car and the pickup.

And shoved Dylan down.

Rocks bit into his knees.

Hoodie walked over and stood in front of him. Then reached down and ripped the duct tape off Dylan's mouth.

"Hello, Dylan," Hoodie said.

"Weezer," Dylan said.

"Nice homework," Petrie said. He got down on one knee so he was face-to-face with Dylan. "I'm impressed. Really. Not as impressed as you're going to be with me. But I want you to know your ex-wife is fine. She's going to be well taken care of. I guarantee it. For years and years and years."

Dylan wondered if he could get one, clear bite on Petrie's neck. It was animal time.

"Did you ever see a movie called *The Great Moment?*" Petrie said. "It was written and directed by Preston Sturges, the guy who did classics like *Sullivan's Travels* and *The Lady Eve*. Did you ever see those, Dylan?"

The headlights from the car made half of Petrie's face a shadow.

"Those were screwball comedies," Petrie said. "But *The Great Moment* was a more serious film, about the dentist who discovered that ether could be used as an anesthetic. What a great moment that was for anybody who needed a tooth pulled, huh? To take away pain like that?

Well, this is my great moment, Dylan. Except I'm going to give pain. You're going to see your son again. He's sitting there in the truck, just waiting for his great moment with you. And then he's going to kill you, Dylan. Pow, right to the head. Your own son. You've got to love that. And then I'll have Erin all to myself, and the things we'll do together!"

Petrie smiled at him, like he was expecting Dylan to wail or plead. But in his head right then Dylan heard the gentle rushing of a stream, and saw a picture, of himself, transported back to the one time he took Kyle fishing, showed him how to bait a hook and how to be patient, and they didn't catch a single fish but it was a perfect time, both of them happy, warm in a moment. That he should be thinking of that now was, Dylan realized with obvious irony, like the ether this scumbag just talked about. A memory given to him to anesthetize his soul. Given to him by whom? By the five-year-old Kyle, somehow. The real Kyle. The only Kyle.

"You lie," Dylan said. His body felt light.

"Oh no, my lad."

"All lies," Dylan said. "That's not my son."

"Let's go," Carbona said from behind.

Petrie punched Dylan in the face. Knuckles dug deep into his cheek.

Dylan put poison in his smile. "Loser," he said.

Petrie hit him on the other side of the face.

Dylan fell sideways, his head thudding on the sand. But there was no pain, none at all, and he heard the soft rush of the stream, and saw Kyle's hands on the fishing pole.

He heard Carbona say, "Hurry it up."

"Don't tell me what to do," Petrie said.

"Such a liar," Dylan said.

"Give me the gun," Petrie said.

"That's not part of it," Carbona said.

"I'm gonna shoot his knee," Petrie said. "He has to focus."

"Make it quick, will you?"

"Not too quick," Petrie said.

Dylan, in a bound and fetal position, saw movement of legs and assumed Petrie was being handed a gun. He prepared for the shot.

He saw young Kyle in his mind, holding the pole like Huck Finn.

We'll be together, son. Somehow. Somewhere.

Dylan heard a crack, a distant snap in the night.

Petrie fell, screaming, a wail of pain and something more, something deep and primal, like a man falling into a pit and knowing it had no bottom.

Another crack, and the sound of pinging off metal.

Then feet running on scrappy ground, the sound of the pickup truck starting, the grind of tires on gravel, another starting, roar of engine.

Light receding, and Petrie in the dirt in front of Dylan, writhing.

The gun lying on the ground near Petrie.

Dylan got to his knees, then his feet.

He kicked the gun.

Petrie, grunting now, started to crawl.

With the last of the light Dylan calculated where Petrie's head was and kicked it like a soccer ball.

A soccer ball made of bone. Dylan's foot exploded with hot pain.

Petrie stopped moving.

But why did he fall in the first place, like he'd been shot?

The answer came roaring up a minute later. An off-road job. Maybe a Jeep. No headlights.

It skidded to a stop.

Somebody got out. In the darkness Dylan saw only a gray shadow.

The shadow came to him. It had an alien face, with eyes bulging out.

No, they were goggles.

A hand flipped them up.

101

Gadge Garner said, "You okay?"

He had a rifle with a scope in his left hand.

All Dylan could say was, "How?"

"We have to move fast," Garner said.

Garner took something off his belt. A flashlight. He put the beam on Petrie's inert body.

"I kicked him in the head," Dylan said.

"Good," Garner said. "Goes with the wound to the articulation of the shoulder joint."

"How do you know that?" Dylan said.

"Because that's where I shot him," Garner said.

"You meant to hit him there?"

"You kidding? Of course. We need him."

Garner put the rifle on the ground and took a knife off his belt and cut the zip ties on Dylan's wrists. Dylan brought his hands in front of him with sweet relief, and rubbed the burn marks on his wrists.

Garner said, "Let's patch him up."

Within two minutes Garner had illuminated an LED lantern, retrieved a first-aid kit, and put a quick but solid dressing on the unconscious Petrie's wound.

In thirty more seconds he had Petrie's hands secured behind his back with metal handcuffs.

"Help me get him in the back," Garner said.

With Petrie in place in the Jeep, Gadge Garner added a gag made of red cloth.

Then Garner went over to the handgun Petrie had held. Using his knife, he lifted it by the trigger guard and dropped it into a plastic bag he'd pulled from his pocket. Then he swept up the lantern and ordered Dylan into the Jeep and told him to strap himself in.

As the Jeep made its bumpy way toward the highway, Dylan said, "Where we going?"

"Our friend here owns a movie theater," Gadge Garner said. "Found it through a real estate database. It's one of those old, restored jobs. May be where Erin is, or where those other guys are heading. Or both."

"But how did you find me?"

"Tracked you. GPS."

"But they found it. At the 7-Eleven. It was in the knife you gave me, which you didn't tell me had tracking, by the way."

"When I put the knife in your sock I pinned another tracker to the inside of your pants."

"What?"

"Misdirection. I figured they pat you down and they might find the knife in the same location. They take out the knife because they felt it, leaving the other tracker in place."

Dylan reached down and patted his pant leg near the ankle.

"It's on the inside," Garner said.

Dylan felt it. A small disk of some kind, held there by a simple pin.

"And you knew that was going to work?" Dylan said.

"Maybe eighty-five percent, which is a go for me in these situations," Garner said.

"But where were you?"

"About two hundred yards behind. No headlights. Night vision. When they stopped I had to hoof it to a good spot. When they gave Petrie a gun, I had to shoot."

"He said the guy in the truck was Kyle. That he was going to shoot me."

"I doubt it," Garner said.

"That he'd shoot me?"

"That it was really your son."

They made it to the highway and headed west. Gadge Garner took up a radio handset and pressed a button. "Fish Fry One, Fish Fry One this is Garner's World, come in. Over."

A voice came through the speaker, "Garner's World, this is Fish Fry One. Go ahead. Over."

"Two plates, emergency pursuit. Attempted murder. Armed and dangerous. Hold for questioning. Are you ready? Over."

"Go ahead, Garner's World."

Gadge Garner gave out two license plate designations and described the vehicles. That he had done all this in the dark of night was more than amazing. Dylan allowed himself to believe the amazement would continue.

To Erin.

Garner said, "Send a car to the Bijou movie house on Market. Have reason to believe hostage situation. Over."

"Roger that," the voice said.

"Over and out." Garner replaced the handset. "Connection at the Sheriff's Department," he said. "They'll notify CHP, too. We'll need some luck."

"How about a miracle?" Dylan said.

"I'll see what I can do," Garner said.

102

When they got to the Bijou there was a sheriff's car and two male deputies outside the glass doors of the darkened building. An old-fashioned ticket kiosk sat there like a sepulchral sentinel.

Dylan followed Gadge to the deputies. "I'm Garner, I made the call."

The older of the deputies said, "Place is locked up."

"I can take care of that," Garner said, producing a folded cloth from his back pocket.

"You mean pick the lock?" the deputy said.

"Better than smashing the glass."

"I can't let you do that."

"You certainly can," Garner said. "Exigent circumstances, an exception to the warrant requirement. There's a potential victim inside. You got the information from a reliable citizen, who would be me."

"Yeah, but information based on what?"

Garner sighed. "I heard a scream. Did you hear it?"

The deputy smiled. "All right. Unlock the door."

As Garner went to work with a lock pick, he said to the other deputy, "In the back of my Jeep is the guy who tried to kill my friend here. He's got a bullet wound but I patched him up. He's a little woozy. Arrest him and put him in your squad car."

The lock clicked. Gadge Garner opened the door.

Both Garner and the deputy had flashlights. Dylan followed them in and saw the beams revealing a lobby with a glass concession counter and framed posters. Not current movies. They looked old, like from the silent days.

One of them was *West of Zanzibar* with Lon Chaney.

Dylan's entire body went cold. He felt like he was in the dark castle of a madman.

And then, as if on cue, a scream cut through the silence.

More like an animal's screech, long and closing in on them from the shadows.

The deputy whipped his flashlight around and Dylan saw the white face in the beam.

A young man's face, teeth bared, flying at the deputy sheriff.

Who backhanded the face with his flashlight. An ugly cracking sound, and the young man's body hit the floor.

Lobby lights came on. Gadge Garner was standing by a wall switch near the concessions stand.

The screamer was now a moaner, flat on his back. He was dressed in jeans and black Converse tennis shoes and red T-shirt that was too short for him. Part of his stomach pooched out, white as porcelain.

"What goes on here?" the deputy said.

Gadge Garner came and leaned over the kid. He patted him down quickly, expertly, then detached a keychain from the kid's belt. At least ten keys jangled off it.

"Give me ten minutes," Garner said to the deputy.

"What about this guy?" the deputy said.

"I suggest you cuff him." To Dylan, Garner said, "Come with me."

Garner led him to the exits, popping the doors and looking through.

Then, using a flashlight, Garner went down the aisle of the theater to the left side of the screen and through a curtain.

Over on the right side, they found two doors—one an exit, the other marked *Electrical. Do Not Enter.*

"We're entering," Garner said. "Hold this."

He handed Dylan the flashlight, then looked at the keys he'd taken off the wild young man. He tried one, then another in the lock.

When that didn't work he looked more closely at the keys on the chain. He selected one and inserted it.

The door opened.

"I'll take that," Garner said, and took back the flashlight.

It was a small, closet-sized space, dominated by a bank of circuit breakers and breaker boxes.

Nothing special.

But Garner was giving it all a strong look.

"Well look at this," he said. "Fifty-amp, double-pole breakers."

"I have no idea what that means," Dylan said.

"It means inadequate for this usage," Garner said. He began to flip the switches. There were no loud clicks, as one would expect with a real breaker.

"Well how about that?" Garner said. "A facade."

He began to pull and jiggle at switches and boxes. Down one row, up another.

And then one of the switches moved. Garner pulled it, and it opened like a little door on a hinge. Behind it, in the flashlight beam, Dylan saw a cylindrical lock body.

"Ingenious," Garner said.

He tried one of the keys in the lock.

Nothing.

Another, and another.

On the fourth try, the lock turned.

Garner pushed and the entire panel opened like a door.

Because that's what it was.

It led to a stairway of iron. Dylan's heart spiked into overdrive as Garner led the way.

At the bottom of the stairs was flooring about ten-by-ten, and another door—industrial, probably aluminum.

And another lock.

Garner used a key, presumably the same one that had just opened the secret door, to flip the lock.

They entered the darkness.

In the initial flashes of light Dylan saw a row of theater seats and what looked like a table that had been set for a dinner. He waited just inside the door until Garner found a light switch.

It was some kind of movie viewing room. A projector was set up behind the theater seats. A big, white wall would have been the screen. Beyond the projector was an open doorway leading to another room.

That was where Gadge Garner headed.

Dylan was drawn to the table. He had the disquieting idea that Petrie had been the one to set it.

He smelled garlic and saw lettuce spread out on the floor in front of one of the seats.

"She was here," Dylan said.

"What's that?" Garner said from the other room.

"I'm sure of it," Dylan said. "She was here!"

Garner came back to him. He examined the scene, the table, the scraps. "And not very long ago."

"What do we do?"

Gadge Garner said, "Let's go talk to our boy."

103

It was unbelievable.

She was in a pickup truck, handcuffed. And driving the truck was the man she had thought was her son.

A man holding a revolver in his left hand, steering with his right.

Was he really Kyle? Doubts were creeping in. She was exhausted, pushed to the limits. Petrie had done a number on her mentally. Was she projecting? Was she so spent and desperate that she made this driver, this obvious criminal, into her flesh and blood?

He had taken her roughly from her prison, uncuffing her from the seat but securing her hands again in front of her.

He told her to shut up as he practically dragged her up the iron stairs, then out an exit to where his idling truck was.

Shoved her in from the driver's side. Didn't put a seatbelt on her, which made her think he was going to shove her out the door at some point.

As soon as he got on the 5 freeway, heading north, he said, "Talk! What was T. J. doing with you?"

Erin fought for coherence. "He kidnapped you. From me and from your father."

"You are crazy with that! He adopted me when I was a baby, my mom was a drug addict. T. J. was trying to help her."

"How do you know all that?"

"He told me about it. Showed me papers and stuff. Where do you get off with this?"

"Where are you taking me?"

"I don't know!" he said. "T. J.'s dead and you got something to do with that."

"He was going to have you kill your father!"

"That's a lie."

"Your real father, my husband. That was his plan—"

"Shut up with that!"

"Don't you remember anything from your childhood? Harry Potter? Baseball? The Cubs. You were on the Cubs, don't you remember? Coach Mike. Your friends, Jayson Gillespie, Sergio Varela—"

"I don't know any of that! You better start talking straight."

The possibility of this man being Kyle began to fade. It was a million to one shot, always had been. Most likely, Petrie had set up a ruse. He concocted a wild scenario. And she fell into it. He wanted her to want to see Kyle, he'd made her want it too much.

"I'm giving you one last chance," the driver said. "You tell me straight or I'm gonna blow you away."

104

The other deputy was standing by the sheriff's car. Petrie was seated in the back.

When Dylan and Gadge Garner approached, Petrie snapped his head toward them and looked Dylan in the eye.

Gadge Garner said to the tall, lanky deputy, "Open up. I need to question him."

"He's under arrest," the deputy said.

"We have a potential victim out there," Garner said. "Open the door."

The deputy complied.

Dylan listened as Garner leaned down and said, "Where is she, Petrie?"

A half-smile crept onto Petrie's face. "Who?"

"You know you're going down. You've got one chance to help yourself."

"May I have a glass of wine?" he said.

"We've got 'em all," Garner said. "Somebody's going to flip on you."

Petrie squinted, as if trying to determine if Garner was telling the truth. The half-smile stayed.

"I show movies," Petrie said. "Why did you shoot me? Deputy! This man tried to kill me!"

Garner straightened, looked at Dylan, shook his head.

Petrie said, "Dylan! Buddy!" He motioned with his head for Dylan to approach.

Dylan looked at Gadge Garner, who nodded. Dylan stepped up to the squad car.

"Not your son," Petrie said. "Your son is dead. You'll never see him again."

"Where is my wife?" Dylan said.

"Who?" Petrie said.

Dylan readied a fist to put through Petrie's face.

"I'm talking about your son," Petrie said. "I made the whole thing up. It was a game. I won. And for that you tried to *kill me!*"

A second before Dylan sprang, the deputy pulled him away from the car. And shut the door.

Dylan yanked out of the deputy's grasp. "My wife is missing."

"I sent out a couple of plates," Gadge Garner told the deputy. "Do the same."

105

"We can work this all out," Erin said. "Let's go to the police."

The driver snorted a laugh.

"You're not guilty of anything yet," she said.

"You stupid ... they got me for kidnapping right now."

"I won't say you did it."

"I'm not the stupid one."

"I just want to *know*. I need to know. *We* need to know."

"All I want from you is the real deal." He lifted the revolver in his left hand and pointed it at her over his right arm. "I'm giving you one more chance."

"You're not a killer," Erin said.

"No?"

"No."

"Talk!"

"Then listen!" Erin was shocked by her own voice, but it exploded out on a river of adrenaline. "Your T. J. is a punk! He always was. I went to high school with him. He puts his hands all over me once, tried to push me up against a wall. Dylan, the man you were going to shoot tonight, beat the snot out of him. And then Weezer, that's what he was called, got kicked out of school."

The driver pressed harder on the gas as he looked in his rearview mirror.

Erin said, "Then he comes along all these years later, says he has our son. Our son who was taken when he was—"

"Shut up!" the driver said.

"You listen!"

"There's a cop behind us!"

Erin spun to look through the cab's back window. Flashing lights were closing in.

Mumbling curses, the driver pulled over to the right-hand lane. He put the revolver down on the floorboard. He lowered his window, stuck out his arm, and gave a wave to the vehicle behind him.

They were coming to an offramp.

The driver took it. At the end of the ramp was a STOP sign but no light, indicating a road that was not highly trafficked. He put on his turn signal, turned left, went under the freeway.

The flashing lights were right behind as he slowed to a stop on the side of the road.

Then reached up behind him and pulled down something Erin had not noticed before.

A rifle.

"No," she said.

"Shut up," he said.

"We can work this out."

He opened his door a small crack and put the barrel of the rifle up to it.

In the next split second, Erin knew nothing verbal was going to stop him, and screaming an alert to whoever was approaching would be too late.

The driver was going to jump out and start shooting.

The physics of her body and position became clear in that split second, and without reflection she pulled her knees up to her chest and leaned right, spinning herself on the bench seat of the cab.

With all the force she could muster, with legs strong from her running years, she pile-drove both feet into his back, sending his upper body into the slightly opened door.

She drew her legs back again and gave him another shot, this one sending him outside the cab. He went forward, face down.

Using her heels she scooted to the end of the bench seat, put her head down, and dove on top of the driver just as he was scrambling to get up.

Her jaw hit the back of his head, made a cracking sound, and she heard a voice shouting and what sounded like a gunshot.

Then her body shut down, and all was darkness.

106

On the first Tuesday in May, Dylan Reeve picked up Erin at DeForest University a little after one o'clock in the afternoon. As soon as Erin was in Dylan's car, she said, "I didn't get any sleep last night."

"Me either," Dylan said.

"Are you as scared as I am?" Erin said.

"Nervous," Dylan said.

Erin exhaled, long and slow. "Let's go."

They drove mostly in silence. Dylan took the 101 downtown and parked in the lot near Sam Wyant's building. He didn't care that it was going to cost him twenty bucks. Money was of no concern now.

Not with the final answer waiting for them in Wyant's office.

Pete Parris met them in the reception area. "Mr. Wyant is waiting for you in his office. Dr. Haslam is with him."

Dylan tried to read Pete's face, but it seemed just like its normal, smiling self.

As Pete walked them toward the corner office at the end of the long hallway, Erin took Dylan's hand. It was warm and trembling in his.

Pete ushered them through the door and into Sam Wyant's office. Wyant stood up behind his desk to greet them.

A tall, gray-haired man in a charcoal suit stood behind one of the client chairs.

"This is Dr. Jonas Haslam," Sam Wyant said.

The gray-haired man shook hands with Dylan and Erin. They all sat. Dylan hardly felt the chair underneath him.

"I don't want to warm up," Sam Wyant said. "The charges against you have been dropped."

The relief Dylan felt was only partial.

Sam Wyant knew why. "And the man they are holding as James 'Jimmy' Petrie is, definitively, your son."

Wyant slid a paper across his desk. Dylan picked it up. It was a report with medical jargon and numbers.

"The DNA test is conclusive," Wyant said.

Dylan felt light in the head. After all they'd been through, it was true.

His son was alive.

Their son was alive.

He reached for Erin's hand and saw that her eyes were moist.

To Wyant, Dylan said, "Can we see him?"

"That's what we need to talk about," Sam Wyant said.

"What's there to talk about?" Dylan said.

Wyant folded his hands on the desk. "There is nothing that can compel him to see you. I will of course do everything in my power to convince him."

"You?"

"I've decided to represent him."

Erin squeezed Dylan's hand. Dylan was glad she was holding it, because he had no words.

Sam Wyant said, "I'm taking this case pro bono, in part because of what you two have been through. But in greater part because I believe James has been—"

"Kyle," Dylan said.

Wyant nodded. "He has been operating under an extreme form of duress for many years. I'm going to let Dr. Haslam explain. But on the legal side, James ... Kyle possessed loaded weapons, but he didn't discharge them." He looked at Erin. "When you kicked him out of that truck and jumped on him, you saved his life."

Erin closed her eyes.

Wyant put his hand on some papers on the side of his desk. "I just received this morning the statement by the deputy sheriff who stopped the truck. He was about to shoot to kill. If you hadn't done what you did, the shot he fired would have found ... Kyle, instead of the ground next to him. Things could have gone the other way. You also saved that deputy's life."

"What is Kyle facing?" Erin said.

"He's charged with two counts of carrying a loaded firearm, of brandishing a weapon, criminal threat to a law enforcement officer, and conspiracy to commit murder."

Dylan tried to process his thoughts, now raw and swirling. His son was alive, but could spend years in prison.

"But we have a basis for a reduction," Wyant said. "The woman, this Terri Boyce, she's flipped on her partner, Carbona. They're a real winning pair, these two. With the money Petrie was paying them, they were getting set to leave the country. They were caught trying to get into Mexico, and I don't think they're going to be playing house anytime soon."

"What does that mean for Kyle?" Dylan said.

"I've been approached by the prosecutor, he's somebody I know, worked with a long time ago. If Kyle cooperates against Petrie, he's willing to drop the conspiracy count and the felony weapons charges. Kyle would plead to a misdemeanor and have to do some county jail time."

"Is he going to do it?" Dylan said. "Cooperate?"

"I don't know," Wyant said. "His mental condition is tenuous. Which is why I asked Dr. Haslam to join us. He examined Kyle on Friday. He has some things to tell you."

107

Dr. Jonas Haslam stood as he spoke, almost like he was giving a lecture. He said, "Based in part on what this woman, Boyce, has said, and in part on my questioning of Kyle, what he went through is similar to the brainwashing the communist Chinese experimented with on U.S. prisoners of war during the Korean conflict."

"Brainwashing," Dylan uttered, to himself as much as to the room.

"Serious, methodical. And on a young child. It is possible, indeed easy when one knows how to do it, to replace real memories with false ones. What Petrie did is likely just as you have supposed. He could certainly have raised your boy to be a criminal, for the purpose of ..."

He didn't finish the sentence.

"It's all right, doctor," Dylan said. "Just tell us. Can what was done be undone?"

"Given the right circumstances and the right attitude on the part of the subject."

"Meaning Kyle has to buy into it," Dylan said.

"Exactly. To do that he'll need a trust anchor."

"What's that?"

"Someone he can trust with complete confidence. In Kyle's case, that is a difficult proposition. He does not trust me, or Sam, at least not yet."

The obvious next question hung in the air, and it seemed to Dylan they were all thinking it at the same time.

Dylan squeezed Erin's hand and said, "Might we be that anchor?"

Dr. Haslam tapped his fingertips together. "If he can be convinced to take that risk. It is a risk because of what he's been through. He's confused. And he doesn't know yet that Petrie wants to communicate with him."

Dylan jumped from his chair. "No!" He looked at Sam Wyant. "He can't, can he?"

"Not if we can get through to Kyle," Wyant said. "If we can establish that trust."

"Then we have to do it," Erin said.

"Let's spend some prep time," Dr. Haslam said. "And then we can set up a meeting."

108

Thomas Jefferson Petrie, inmate #4862195, looked at his tray, at what they called a meal. He looked at the orange mash of indeterminate origin, and shook his head. What he wouldn't give right now for a good theater hot dog and some popcorn.

But it would come soon enough. He'd get out. He'd beat this. No one was ever smarter than Thomas Jefferson Petrie.

Yeah, he'd let himself slip, and now he had his arm in a sling. But he chalked that up to passion. He'd underestimated his desire for possessing Erin. Women were not to be trusted.

Like Terri Boyce. After all he'd done for her! She was pure rat now.

He had a plan for her. It would take some doing. But he'd get her in the end.

Her and Carbona both.

He had enough money to spread around, and contacts with associates, so it would be easy to contract hits on that happy couple from high school.

He would make sure they knew it was coming, that it was coming from him, and that he would do the same to Jimmy.

Oh yes. He'd finish off Jimmy, too. No more Kyle for the world.

Then he could do his time as a happy man, could Thomas Jefferson Petrie. They didn't execute anymore in California. He'd have a long life. And with the help of the ACLU, he was sure he could make the state pay for a DVD player, or maybe even Netflix streaming right to his cell.

He didn't like the flicker of remorse he had for William. But the half-wit was loyal, you had to give him that. He kept those bathroom floors clean enough to eat a salad off of. He'd probably be dead now if Petrie hadn't found him homeless and wandering around a park five years ago, and turned him into a productive slave. William responded to discipline and food and the occasional woman Petrie supplied him. Now they'd probably put William in an institution. Or maybe, because this was California, they'd just toss him out on the streets.

You're on your own now, kid. Just like the rest of us. Good luck.

Another inmate sat opposite him. He was thin with slicked-back black hair and dark tats on his neck. One of the tats was Spanish script. *Vida* was one of the words. "Hey, man," the guy said. "Lemme have your brownie."

Petrie felt and loved the ice water in his veins. "Get lost, jalapeño."

The guy didn't move or even twitch. He'd have to be dealt with soon. Petrie had some ideas about that.

"You tried to take out my friend, the doctor," the guy said.

"You speak good English, chico. What part of get lost don't you understand?"

"You gonna give me that brownie?"

Petrie picked up the chocolate square and shoved it in his own mouth. The whole thing. It was dry and chalky, but he smiled as he chewed.

109

Friday afternoon.

Erin was seated with Dylan in an attorney interview room at the Men's Central Jail, downtown. Sam Wyant sat with them, looking casual in a sport coat and slacks.

The air was stale. Erin didn't want to take a deep breath lest a disturbance in the atmosphere throw off the delicate hope she had been carrying around for the last four days.

The entire course of her life from this point on would turn on what happened in the next fifteen minutes.

Fifteen.

Help me, help me, help me.

The door opened, jarring her. The jangle of a chain awakened her to the reality of the situation.

Kyle was dressed in an orange jumpsuit, waist-chained and handcuffed. A large deputy sheriff wordlessly led him to the chair on the other side of the table and sat him down. In the center of the table was an iron ring. The deputy attached Kyle's handcuffs to the ring with another set of shackles, and left the room.

Kyle looked at his hands.

"Jimmy knows why we're here," Sam Wyant said. His use of that name disturbed Erin, but reminded her of what Dr. Haslam had said. It had been agreed that Dylan would ask permission first.

Dylan said, "May we call you Kyle?"

"This is all bogus," Kyle said, not meeting their eyes.

"Can we at least try?" Dylan said.

"Your time," Kyle said.

"You heard about the DNA test?"

"Those things get messed up," Kyle said.

"You don't really think that, do you?" Dylan said.

Kyle's eyes were cold, almost lifeless. Erin tried to pour love out of her own eyes. Could he see it?

Dylan said, "You've been filled in on all that's happened."

"What they say happened." Defiant.

"What I wanted to say, Kyle, is—"

"Name's not Kyle."

"All right," Dylan said. "Let me say it this way. We want to stand by you."

Kyle's eyes, empty of warmth, looked between them. Then at his hands.

"Why?" he said.

"We are your parents," Dylan said. "We loved you more than we can say, and that hasn't changed since the day you were taken away from us."

"Never happened," Kyle said. "My parents are dead. I remember 'em."

"What if that's not true?" Dylan said. "Wouldn't you want to know?"

"No," Kyle said.

"All we're asking is for you to trust us a little, and let Dr. Haslam work with you."

"Got no time for that," Kyle said.

Dylan opened his mouth. No words came out.

110

Captain Moses Jurado rubbed his temples. Normally at this time he'd be cleaning up a few emails before heading home to a nice weekend in Simi Valley with his wife and two kids.

Instead, he was going to be here at the jail for at least another two hours, owing to the news that had just been delivered by Deputy David Eslick.

"How did he do it?" Jurado said. He was sitting at his desk, looking at the report, while Eslick stood at attention.

"Sir?" Eslick said.

"Hang himself. According to this he only had one good arm."

"He used his arm sling," Eslick said.

"You believe that?"

"If you're determined enough, anything's possible."

"It doesn't smell right," Jurado said. "Petrie was psyched a 2A. No reason for a suicide watch." He ran his finger down the report. "He have any incidents?"

"Nothing reported," Eslick said.

"Anybody he was on the wrong side of?"

"Again, no reports. There was some shoving at dinner a couple days ago. Something about a brownie. But that happens all the time."

Jurado pulled at his earlobe. "And sometimes it leads to something. Maybe that's the guy that offed him."

"You want me to run an ISR?"

Jurado shook his head. "We don't need an investigative session on this one. Yet."

Eslick said, "We can revisit it."

"He have any next of kin?" Jurado said.

"That's the funny thing," Eslick said.

"Funny?"

"He insisted he had a son."

"Does he?"

"I haven't been able to find any evidence of it," Eslick said. "Want me to keep looking?"

"Tomorrow," Jurado said. "I want to go home."

111

Erin sensed Dylan felt the same way she did. That they were losing Kyle again. She'd known Dylan, loved him, been with him through the worst part of both their lives. She knew his body language, and right now it was crying out.

What was it he'd once said about hope? That he couldn't afford it? That it would tear him apart?

Sam Wyant leaned against the wall, arms folded. He was letting them talk but she could sense his skepticism that this would lead to anything.

Kyle's head was still down. His hair was mussed, beautiful. And then all the words Dr. Jonas Haslam had prepped Erin to say flew out of her mind.

"Kyle *is* your name," she heard herself say. "When you were sick with a fever, and could hardly breathe, I sat up all night with you in a reclining chair. You slept on my chest so I could hold you upright. Your father did the same with you the next night. We did that five nights in a row. When you got night terrors, I would come into your room and sing you back to sleep. It was called the 'Star Carol'."

Kyle's head did not move.

Softly, Erin sang, "*Long years ago, on a deep winter night, High in the heavens, a star shone bright ...*"

She paused, hoping he'd at least look at her. He didn't.

"You always wanted me to sing that to you," Erin said, "all the way to when you were five years old."

Kyle kept his gaze down.

"Try to remember that," Erin said. "Can you?"

No response.

"When you were five you were taken from us. What we went through was something I wouldn't wish on anyone. Not knowing if you were alive or dead. And now we do know. Alive. We don't want to lose you again. We will never let you go, if you will only let us ... stay ... in your life."

Silence.

"Will you just let us try?" Erin said. "We've come so far ..."

She couldn't continue. But she knew. The next moment would bring the answer. Kyle would look at her and she would see his eyes, be able to read them, and they would tell her whether she was granted life or living death.

For a long moment no one spoke, or even moved.

Then Kyle raised his head.

112

In the parking structure of the jail, sitting in the car with Erin, Dylan had no thought of starting the engine. This was the first place they could be together in private, out of the gaze of jail personnel.

Before saying a word Erin put her head on his chest. He put his arms around her. Her tears soaked his shirt. He tried to hold back his own.

He fell into the rhythm of her breathing.

And then, into his chest, Erin said, "Thank you, thank you, thank you."

"Yes," Dylan said. "Thank you, thank you, thank you."

She sat up and wiped her eyes with the back of her hand. Dylan reached past her, to the glove compartment, got out some tissues. He handed her one and took one himself.

"It's going to be a long road," Dylan said.

"Like a marathon," Erin said.

"He'll be there at the finish line," Dylan said.

"We've got to believe that."

"Do you?" Dylan said.

"I do," Erin said.

"Me, too," Dylan said. "And ..."

"Yes?"

"I was just ..."

"What is it, Dylan?"

"It may sound, I don't know, crazy."

"Nothing is going to sound crazy after all this."

Dylan smiled. "Okay then. What would you say if I told you I wanted something I once had?"

"Like?"

"To be," he said, "your density."

Erin laughed then. Short and sweet. "I think we can take that one step at a time."

"I can deal with that," Dylan said. "One step at a time. For you and me and Kyle."

"Yes," Erin said. "For you and me and our son."

AUTHOR'S NOTE

Thank you for reading *Your Son Is Alive*. Suspense is what I love to write , and there's always more in the pipeline.

If you'd like to be on my email list and be among the first to know when the next one's coming, please go to JamesScottBell.com and navigate to the FREE book page. I won't share your email address with anyone, nor will I stuff your mailbox with spam. It's just a short, to-the-point email from time to time.

MORE THRILLERS BY JAMES SCOTT BELL

The Mike Romeo Thriller Series

Romeo's Rules
Romeo's Way
Romeo's Hammer
Romeo's Fight

"Mike Romeo is a terrific hero. He's smart, tough as nails, and fun to hang out with. James Scott Bell is at the top of his game here. There'll be no sleeping till after the story is over." - **John Gilstrap**, New York Times bestselling author of the Jonathan Grave thriller series

The Ty Buchanan Legal Thriller Series

#1 Try Dying
#2 Try Darkness
#3 Try Fear

"Part Michael Connelly and part Raymond Chandler, Bell has an excellent ear for dialogue and makes contemporary L.A. come alive. Deftly plotted, flawlessly executed, and compulsively readable, Bell takes his place among the top authors in the field. Highly recommended." - **Sheldon Siegel**, *New York Times* bestselling author

Stand Alone Thrillers

Blind Justice
Don't Leave Me
Final Witness
Framed

ABOUT THE AUTHOR

JAMES SCOTT BELL is a winner of the International Thriller Writers Award (*Romeo's Way*) and is the author of the #1 bestseller for writers, *Plot & Structure*. He studied writing with Raymond Carver at the University of California, Santa Barbara, and graduated with honors from the University of Southern California Law Center. A former trial lawyer, Jim writes full time in his home town of Los Angeles.

For More Information
www.jamesscottbell.com

Printed in Great Britain
by Amazon

43940148R00192